D0166827

ALSO BY CHRISTOPHER BUCKLEY

Washington Schlepped Here: Walking in the Nation's Capital

No Way to Treat a First Lady

Little Green Men

God Is My Broker

Wry Martinis

Thank You for Smoking

Wet Work

Campion

The White House Mess

Steaming to Bamboola: The World of a Tramp Freighter

FLORENCE *of* ARABIA

Christopher Buckley

FLORENCE of ARABIA

a novel

Random House New York

This is a work of fiction. All incidents and dialogue, and all characters with the exception of some well-known historical and public figures, are products of the author's imagination and are not to be construed as real. Where real-life historical or public figures appear, the situations, incidents and dialogues concerning those persons are entirely fictional and are not intended to depict actual events or to change the entirely fictional nature of the work. In all other respects, any resemblance to persons living or dead is entirely coincidental. Got that? Any questions? It's all made up. Okay? Whatever.

 Published in the United States by Random House, an imprint of The Random House Publishing Group, a division of Random House, Inc., New York, and simultaneously in Canada by Random House of Canada Limited, Toronto.

ISBN 0-7394-5248-7

Printed in the United States of America

Book design by Barbara M. Bachman

For Bob, Kip, Steve and Tim Forbes

PROLOGUE

The official residence of His Excellency Prince Bawad bin-Rumallah al-Hamooj, ambassador of the Royal Kingdom of Wasabia to the United States of America, perches expensively on $18 million of real estate overlooking a frothy rapid of the Potomac River a few miles upstream from Washington, D.C. The emblem on the front gate of the palatial compound displays in bright gold leaf the emblem of the Royal House of Hamooj: a date palm tree, a crescent moon and a scimitar, hovering over a head. Viewed close up, the head does not bear a pleased expression, doubtless owing to its having been decapitated by the above scimitar.

Historically speaking, the head belonged to one Rafiq "The Unwise" al-Sawah, who, one night in 1740 or 1742 (historians differ on the precise date), attempted to usurp the authority of Sheik Abdulabdullah "The Wise" Waffa al-Hamooj, founder of the Wasabi dynasty and future king. According to legend—now taught as historical fact in the country's schools—Rafiq's severed head attempted to apologize to the sheik for its perfidy, and begged to be reattached. Sheik Abdulabdullah, however, was in no mood to hear these entreaties. Had he not treated Rafiq like his own brother? He ordered the still-blubbering mouth to be stuffed with camel dung and the head tossed to the desert hyenas.

The event is commemorated every year on the anniversary of the Perfidy of

Rafiq. Adult male citizens of the kingdom are required to place a token amount of camel dung on the tongue, as a symbol of the king's authority and a reminder of the bitter fate that befalls those who attempt to undermine it. In practice, only Hamooji royal palace staff and the most conservative of Wasabis reenact the ritual literally. A hundred years ago, an enterprising confectioner in the capital city of Kaffa devised a nougat that gave off the telltale aroma of the original article, enough to fool the *mukfelleen*, the religious police who sternly enforce the precepts of the *Book of Hamooj*. Wasabis could pop one onto the tongue and walk about all day with a showy air of piety. Alas, the trickery was discovered, and the unfortunate candy-maker forfeited not only his license to manufacture sweets but his tongue, right hand and left foot. On assuming the throne in 1974, King Tallulah decreed that a symbolic piece of dung would suffice. This caused much grumbling among the Wasabi mullahs and *mukfelleen* but vast relief among the adult male population.

A few minutes past midnight on the crisp fall night of September 28, the gates on which the royal emblem was mounted swung open and let out the car driven by Nazrah al-Bawad, wife of Prince Bawad.

Nazrah's exit would have gone more smoothly had she spent more time behind the wheel of an automobile. Wasabi women were not permitted to drive. However, being both enterprising and spirited, Nazrah had, since she was a teenager, been begging various males, starting with her brother Tamsa, to teach her the mysteries of steering, brake and gas. Taking the wheel of their father's Cadillac in the open deserts of Wasabia was not so complicated. In Washington, she would importune (that is, bribe) reluctant Khalil, her chauffeur-bodyguard-minder, to let her drive on certain half-deserted streets, and in the parking lots of such royal hangouts as Neiman Marcus and Saks Fifth Avenue. She had progressed to the point of almost being able to park a car without leaving most of the paint on the fenders of the ones in front and behind. Khalil had, in the process, earned a reputation within the residential household as a driver of less than perfect reliability.

Here, tonight, Nazrah found herself maneuvering with difficulty. Exiting the gate, she sheared off the rearview mirror and left a scrape down the side of the $85,000 car that would cause the most stoic of insurance adjusters to weep. Her intention had been to turn left, toward the city of Washington. But, seeing the headlights of a car coming up the country lane from that direction, she panicked and turned right, deeper into the deciduous suburb of McLean.

In truth, Nazrah was not thinking clearly. In truth, she was drunk. Drunk, as one might explain to a magistrate, with an explanation.

After more than twenty years in Washington, her husband, the prince, had announced his intention of returning to Wasabia, along with Nazrah and his three other wives. His uncle, the king, had decided to reward his decades of smooth service by annointing his nephew foreign minister. This was a big promotion that came with an even bigger palace and share of Wasabia's oil royalties.

The news was less than joyous to Nazrah, the youngest, prettiest and most independent-minded of the prince's wives. She did not want to return to Wasabia. Her years of living in America—even under the watchful eye of Shazzik, Prince Bawad's stern, neutered (so it was rumored) chamberlain—had left Nazrah with an appreciation of the role of women in Western society. She was in no hurry to return to a country where she would have to hide her lovely features under a veil, and in even less of a hurry to return to a country where women were still being publicly flogged, stoned to death and having their heads cut off in a site in the capital city so accustomed to the spectacle that it had earned the nickname "Chop-Chop Square."

Nazrah had been planning to inform the prince of her decision to remain in the United States that night after he returned home from his dinner with the Waldorf Group, a very influential group indeed, consisting of ex–U.S. presidents, ex-secretaries of state and defense, ex-directors of the Central Intelligence Agency, excellent folks, all—and what contacts they had! Since its founding ten years before in a suite at the Waldorf-Astoria Hotel in New York City, the Waldorf Group had invested over $5 billion of Wasabi royal money in various projects. This made for close relationships all around. Many of the Waldorf's board of directors also sat on the boards of the companies in which all the royal Wasabi money was being invested.

Today's Waldorf board meeting concerned a desalination project. Desalination was always a hot topic in Wasabia, owing to its geographical peculiarity. The country was entirely landlocked. Its lack of a single foot of shoreline was a grating historical vestige, the result of a moment of bibulous pique on the part of Winston Churchill when he drew up Wasabia's modern borders on a cocktail napkin at his club in London. King Tallulah had been uncooperative during the peace conference, so with a few strokes of his fountain pen, Churchill had denied him seaports. Thus do brief brandy-saturated moments determine the fate of empires and the course of history.

Wasabia's population was booming, owing to the fact that every man could take up to four wives. You were hardly considered manly unless you had twenty children. As a result, it was an increasingly young and thirsty nation.

At the board meeting, Prince Bawad told the assembled Waldorf directors, dear friends all, that the kingdom would be pleased to invest $1.2 billion with the group. The group would in turn hire the necessary Texans—kindred desert people—to build more desalination plants and the requisite pipelines into perennially parched Wasabia. At the critical moment during the meeting, the chairman of the board, an ex-president of the United States, would scribble a number on a piece of paper and slide it over to Prince Bawad. The number on the piece of paper represented Prince Bawad's "participation"—such a nicer word than "skim" or "take"—in the profits.

This ritual usually went smoothly. But this time Prince Bawad, who was building a 150,000-square-foot ski lodge in Jackson Hole, felt that the sum was, well, inadequate. He stared at the ex-president.

They had a good relationship, the ex-president and Prince Bawad. The former had been a guest, while president, at Bawad's present hundred-thousand-square-foot ski lodge in Aspen. Normally, he would have scratched out the number and written a slightly bigger one on the paper. But this time he did not. There had been grumbling among the Waldorfians. The kingdom had been getting a bit frisky lately in its demands. Business was, after all, business.

The ex-president merely smiled back. Finally, Bawad, with a trace of a scowl, nodded his agreement to the number on the paper. The ex-president beamed and made a little joke about what a tough businessman the prince was. The meeting was adjourned, the doors opened and in came the refreshments, and such refreshments. It was a very pleasant group with which to be associated, the Waldorf. Never in the field of human profit was so much made by so few for doing so little.

—

BACK AT THE RESIDENCE, Nazrah took a nip from the prince's bottle of 150-year-old French brandy. When, at eleven o'clock, the prince still had not returned, she took another nip. Then another. By the time the prince did arrive home at 11:40, she was feeling no pain.

The speech that she had so carefully rehearsed tumbled off her benumbed tongue without eloquence or coherence, and heavily redolent of Napoleon brandy. The prince, moonfaced, goateed and imperious, and still fuming over his inadequate participation in the desalination project, brusquely ordered Nazrah to her room.

A late-night argument between an indulged royal prince and a tipsy junior wife is not an occasion of ideal dialogue. It deteriorated into shouts and terminated all too quickly and dramatically with the prince dealing Nazrah a cuff across the chops with a meaty, cigar-smelling hand. With that, he stormed off, loudly cursing Western corruption, to the bedroom of one of his less troublesome wives.

Nazrah, smarting and furious, went to her bedroom but not to bed. She hurled a few things into an Hermès overnight bag and made her way to the garage, where she could choose from eleven cars. (The prince loved to drive and was known personally to most of the Virginia state troopers.) She decided not to take the Maserati, Lamborghini, Maybach or Ferrari, these having too many buttons of uncertain provenance on the dash, and settled instead on the Mercedes in which Khalil usually chauffeured her, with whose controls she was quite familiar, including the special button on the walnut dash that overrode the guards' control of the front gate.

So it was that Nazrah found herself roaring out the gates past alarmed guards, with the grim Shazzik and two of his men, fierce Warga tribesmen in blue suits, in hot pursuit.

But where to go? She'd missed the turn to Washington.

After nearly colliding with several trees and going through a succession of red lights, she found herself turning north on Route 123 at a speed triple the legal limit, a fact not lost on Virginia state trooper Harmon G. Gilletts.

It was at this point, with Trooper Gilletts's red-white-and-blue flashing lights and urgent siren behind her, that she saw the sign announcing GEORGE BUSH CENTER FOR INTELLIGENCE. Any port in a storm.

The sight of a car approaching at high speed, followed closely by a state policeman in apparent hot pursuit, is not a welcome one these days at U.S. government installations. By the time Nazrah had reached the front gate of the CIA headquarters, a steel barrier had swiftly risen up from the cement. This abruptly and loudly terminated her forward progress, in the process activating so many airbags inside her vehicle that the princess disappeared from sight altogether, concussed into unconsciousness.

As Nazrah dreamed of turquoise antelopes flying over a boundless black desert, pursued by giant scarlet crabs with snapping golden claws—adrenaline, cognac and the punch of air bags produce the most vivid visions—the United States government was waking to the reality of an incident of epic dimension.

FLORENCE *of* ARABIA

CHAPTER ONE

While Nazrah was still dreaming of psychedelic antelopes, the CIA guards and Virginia state trooper Harmon G. Gilletts, weapons drawn, examined their catch through the car's windows. All they could see, amid the myriad air bags, were two distinctly feminine hands, the one on the left bearing enough diamonds to put all of their children combined through Ivy League colleges and law school.

Another expensive German car drove up, this one bearing Shazzik, looking even more grim than usual, and his two *mukfelleen*. The CIA guards and Trooper Gilletts noted the diplomatic license plate but did not holster their weapons.

Shazzik emerged from the car and, in his accustomed peremptory manner—Hamooji retainers are not renowned for their courtesy to nonroyals—announced that the vehicle contained a member of the household and asserted his rights of extraction.

This was too much for Trooper Gilletts. As a Marine Corps reservist, he had spent time in Wasabia during one of America's periodic interventionist spasms in the region. As a result, he could not stand Wasabis (a common enough sentiment among foreign visitors). Six months at the Prince Wadum Air Base had left Gilletts, a reasonable man of no particular bias, hating even the name "Wasabi."

He dispensed with the usual "sir," with which he addressed even the most wretched of his highway detainees, thrust out his impressive marine reservist pectorals at the chamberlain while tightening his palm around the grip of his Glock nine-millimeter, and counterasserted jurisdiction on behalf of the sovereign commonwealth of Virginia. Stonewall Jackson at First Bull Run, just down the road from here, had been no less unmovable than Trooper Harmon G. Gilletts.

The CIA guards, meanwhile, had pressed buttons summoning backup in the form of an armored vehicle capable (should any gate situation deteriorate seriously) of launching missiles; also of passing impressive amounts of electrical current through the bodies of the undesirable. A helicopter with snipers was also put into play. Why take chances? Why screw around?

Amid this bruit of riot vehicle, rotor blades, drawn guns, male barking and bantam outthrust of chests, Nazrah's hallucinations ended. She stirred inside her bulbous polystyrene cocoon. The air bags deflated sufficiently to allow her wriggle room. She peered with horror at the standoff taking place outside her car windows and did what anyone would in such circumstances. She reached for her cell phone.

FLORENCE FARFALETTI HAD been in the U.S. Foreign Service long enough to know that when a phone rings after midnight it is A) never a wrong number and B) never a call you want to get. But being a deputy to the deputy assistant secretary of state for Near Eastern Affairs (DASNEA), she C) had to take the call.

"Farfaletti," she said with as much professional crisp as she could muster in the middle of a ruined REM cycle. Even though her last name had been spoken aloud for thirty-two years, it still sounded like too many syllables. But having changed her first name, she felt she couldn't change her surname. It would crush her grandfather, who remained defiantly proud of his service in Mussolini's army in Ethiopia in the 1930s. Perhaps after he died. He was in his nineties now. Or if she remarried. Meanwhile, she was stuck with the patronymic embarrassment of vowels.

"Flor-ents!"

Florence struggled against the glue of sleep. She recognized the Wasabian difficulty with soft C's. The voice was young, urgent, scared, familiar.

"*Nazrah?*"

"It's me, Florents! It's Nazrah!"

Florence flicked on the light, grimaced at the clock. What was *this* about?

She knew Nazrah Hamooj. They had met back in Kaffa, the Wasabi capital, when Florence lived there. Nazrah was the daughter of a lesser sheik of the Azami tribe, quite lovely, intelligent, self-educated—the only education a Wasabi woman could acquire, since they were barred from schooling above age fifteen. Nazrah was irreverent about the other wives, whom she referred to with delighted sarcasm as "my *dear* sisters." During her dismal time in Kaffa, Florence heard the gossip: Prince Bawad had married the much younger Nazrah to annoy his snobbish second wife, Bisma, who felt that Nazrah was socially several rungs too low down the ladder.

Florence and Nazrah had reconnected socially in Washington, at an embassy reception, one of the few occasions when Wasabi wives were on public display. They had managed to get together for a half-dozen lunches in French restaurants, where Nazrah ordered expensive wines in view of the frantic Khalil. Florence liked Nazrah. She laughed easily, and she was deliciously indiscreet. Nazrah knew of Florence's own experience with Wasabi princes and confided in her. Florence dutifully filled out the requisite State Department report after each encounter. Out of decency and respect for her friend, she left out certain details, such as those concerning Prince Bawad's amatory practices. If Nazrah had confided anything of strategic value or necessity to the United States, Florence would, of course, as an officer of the government, have vouchsafed it to the relevant authority. So why was Nazrah calling at this hour?

"Flor-ents. You must help me—I need asylum! Now, please!"

Florence felt her chest go tight. Asylum. Within the State Department, this was known as "the A-word." A nightmare term in a bureaucracy consecrated to stasis and inertia. "I want asylum" sent shudders down a thousand rubber spines. It summoned hellish visions of paperwork, cables, meetings, embarrassment, denial, restatement and—*invariably*—clarification. "I want asylum" ended in tears, approved or denied. Denied, it usually ended up on the evening news, a nation's shame, the anchorman asking, in tones sepulchral, disappointed and trochaic, "*How* could *something* like *this* have *happened* in the *United* States of *America*?"

Florence was now bolt, wide, awake. The wife of the ambassador of the country that supplied America with the majority of its imported fossil fuel was asking her, a midlevel Foreign Service officer, for asylum. Homeland security alert levels come in six color codes ranging from green to red. Florence's own alert levels consisted of just three: Cool, Oh Shit and Holy Shit.

Her crisis training kicked in. She heard a voice inside her head. It said, *Stall.* This was instantly drowned out by a second voice saying, *Help.* The second voice was real and coming through the phone. It was speaking Wasabi.

Florence found herself saying, "Tell them you're injured. Insist they take you to a hospital. Fairfax Hospital. Insist. Nazrah—do you understand?"

She rose and dressed and, even though hurrying, put on her pearl earrings. *Always wear your earrings,* her mother had told her from an early age.

OUTSIDE THE EMERGENCY ROOM entrance, she recognized Shazzik and the two *mukfelleen.* For the first time in her life, she wished she were wearing a veil. During her months in Wasabia, she'd been required to and never got used to it.

Shazzik was furious, making demands of—she guessed—several CIA security officers. What worried her more was the amount of Virginia state trooperage outside. Seven cruisers. Someone was bound to call the media, and once that happened, the options narrowed. Few situations, really, are improved by the arrival of news trucks.

Two armed hospital security guards stood athwart the doors to the ER. Florence pulled her scarf over her head as a makeshift veil, lowered her head so as to look demure, and approached.

"I'm here to see Nazrah Hamooj. I am her family." She made herself seem and sound foreign. With her dark hair and Mediterranean complexion, she looked credibly Middle Eastern.

"Name?"

Neither "Florence" nor "Farfaletti" sounding terribly Wasabian, Florence said, "Melath." It meant "asylum" in Wasabi, a fact that would in all likelihood be lost on a Virginia hospital security guard.

Word was sent in. It came back: Let her in.

"She's all right. Her CAT scan and MRI were clean."

The doctor was young, not quite as good-looking as the ones in television dramas but, from the way he regarded Florence, an appreciator of beauty. Florence had grasped, as soon as boys began to bay outside her windows, that beauty was, in addition to being a gift, a tool, like a Swiss Army knife.

"Could you do another? Just in case?"

"She is your . . ."

"Sister."

"Well, we've established from a medical point of view that your sister is all right. Were you aware that she was drinking?"

"Dear, dear."

"She's lucky to be alive."

"Can you just keep her here? Under observation?"

"This isn't the Betty Ford Center."

"A few *hours* is all I'm asking."

"The insurance company—"

Florence took the doctor by the arm and tugged him to a corner. He didn't resist. Men tend to yield to pretty women dragging them off into corners. She dropped the Wasabi accent.

"I am asking you on behalf of the United States government"—she flashed him her State Department ID—"to keep that woman here in this hospital for a few hours. Surely there are some more tests you can give her?"

"What's going on?"

"Do you know what an honor killing is?"

"This is a hospital, in case you hadn't—"

"Where she comes from, it's what happens to a woman who dishonors her husband or relative. No trial, no jury, no appeal, no Supreme Court, no ACLU, just death. By stoning or decapitation. You with me?"

"Who is she?"

"She's the wife of the Wasabi ambassador. One of his wives, anyway. She tried to run away. If you release her into their custody before I can figure something out, it's probably a death sentence."

"Jesus, lady."

"Sorry to lay that on you." Florence smiled at the doctor.

"How long am I supposed to keep her?"

"Thank you. Just—a few hours. That would really be great. There's a tall man outside, Middle Eastern, very unpleasant-looking, thin with a pencil mustache, high forehead and goatee. Tell him you need to do more tests, and she's in isolation."

"Oh, man."

"You're really, really great to do this. I won't forget it." Florence nudged him toward the swinging doors, then located Nazrah and drew the curtain around her bed.

Nazrah had held it together until now, but upon seeing Florence, she burst. The Great Desert in the interior of Wasabia had not seen such moisture in an entire year. She had, in the manner of women of the region, applied copious mascara, which now ran sootily down her tawny checks. Florence listened and nodded and handed her a succession of tissues. Nazrah explained. It hadn't been planned. She was sorry to have involved Florence. She'd intended to drive to the train station and take the Acela Express to New York City and then . . . whatever the next step was. Then she'd taken the right turn. Then the police car. Then the CIA front gate seemed like . . . Then the crash. And the only person she could think to call was Florence. She was so sorry.

Florence fought the temptation to say something hopeful, there being little reason to hope. At some point she realized she was holding Nazrah's hand.

Eventually, Nazrah's tear ducts gave up from exhaustion. Calm descended on her. She looked up at the hospital ceiling and said, "What will they do with me?"

The curtain parted with a fierce zip to reveal Prince Bawad and his retinue. *He looks like Othello,* Florence thought. *And here's Shazzik in the role of Iago.*

Accompanying them, she recognized State's chief security officer and, oh hell, Duckett. And McFall, CIA's chief for Near East.

Behind this scrum of officialdom Florence heard the doctor manfully explaining that there was some possibility of subdural something, but it was clear that he was being overruled. Bawad, whose finger-snaps could summon a kingdom's resources, had brought his personal physician and orderlies to carry her off. Nazrah was, as far as the United States was concerned, Wasabi national soil.

CHAPTER TWO

Why did she call you?"

"You've asked me that twelve times." Twelve times over the course of three interrogations. Present at this one were: Charles Duckett, deputy assistant secretary of state for Near Eastern Affairs (DASNEA); two frowns from the White House National Security Council; an FBI supervisor and a CIA guy introduced by a name most likely not real who probably worked for McFall. Also a stenographer who coughed. Why, Florence wondered, hadn't they sent along someone from Housing and Urban Development?

"Then I'm asking again. Aren't I?"

"Why don't you just box me?" She would have welcomed a polygraph at this point for variety.

"No one's talking about boxing you. Why did she call you?"

"She'd crashed her car, Charles. She looks out one window, and there are men with guns everywhere. We knew each other. We were friendly. I'm a woman. She found herself in a stressful situation. She probably wanted to talk to a sympathetic person in the U.S. government. Hard as they are to find."

"Why didn't you report it to us immediately?"

"I was going to, once the situation stabilized."

"Stabilized? Sequestering a runaway diplomatic wife—the wife of Price

Bawad. By what earthly definition does this qualify as stabilizing the situation?"

"I was trying to buy some cooldown time. That's all. She was terrified. Call it a human transaction. Just so we're all clear, I'm not running an underground railroad for Wasabi wives. Okay?"

Duckett read from inside a red folder marked TOP SECRET. "You said to her, 'Tell them you're injured. Insist they take you to a hospital. Fairfax Hospital. Insist. Nazrah—do you understand?' Why Fairfax?"

That they had a transcript of Nazrah's cell-phone call to her indicated two distinct possibilities: that the CIA could spontaneously intercept any cell call made on its property. Or—more interestingly—that the government had *already* tapped Nazrah's cell phone.

"It's the closest hospital."

Duckett grumpily opened a green TOP SECRET folder and scanned. "You say you met with her on . . . seven . . . separate occasions."

"That's right. Four lunches, one tea at the Four Seasons Hotel. We went shopping twice. It's all in the folder. The yellow one."

Duckett opened the yellow folder. "Are these reports complete?"

"How do you mean, complete?"

"Did you report everything?"

"Of course. Everything relevant."

"What would you consider irrelevant?"

"Personal stuff."

"Define 'personal.' "

"Girl talk." Probably the best way to explain it to this high-testosterone bunch.

Duckett sighed as only a bureaucrat can, from the very depths of his soul. "Florence, this is not Twenty Questions. *Everything* that she told you is relevant."

Florence looked at Duckett, then at FBI, at the White House pair, at CIA—who seemed to be regarding her with an expression that went beyond strictly business. She turned back to Duckett.

"Okay. She told me that the prince likes to smoke hash, then dress up in cowboy boots and his tribal headdress and nothing else, then line up all four of his wives with their bottoms in the air and, well, I guess the technical term for it would be—"

"All right, that's all."

CIA burst out laughing. The White House mice looked stricken.

Florence said, "Next time a diplomatic wife confides in me, I'll be sure to put everything in writing."

"Would you excuse us?" Duckett said to the others. He added to the stenographer, "You, too."

CIA flashed Florence a grin as he exited.

"God of heaven and earth, *why* would you reveal something like that?" Duckett said, aghast. "In front of *them*? Don't you understand the situation? The Wasabis are madder than hornets. If they find out that *State* has been retailing—to *CIA*—intimate details of . . ." He put his head in his hands. "Oh, what a disaster. They'll use this to crucify us. You know what they'll say, don't you? That you were on a personal vendetta."

"That's absurd. I was trying to help a fellow human being. Ridiculous as that may sound."

"You were married to a Wasabi. And you're Italian. 'Vendetta' is an Italian word."

"I'm as American as you are. And that is just completely out of line. To say nothing of stupid."

"Explain it to their Foreign Ministry!"

Florence had grown up fascinated by her grandfather's tales of the Middle East. At college she majored in Arabic studies and was fluent by the time she graduated Yale. There she met Hamzir, a minor Wasabi princeling, charming, handsome, raffish, rich and, being a reservist fighter pilot in the Royal Wasabi Air Force, dashing. What American girl with a predilection for the Middle East wouldn't have fallen in love? They were married weeks after graduation.

After a honeymoon in the Mediterranean on a 125-foot yacht, Florence arrived in her new home of Kaffa to a succession of discoveries, exponentially depressing. Hamzir had not been straightforward about the realities of life as a foreign Wasabi bride. He'd told her that she would be exempt from the strictures governing Wasabi women. *Not to worry, darling!*

Florence found herself under virtual house arrest, required to wear the veil outside the home and to be accompanied by a male escort. With this much, she resolved to cope. But within three months, she discovered that her birth-control pills had been switched with sugar substitutes—the kind one puts in coffee. Confronted, Hamzir shrugged and grunted that it was time, anyway, that she bore him a child. She retaliated in the Lysistrata fashion by cutting off sex, whereupon he went into a rage and announced the next evening over dinner—as if remembering a dentist's appointment the following day—that he was taking a second wife, a first cousin. *Pass the lamb, would you?*

The next morning Florence drove herself (a flogging offense) to the U.S. embassy and said, *Beam me up, Scotty.* Their response was *You got yourself into this, and now you expect us to get you out of it? Here, read this.* They handed her a pamphlet titled "What American Women Should Understand When They Marry a Wasabi National." The State Department's reflexive response to any American in extremis overseas is to hand them a pamphlet—along with a list of incompetent local lawyers—and say, "We told you so."

Florence was not one to be deterred. She announced firmly that she would not leave the embassy except in a car driven by an embassy staffer, to Prince Babullah Airport. An enterprising young Foreign Service officer, like herself of Italian extraction, worked out a quick and dirty arrangement with the Italian embassy and got her out of the country on an Italian passport, to which Florence was technically entitled.

Back in the U.S.A., she went to work in Washington with a Middle Eastern foundation. One day, bored, and thinking about the enterprising Foreign Service officer in Kaffa who had rescued her, she sat for the Foreign Service exam. She passed. Being fluent in Arabic and an expert on the culture, she was posted to Chad. After 9/11, it was thought that her skills might be better suited elsewhere at State, so she was moved to Near Eastern Affairs.

Florence said to Duckett, "Did they have a tap on her cell phone? Or did they intercept the call on the spot?"

"What does it matter? They have you on tape, urging her to flee. Practically issuing amnesty on the spot."

"But who taped the call? Who gave you the transcript?"

"McFall's person, Brent whateverhisname."

"Ask him how they got it."

"They're not going to tell me that. You know what pricks they are about sources and methods."

Florence whispered, "Tell him that you know what they were up to."

Duckett stared. "Namely?"

"That CIA had a tap on Nazrah's phone long before she drove into the gate. That they were working on her. That they'd targeted her. That they were going to try to blackmail Prince Bawad through her."

Duckett pursed his lips. "Thanks to you, now they do have something on him."

"But they won't be able to use it if you tell them that you've seen through them. That you're on to them. That you've blown their operation. And that you're now going to climb to the top of the Washington Monument and scream your lungs out about it."

"But what if it's not true?"

"Let the director of CIA deny it. To the president's face. In the Cabinet Room."

The lines on Duckett's forehead relaxed, as if he'd suddenly been injected with Botox. He let out a pleased, ruminative grunt. His loathing of the CIA went back to one of his first overseas postings, Ecuador. There, he had overseen the opening of one of State's dreary cultural exchange centers, this one designed to "highlight the historic synergy between the United States and Ecuador." The next day it was blown up, ostensibly by a local guerrilla group, but in fact by the CIA, who wanted to stage an anti–U.S. outrage in order to widen its campaign against the current set of rebels. Duckett had been licking this still-moist wound for decades. He was smiling now.

He called the others back in. "I've questioned Ms. Farfaletti, and I have established to my satisfaction that her version of the events is accurate and truthful. Now"—he picked up the transcript of Nazrah's call—"I'm not going to ask you, or you, how this call came to be intercepted. Because that would not only compromise sources and methods, it would also raise the appalling possibility that one or more agencies of the U.S. government were spying on the wife of a diplomat. Not just any diplomat but the dean of the diplomatic corps—a close personal friend of the president of the United States."

"That's a bunch of shit."

"Which your director, or yours, can scrape off the bottom of their shoes—in the Cabinet Room, after State has presented *its* perspective on the matter."

FBI and CIA stared.

"Alternatively," continued Duckett, lord of the moment, "we can all of us agree that the matter is now closed. Princess Nazrah is, as we speak, on her way back home in a Royal Wasabi Air Force transport. The media is unaware. So, gentlemen, how shall we proceed?"

The White House people whispered with FBI and CIA. FBI said, none too happily, "We're done here." On the way out, the CIA man winked at Florence.

The next morning Florence inserted her ID card into the State Department turnstile, half expecting the display to read CANCELED, like a maxed-out credit card. But it let her in. Apparently, she still had a job in the United States government.

She sought out George. George was a desk-limpet in the Political/Econ section who amused himself during his lunch hour by devising crossword puzzles in ancient Phoenician, one of twelve languages he spoke fluently. He claimed to dream in seven of them, and George was not the sort to boast. His model was Sir Richard Burton, the nineteenth-century polymath-explorer who spoke thirty-five languages and dreamed in seventeen. One of the most daring adventurers of all time, Burton was a curious role model for the agoraphobic George, who had managed to wriggle out of every foreign posting he had been offered, except for one eighteen-month stint in Ottawa, during which he learned Micmac, a complex native Canadian language.

"I had the most vivid dream last night. In Turkish. I was on the Bosporus with Lord Byron and Shelley. We were each in one of those idiotic tourist pedal boats, trying to get from one side to the other, only the continents started moving apart. What do you make of that? You look awful. Did we not sleep last night?"

"George, Nazrah Hamooj asked me for asylum."

"If you think that's more important than interpreting my dream, fine."

Florence told him what had happened, leaving out the detail about Prince Bawad's ride-'em-cowboy fantasy.

"Hmm. I knew something must be cooking. Cables between here and Kaffa have been flying fast and furious. They scrambled a Royal Wasabi transport out of Jacksonville to Dulles. Oh, the humanity, oh, the paperwork."

George caught the look on Florence's face. "That was she on board? Oh, dear. I hear the sound of sharpening steel."

"I'll call Tony Bazell in Kaffa," Florence said. "Maybe he can—"

"What? Storm the palace? Forget it. Maybe they'll let her off with thirty lashes." George peered at Florence. "Are we leaving something out? Are we not telling all? Out with it."

"I . . . Nah."

"In Italian." It was the language they used for office gossip.

She told him.

"*Mamma mia!* All four? Simultaneously? Well, I knew the prince entertained, but I had no idea. Filthy old goat. No wonder the poor thing wanted asylum. She probably dreamed of a nice, boring life in the 'burbs. Apron, gingham frock, pies cooling on the windowsill, golden retriever named . . . Brandy, stretching class on Tuesday, yoga on Thursday, Lord and Taylor's trunk show, *Jeopardy!* every night at seven-thirty during dinner with a husband named Cliff . . . no, Brad. Brad the Impaler. Who would ask for oral sex only on his birthday. Now she's on her way back to Wasabia. Land of fun and sun. Well, darling, you tried. God *knows* you tried."

Two days later, Florence called Bazell at the U.S. embassy in Kaffa, who put her through to the embassy guy who kept the Chop-Chop Square tally. Nazrah Hamooj had been executed that morning at dawn by sword, for the crime of adultery.

"She was pretty calm about it, from what we heard. Sometimes they make a hell of a fuss. Last month they did Prince Rahmal's wife. Man, did she put up a fight. Yelling, screaming, kicking. They finally jabbed her full of Valium so they could get a clear cut. Tomorrow's entertainment is they're stoning a woman to death for schtupping—get this—the black cook. It's the Thousand and One Nights. They can't get over it. Is this a great country or what?"

CHAPTER THREE

If Florence had an office with a door, she would have shut it and had a private cry, but she didn't, so she used the ladies' room. She remained there most of the morning, until George sent someone in to get her. When she emerged, he said, "Frankly, you'd look better under a veil," and put her in a cab and sent her home.

She unplugged the phone and went to bed and had a dream in which Nazrah was lying on the hospital bed with mascara streaming down her cheeks, and Shazzik, dressed in a female nurse's uniform, was administering a lethal injection. Nazrah's body gradually shrank and was sucked into the tube and up into the plastic drip bag, where she was imprisoned, screaming silently for help. Florence started awake, so drenched in perspiration that she got up and took a shower.

She went to work the next morning and stayed at the office until past midnight for the next three days.

When she was finished, she printed three numbered copies, placed them in TOP SECRET folders, gave one to Duckett's secretary, another to George, and sent the other straight to the top.

"So this is what you've been holed up doing lo these three days?" George opened the folder and read the cover page and let out a whistle. He read at the speed it took him to turn the fifty-odd pages.

"Well?" she asked.

"Couldn't put it down. The middle bit could use some buffing. It was Tallulah the second, not Tallulah the third, who instigated the practice among the Hawawi of female circumcision—*qu'isha,* by the way, not *quish'aa.*"

"Other than that?"

"I'm sure it helped to get it out of your system."

"I sent it to Duckett."

George stared. "Why don't you just stab him in the heart with Malal's dagger and get it over with?"

Their boss kept a nineteenth-century gold and silver dagger on his desk, a gift of Prince Malal, Wasabia's minister of agriculture. It was probably the cheapest present ever given by a Wasabi royal, but Duckett was proud of it. He used it as a letter opener, and sometimes brandished it to make a point.

"George, I'm asking you what you think."

"I hardly know where to begin. This goes a bit beyond our traditional brief. You didn't really send this to him? Come on."

Florence nodded. "And to S."

"You sent it to S?"

"Why not? This way Duckett can't stop it. You're the one who's always saying it's easier to ask forgiveness than permission."

"Well," George said. "Well, well, well. Wow."

Florence's phone rang. "Florence? Mr. Duckett wants you. It's urgent."

"Do you want to be cremated," George said, "or do you prefer traditional burial?"

FLORENCE ENTERED DUCKETT'S office without knocking and closed the door behind her. It shut with a portentous *click.*

Charles Duckett was leaning back in his chair, as if trying to distance himself physically from the document in front of him. He was looking at it as though it were a dead animal, far gone in putrefaction, that had been malevolently dumped upon a pristine altar consecrated to solemn rituals and tended to by votaries of an elite cult.

The cover sheet looked up insistently.

FEMALE EMANCIPATION AS A MEANS OF ACHIEVING LONG-TERM POLITICAL STABILITY IN THE NEAR EAST: AN OPERATIONAL PROPOSAL

Submitted by Florence Farfaletti, DDASNEA

Circulation: SecState, DASNEA

"I know you've been under a strain, Florence. I understand that—"

"Charles, the reason I sent it to S before getting your approval was to relieve you of responsibility. And to be honest, I didn't think I'd get your approval. So what do think?"

"What do I think?" Duckett said absently. "Of the fact that one of my deputies, whose actions reflect directly on me, has circulated a proposal calling for the fomenting of revolution in a country that supplies one third of America's energy needs, a country to which we are formally allied, to which we are vitally and strategically linked . . . circulated it and sent it directly to the . . . secretary of state? What do I *think*?"

"I truly believe that—"

"Do you see this phone on my desk, Florence?"

"Yes, Charles, I see the phone."

"Any moment now, that phone is going to ring. It will be S calling. *The secretary would like to see you, Mr. Duckett. Right away.* That's what the voice will say."

"Charles—"

"During my time here, I've endeavored to make my infrequent visits to S occasions of light. Sometimes, given the region it falls to us to superintend, that is not always possible. But at least when the secretary sees me walk into his office, he does not say to himself, *Why, here's Charlie Duckett! Say, isn't he the one whose staff sends me cockamamy proposals to undermine the social structure of America's most strategic partner in the Middle East? Why, come on in, Charlie boy! What's that Skunk Works of yours cooked up this time? Ho ho. Certainly hope* The Washington Post *doesn't find out I've been reading proposals to overthrow Wasabia. Ha ha. Might makes things a bit sticky at the dinner I'm giving for Prince*

Bawad next Thursday at my house. Oh, and by the way, Charlie old bean, what's this about one of your people operating an underground railroad for his runaway wives? Gosh, why didn't I think of that? What better way to promote harmony between our two countries! Let's give that girl of yours a promotion! Are you out of your fucking *mind,* Farfaletti?"

"I made it clear to the secretary in my cover letter that you hadn't signed off on it."

Duckett rubbed his forehead. The lines were back. "I protected you. I went the extra mile. Now I'm beginning to think you're working for them."

"Them? Who are you talking about?"

"*Them.*" Duckett did the Langley Hook.

"CIA? Charles, I work for the State Department. I work for you."

"No, no. This could only be an Agency operation. To destroy State—from within. It's happened before, you know. In Quito."

"Charles, I'm on your side. I'm just trying to think outside the box."

"What box? Pandora's?"

"If we want to bring about change in the Middle East, this is the way to do it. I'm convinced of it. It might be the only way."

"How do I explain? Where do I begin? It is not our job to bring about change in the Middle East."

"It's not?"

"No, it is not. Our job is to manage reality."

His phone rang. The shadow of the angel of death passed over Charles Duckett's features as he answered. "Yes," he said grimly, swallowing. "Yes. Right away." He hung up. "Satisfied, Florence?"

"Let me go with you. Let me make the case. I can."

Duckett rose slowly. His eyes had gone glassy. "I was up for the ambassadorship, you know. It was mine. It was all set. They told me."

He shuffled out of his office like a mental patient in slippers going off to get his noon meds.

George was waiting for her. "Where would you like me to ship your remains?"

—

THE NEXT MORNING Florence received by interoffice notification that her request for transfer to the visa section of the U.S. consulate in the Cape Verde Islands had been approved, effective immediately.

"You might have told me you'd applied," George said. "I thought we had a relationship."

Florence started glumly at the paper.

"Well, let's look on the bright side," he said. "Bracing sea air on all sides, steady climate, especially during hurricane season. And whale-watching second to none. A lot of the harpooners on the Nantucket whale ships were Cape Verde men."

"Shut up, George."

"I thought it was a damn slick proposal. Oh, hell. I'll miss you."

"I'm not going to Cape Verde. For God's sake."

"You're not going to quit? Just go, put in a few months. Duckett's due for a rotation, he'll be gone before you know it. Think of it as a vacation. Couple of months on the beach in Cape Verde, nights hobnobbing with the local gratin. You'll be back before you know it, tanned, rested and ready. Come on, Firenze."

George was the only one outside her family who called her that. And he'd guessed it. It was the baptismal name her father, a native of Florence, had insisted on. The priest had initially refused, there being no Saint Firenze, but there are few theological issues that can't be resolved with a hundred-dollar bill. Florence Americanized the name in the fifth grade after she'd had enough abuse from classmates. But George much preferred Firenze to Florence, which he said sounded like the cleaning woman's name.

"I'm out of here," she said. She kissed George on the forehead and collected her things and left. What now? There were a dozen foundations in Washington where her knowledge of the Middle East would be better used than on an archipelago off the coast of Senegal. Where better, she figured, to sink back into the earth than a foundation? But what a shame, what a waste.

—

IT WAS A STUNNING, crisp fall day, and feeling liberated after dropping off her letter of resignation, Florence zipped up her black leather jumpsuit—the sight of which caused cricks in many a male neck—tied her hair in a ponytail, donned the red helmet, flipped down the visor, pressed the start button on her motorcycle and screamed out of the city at a deliciously breakneck speed.

At the end of River Road, she turned left and roared deeper into country. She glanced down at the speedometer and saw that she was going almost ninety miles per hour, too fast, but what bliss! The fall leaves went by in a lush slipstream blur of gold and red and orange.

Another color suddenly appeared in her rearview mirror, not found in nature, electric blue and flashing. For a moment she considered trying to outrun it, but then she let up on the throttle and rumbled over to the shoulder to await the inevitable *Do you have any idea how fast you were going, ma'am?*

The man who got out of the unmarked car was not in uniform. The first discordant note that struck her was his age. He was in his mid-sixties, at least. He was trim, with the body of someone who had once been an athlete or in the military, gray about the temples, with wire-rimmed glasses perched on a sharp nose. The eyes, now close enough for her to see, were bright blue and twinkled. His lips were pursed, but pleasantly, in something like a smile. It didn't compute. Florence looked at the flashing blue light mounted on his dashboard. Some county supervisor or sheriff?

"Goodness gracious, young lady. Ninety miles an hour—on a road teeming with deer? You could have been killed."

It was said in an avuncular way.

"And what a waste *that* would be." He was grinning at her.

"Excuse me," she said, "who are you?"

"That's the question, isn't it?" He chuckled. "That's quite a machine you have there. Used to do a bit of motorcycling myself. Oh, yes, yes."

Still astride the bike, Florence moved her thumb over the starter button.

"Oh, now, don't be in such a big rush. I should think you'd be very interested to hear what I have to say. Very interested."

Something kept her from pressing the button. "Could I see some identification?" she said gently.

The man seemed to find this amusing. "Oh, certainly, certainly. What sort did you have in mind?"

"Look, sir—"

"We read your proposal, Florence."

Florence stared.

"On achieving stability in the Middle East? Very interesting, original. And, by gosh, out of the box. Not at all your usual State Department pap. No wonder they wanted to transfer you to Cape Verde! I had to look it up on a map. My goodness, it's a long way from nowhere. May I buy you a cup of coffee? This must seem very forward, I know."

"Are you *with* the State Department?" Florence asked.

"Hardly. Come on, I'll buy. There has to be a Starbucks around here."

"I don't—"

"Do you remember the Starbucks in Kaffa?"

"What?"

"The one at the corner of Alkakazir and Ben Qatif? How the *mukfelleen* made them cover the mermaid's boobs on the logo? Now, whenever I go to a Starbucks, I check for her boobs. Silly, I know. Do you want to follow me, or shall I follow you?"

"I . . ."

"I know. You came out here to feel the wind in your hair, the road rise up to greet you. But all I'm asking for is ten minutes of your time at a neutral, well-lit public place. If, after that, you want to walk away, no one's going to stop you, and I'll still pay for the latte. You like tall nonfat double-shot, yes? And sugar substitute, preferably not in lieu of birth-control pills?"

The only human being to whom she had confided that detail was the State Department polygraph operator during her background check. She didn't know what to say, so she followed him on her motorcycle to a suburban Starbucks.

They sat outside, by a parking lot full of expensive cars driven by people who looked like they had something to do with horses.

"Look, before we go any further, who are you?" she asked.

The man appeared to consider the question. He said thoughtfully, "Why don't you just call me Uncle Sam?"

"I take it you're with the government. What is it you want?"

"Quite possibly, the same thing you do. Long-term political stability in the Middle East. Now, *there's* a goal. Oh, yes."

"You agree with my proposal?"

"We've tried pretty much everything else, haven't we? And *what* a pig's breakfast we've made. Dear, dear, dear. Well, I always say, if you can't solve a problem, make it larger. The remarkable thing is how *well* we mean, America. And yet it always turns out so—badly. But I didn't come out here to bore you to death, no, no. I suppose you'll be wanting some bona fides. You'd be foolish not to. And we know you're not that. Let's see. I know—given the region we're dealing with, why don't we use the Thousand and One Nights as a model. I'll be the djinn in the lamp. Ask me for three things that only the good old U.S. government could provide. If you're still not satisfied, then you're still one tall latte ahead, right?"

Florence considered. "Tomorrow's PDB."

Uncle Sam chortled. "Ouch."

Every morning, the president of the United States received the presidential daily briefing, the most highly classified document in the government, seen by fewer than a half-dozen pairs of eyeballs.

"Thank you for the coffee."

"Drive safely, young lady."

THE NEXT MORNING Florence rose as usual at five-thirty for her five-mile run. On her way out, she saw that an envelope had been inserted under the door. She opened it and saw across the top page: FOR THE PRESIDENT'S EYES ONLY. The date was today's.

She read. The Kremlin was planning to use nerve gas on a Chechen stronghold. The president of Venezuela was . . . Florence's eyes widened. In the Sea of Japan, a U.S. submarine was shadowing a North Korean freighter thought to be carrying . . . Jesus. And yet there was no way of knowing whether the document was a fake. She regretted, like so many who have rubbed the lamp, having thrown away a perfectly good wish.

Two days later, she picked up her morning newspaper and saw the headline:

NAVY INTERCEPTS JAPAN-BOUND
NORTH KOREAN FREIGHTER
CARRYING NUCLEAR DEVICE

An hour later, while she was still digesting this along with her bran muffin, her phone rang. It was Uncle Sam.

"Could you make your second wish just a tad easier?"

"All right," she said. "Ten million dollars in Wasabi gold sovereigns."

"You'll give them back, yes?"

"Maybe."

The next afternoon there was a knock on her door. She looked out the peephole and saw a FedEx man with three large boxes on a hand dolly.

"Farfaletti? Sign here, please. They're kind of heavy."

Florence was in her living room staring at piles of gleaming gold Wasabi sovereigns bearing the royal crest when the phone rang. Uncle Sam.

"FedEx. Nice touch, don't you think?"

"All right," she said. "I'm convinced."

"Don't you want your third wish?"

"Why don't I save that."

"*That's* a relief. I thought you might ask for a nuclear warhead. You're a very demanding young lady. Welcome aboard."

"Aboard what, exactly?"

"Don't ask, don't tell. All you need to know is that you now have the best job in the United States government. No Charlie Duckett looking over your shoulder, no endless reports and memos and all that razzmatazz. No inspector generals, no Senate committees. Anything you need to do the job, you just ask your uncle. Within reason, please. I don't want to be getting bills from Maserati or Chanel or Van Cleef and Arpels, thank you very much."

"What *part* of the government am I working for?"

"The Department of Outside the Box."

"Come on. I want to know."

"Young lady, you've been handed the ultimate credit card. Why question it?"

"What if I'm caught?"

"Well"—he chuckled—"exactly my point. Not to make light of it."

"For a second there, you sounded like Satan."

"Satan? That's a terrible thing to say. I'm one of the nicest people you'll ever meet."

"Why me?"

"It was your idea, wasn't it? You know the language. The region."

"So do a lot of people."

"It's a vendetta. You're Italian."

"I'd file a discrimination complaint, if I knew where to find you."

"Oh, all right—you're passionate to emancipate women throughout the Arab world. As a means toward achieving lasting political stability in the region. Does that assuage your outraged ethnic pride?"

"It's a start."

"I'll pin ten dollars on the Virgin Mary at the next wop street fair I come across."

"That will cost you twenty bucks."

"For someone whose grandfather helped Benito Mussolini try to conquer North Africa, you pack plenty of attitude, young lady. All right, let's talk about your team."

CHAPTER FOUR

Rick Renard had learned his trade under the best—or worst, depending on where you set the bar integrity-wise—public relations man in the business: Nick Naylor. Naylor had gained notoriety as chief spokesman for the U.S. tobacco industry during its last Herculean struggle against the armies of neo-puritanism. He ended up serving a twenty-month sentence in a federal prison—minimum security, he would point out as a matter of pride—for allegedly arranging his own kidnapping by anti-smoking terrorists. Now Naylor ministered in the rich loamy pastures of Hollywood, tending to the vanities of the celluloidariat, a type of client whose needs could never be met and thus guaranteed lifetime employment. Lobbying to get your client nominated for an Oscar, or planting a prejudicial item in the gossips about the spouse currently being dumped, was not, Nick confided to his protégé, the heroic stuff of Washington lobbying, yet it was pleasant enough in L.A.'s balmy, moisturized clime. Whenever he reached Nick on his cell phone, Rick could hear the soft, high-pitched whine of German automotive engineering idling on the freeway. "I spent a hundred and twenty thousand on this car," Nick would say. "And do you know, it can go from zero to four miles per hour in twenty minutes."

Nick had been trying to persuade Renard to come join him. The money! The pools! The women! But Rick was not yet ready to surrender to those blandishments, to have his still-sharp edge be filed down by pedicurists in striped cabanas by turquoise rooftop pools. He had apprenticed well under Nick Naylor. At this point in his career, he was acknowledged by even the most grudging of his peers to be the capital's premier champion of causes so devoid of hope, so lacking in integrity, there was a kind of gallantry to it that aspired to the level of grandeur.

For instance, it was to Renard that the American College of Princes of the Church had turned, hoping to put behind it—to use an apposite word—the altar-boy-groping scandals. They had quietly engaged him to get an American cardinal elected pope. Rick did not succeed at this quest. Being arrested by the Swiss Guard, escorted to the limits of Vatican City and barred ever from reentering the holy city cannot be said to constitute a public relations triumph, especially when the next pope hailed from Madagascar. And yet he succeeded at changing the conversation back home. No longer were pallid, twitchy former altar boys and their posse of expensive lawyers Topic A.

But it was Renard's handling of another steaming-hot religious tuber that had gotten Florence's attention.

A year before, the Reverend Roscoe G. Holybone—"the G stands for God," as his literature humbly put it—spiritual leader of several hundred thousand devout and fanatically devoted Southern Baptists, declared from his televised pulpit in Loblolly, Georgia, that the prophet Mohammed was a "degenerate." It was the consensus, even among the stiffer evangelical element, that the Reverend had gone off his meds, but this was scant comfort to the prophet's 1.5 billion followers. Fatwas were issued from a hundred minarets, which seemed only to inflame the Reverend Holybone and his minions, who, like mailed crusaders on the parapets of Acre, responded with burning pitch and missiles, shouting defiance.

This hugger-mugger took place inconveniently in the middle of a presidential primary race. This required all the various candidates to spend precious airtime denouncing the Reverend instead of detailing their bold visions for America's future. Events reached a crescendo when the governor of Georgia was forced into the unenviable position of having to call out the National Guard to protect Reverend Holybone, who had responded to the latest assaults on his person by barricading himself inside his $12 million Holybone Tabernacle with a die-hard remnant of acolytes, fearsomely armed.

Into this radioactive swamp, few public relations types would dare to wade. Yet only hours after the Reverend's helicopter was brought down by a shoulder-fired missile, there was Rick Renard on practically every TV channel, issuing statements on behalf of the Reverend's heirs, calling for an end to hostilities and for the healing to begin; moreover, pledging $5 million to build a Baptist-Muslim intercultural center on the campus of Holybone University, featuring five basketball courts, each facing east for spontaneous midgame prayer. Today relations between Holyboners and Georgia's admittedly not numerous Muslims are immeasurably more tranquil than during the Days of Rage. Credit for that went not only to whoever had fired the fatal SA-7 at the Reverend's chopper, but also to the deft spinnings of Rick Renard. A man as fearless as that, Florence thought, she wanted on her team.

THE OFFICES OF Renard Strategic Communications International were two blocks from Washington's Dupont Circle, far enough from K Street to be geographically distinct from that porcine corridor—oinking trough, some might say—of American enterprise, and yet close enough so that Rick could have lunch with his friends and soul mates who worked there.

Florence had made the appointment, stating only over the phone that she represented a "significant institutional client." No sweeter syllables existed to a PR man's ear. Renard went through the motions of pretending that he was all booked up that day, then pretended to spot a cancellation. Why, he could see her that very afternoon.

Upon walking into his office, she saw that he had dispensed with the customary Washington Wall of Ego, consisting of framed photographs of the politicians being offered for sale. The price of the politician was indicated by the size of the photo. If the photo showed the politician golfing with the lobbyist, or smoking a Cuban cigar, the client could expect a 10 percent surcharge, as the lobbyist and politician were quite chummy.

Instead, Florence saw behind Renard's desk a floor-to-ceiling mural. It was a version of a famous *New Yorker* magazine cover showing that the world west of New York City was rather small and not really worth bothering with. In this case, the boundary waters were the Potomac River. Beyond it, where the Pacific

Northwest would normally be, was the word MICROSOFT. Beyond the Pacific Ocean was a land labeled SONY. A lobbyist's *tour d'horizon*. Of course, neither of these corporate titans was a Renard client, nor in all likelihood would either ever be. His clients by and large lurked in the shadows rather than the bright sunlight. This was hardly cause for shame, for his profession knew none and acknowledged even less.

A row of clocks mounted on the wall indicated the time in various world capitals. This was intended to proclaim Renard Strategic Communications International's global reach. It might be four A.M. in Jakarta, but that fact would not be lost here at world headquarters.

All this Florence took in as Rick Renard rose, smiling, to greet her.

"Ms. Farfaletti," he said, as though it were the most important name in the world. He tried not to stare, but his eyes couldn't help lingering on the unexpected loveliness before him. She reminded him of whatwashisname, the Italian painter—he really must remember the names, it always impressed a certain type of client—Modig-something, the one who painted women with their heads slightly cocked to one side, looking like they were asking the painter, "Won't you *please* have sex with me?" Sometimes they were nude, which made Renard wish he'd been there in the studio when the paint was still wet.

"Mr. Renard?"

"Sorry. You reminded me of someone. Have we met, Ms. Farfaletti?"

"No. But I'm a great admirer of your work."

"Farfaletti. That would that be . . ."

"Finnish."

Renard smiled. Always smile when a prospective client makes a joke. "I would have said Danish."

"It means little butterfly. More or less. In Italian."

"Is that your married name?"

"No, Mr. Renard."

"So, how can I be of service? You said over the phone it involves the Middle East." Rick gestured somewhat grandiosely toward his Wall of Clocks. One gave the time in Dubai. "We maintain offices throughout the region."

"Mr. Renard"—Florence smiled—"you have mail drops 'throughout the region.' Post office boxes. I'd hardly call them offices."

Rick blushed. "Modern communications these days, you don't really need offices. Per se. But I assure you we're wired in that part of the world. Just this morning I was on the phone to Dubai."

"Really? And what did Dubai have to say?"

"Of course, I can't talk about specific clients. But I think it's fair to say that the situation is far from terrific. Well, what *is* terrific in that part of the world?"

"Are you still working for the government of North Korea?"

"No, Ms. Farfaletti. That was just one project. And it was before the Japanese thing."

"The launching-the-missile-at-Japan thing?"

Renard cleared his throat. "I am not currently in a business relationship with the government of North Korea."

" 'Field of Screams.' Isn't that what the newspapers called it?"

"I was unaware that the golf course in question had been built with so-called slave labor." Rick sighed. "Slavery's a subjective term, isn't it?"

"Not especially."

"They asked to put on a celebrity pro-am golf tournament. To promote international peace understanding. At the time I thought, *Why not?* Would I do it again?" Rick shrugged. "Probably not. But my job is not to make judgments on clients. My job, as I conceive it, is to help them get their message across. This is the strategic part of strategic planning. Now"—he smiled—"did you come here to talk about golf in North Korea?"

"No. I came because I want to bring about permanent stability in the Middle East."

"Hmm." Renard nodded pensively, as if he had been asked for his thoughts on promoting a new brand of toothpaste. "And what sort of budget did you have in mind?"

"Money would not be a factor. Within reason, of course."

"In my experience, Ms. Farfaletti, 'within reason' is exactly where money becomes not only a factor but *the* factor."

Florence placed her briefcase on Rick's desk and smartly snapped open the spring-operated clasps. Inside were two bricks of crisp new thousand-dollar bills. She placed them on his desk.

Renard tried not to drool. "You said you were with . . ."

"The United States government."

"Oh."

"Do you always sound that disappointed when a client places two hundred thousand dollars in cash on your desk?"

"No, no. My inner child is definitely doing somersaults. What sort of 'permanent stability in the Middle East' are we talking about? And may I ask, what branch of our wonderful government do you represent?"

"The State Department."

"So, CIA. Wonderful. I'm a huge fan. Your colleagues were extremely helpful to me over there in North Korea when the mine exploded on the golf course."

"I didn't say I was with the CIA, Mr. Renard."

"No, you didn't. So I would be working for the State Department. Umhum."

"You understand the confidential nature of all this."

"Ms. Farfaletti, here at Renard Strategic Communications, discretion rules."

"That's very reassuring, Mr. Renard."

"Well"—Renard smiled and picked up the bricks of cash, tossing them playfully into the air—"I've always wanted to give something back to my country."

"It's a pleasure dealing with such a patriot, Mr. Renard."

"When your country calls, I mean, you pick up the phone, right?"

CHAPTER FIVE

Florence and the curious person who called himself Uncle Sam had been sequestered in a small safe house in Alexandria, Virginia, for two days, going through personnel files. The house was normally used to debrief, or entertain, defectors. To judge from the acrid reek of old cigarette smoke, the defectors must all have died of lung cancer.

They examined the files on Uncle Sam's laptop computer, which appeared to have the most intimate access to the files of U.S. government intelligence officers and covert operators. Whatever doubts Florence might have had about Uncle Sam, he was certainly wired.

"What if you left the laptop on a bus?"

"I don't ride buses," he sniffed.

"Then what if someone took it from you? Would they be able to access all this?"

Uncle Sam sighed. "Anyone who turned this machine on without pressing the right sequence of keys would find himself in a very unhappy position."

"You mean it would explode?"

"Yes, Florence. Now what about this one," he said as another file popped onto the screen. "He was station chief in Karachi. Military background. Might be just the ticket."

Florence scrolled through the file. "No," she said.

"What's wrong with him?"

"I want someone with a grudge."

"Bias, you mean. How many times do I have to point out—*everyone* hates Wasabis."

"You're the one who's biased."

"They're so eminently detestable. You should know. You married one."

Florence wasn't inclined to tell Uncle Sam that she didn't want anyone he recommended. He'd made a fuss over her choice of Rick Renard. "What is this, the Dirty Dozen?" She put her foot down. This was either going to be her team or not. "Let's keep looking."

Uncle Sam groaned. "How many files have we *been* through?"

"If you're bored, why don't you go for a walk? Leave this here with me."

"You'd only blow yourself up. Heavens to Betsy, are you looking to make a purchase, or just browsing?"

Finally, he went upstairs to lie down, leaving Florence to scroll the personnel files of America's armies of the night. They began to blur. Then she realized that she was hunting according to looks. An hour into this phase of the search, she stopped scrolling.

He was in his army uniform, the black beret tipped jauntily over his forehead. Florence examined the ribbons on his chest and looked again at the face. She could tell right away, without reading any further, that he was a southerner. He looked pleased with himself, as though the night before, he had nailed the homecoming queen on the Astroturf in the back of his Ford pickup, under the stars. Or maybe he was pleased with his decorations. She checked his place of birth, and there it was: Mobile, Alabama. The photograph had been taken twelve years ago. She scrolled in search of a more recent photograph and found it. The grin was gone. She read the file and saw why. No longer the young eager warrior. Yes, this one.

"I've found him," she announced to Uncle Sam as he returned.

He scanned the file. "Good Lord, he's completely unsuitable."

"That's why I want him."

"Young lady, I am not running a dating service here."

"I'll try to keep my hands off him. I have to say, why is a sexist pig like yourself interested in women's emancipation?"

"Look at this file." Uncle Sam snorted. "I'm surprised he's even still in government employ. Did it escape your notice that he's the one who called in that cruise missile strike in Dar es Salaam last year—the one that destroyed the residence of the Indonesian ambassador?"

"No, I happened to note that," Florence replied. "And it was a good target."

"Florence, the secretary of state had to personally apologize to the Indonesian prime minister."

"You're starting to sound like my boss. So what if the secretary of state had to apologize to the Indonesian prime minister. The strike destroyed a Qaeda chem-weap plant. They put it put it right next to the ambassador's residence, disguised as a 'children's prosthetic limb factory.' Good for him for calling in the strike. And shame on us for making him take the fall for it, just because some grandstanding senator running for president decided to make an issue of it. Sometimes I think the U.S. capitol is a giant Jell-O mold."

Uncle Sam sighed dramatically and scrolled. "What about this? When he was station chief in Matar, he had an affair with the wife of the U.S. ambassador. What does that tell us?"

"That he was horny. That sort of thing goes on all the time."

"Not in my day. Not in my shop."

"It's of less importance that he was doing the Macarena with the ambassador's wife than that he was station chief in Matar. He must have the place wired seven ways from Sunday. Look at his file. Station chief Amo-Amas, three years. Deputy chief Kaffa, two years. Fluent in Arabic and French. Look at these terrorist renditions. He's the one who got Adnan Bahesh, arguably the worst human being on the planet. He's the one who found out that Saddam Hussein was plotting to assassinate Bush in '93. Look at his chest. Three Bronze Stars, two Purple Hearts. *This* isn't good enough for you?" Florence closed the lid of the laptop, slid it away from her and crossed her arms over her bosom. "Search over."

"Fine. Fine," Uncle Sam said poutily. "But listen here, young lady, it would be disastrous to this entire operation if you had a personal liaison with this man."

"I'm not even going to dignify that with an answer."

"He's a southerner. It's all they think about—sex. And stock-car racing."

"I take it your ancestors came over on the *Mayflower,* or did they arrive earlier, with the Vikings?"

"May I suggest that you save some of this righteous indignation for when you get over there?"

THERE WAS ONE last person to recruit, and he would be the hardest. He arrived at the Alexandria safe house at the appointed time on the dot. He was always prompt.

"Firenze? What is all this? Oh my God, it's *foul* in here."

George looked around the apartment, which had been furnished by some color-blind gnome who worked in a subdivision of a subdivision of a sub-bureaucracy whose job was to furnish and decorate safe houses for U.S. intelligence agencies. The paintings, if they could be called that, had been bulk-purchased at Wal-Mart and were only one step removed aesthetically from paintings of bulldogs in visors playing poker.

George said, "I see you've been to Sotheby's."

"Do you want something to drink?"

"What are you pouring? Wine in a box? Malt liquor?"

"George, you and I together are going to accomplish something really big. Really, really big."

"Can I think it over? No."

"Don't you want to hear about it?"

"Not particularly. Is this where we stash the North Korean defectors? So they'll feel at home?"

Florence explained, insofar as it could be explained, about Uncle Sam, the PDB, the $10 million in gold, the operation, the carte blanche, the fact that he had been able to pull the strings that got George himself reassigned. George listened with deepening gloom, uttering dismissive grunts: "Um-um. Um-*um.*"

"George," she said, "do you remember the conversation we had about what if we were in charge for just ten minutes?"

"Vividly. You recall my saying that I didn't want to be in charge for ten minutes? I vant to be left alone, Firenze."

"Thank you, Greta Garbo. Is that why you joined the State Department?"

"You know perfectly well why I joined the State Department."

"Because of one remark by your mother at a Thanksgiving dinner?"

George's great-great-uncle was Adler Fillington Phish, the American diplomat, then ambassador to Bogotá, to whom President Theodore Roosevelt famously cabled in 1902: SECURE ISTHMUS BY CHRISTMUS. This led to the "secession" of Panama from Colombia, the building of the canal and the further enrichment beyond wild dreams of Cleveland industrialist Mark Hanna, New York financier J. P. Morgan and William Cromwell, founding partner of the law firm of Sullivan & Cromwell. The gilded trio later expressed their gratitude to Ambassador Phish by retaining him as counsel in numerous transactions, inaugurating the Phish family fortune.

By the time George arrived, four generations later, the family fortune had dwindled to Phish House, a once handsome redbrick Federal in Georgetown, now in dire need of maintenance. George's mother, Philippa Phish Tibbitts, had never gotten over the disappointment of not being richer, or the departure of her husband, Jameson "Bucky" Phish, for an Argentine polo player named Esteban, a close friend of the Kennedys', which only made it worse. She had been nursing these grievances for many years with increasing dosages of vodka (now mixed with buttermilk). One particularly gruesome Thanksgiving dinner, she announced in front of all the guests that George, seated at the table and as usual staring glumly into his mushroom soup—trying not to lunge across the table and concuss his mother with the silver tureen (a gift from the newly installed governor of Panama, and the last item of any real value remaining in Phish House)—that her son would never have "the gumption" to join the Foreign Service; moreover, that he would probably end up "arranging flowers for a living." George signed up for the Foreign Service exam the following Monday. Here he was, sixteen years later. It remained unclear who had won.

"George," Florence said, "you're one of the most brilliant men I know. You're wasted behind that desk. Look at this chance we've been handed. It'll never come this way again."

"You don't know the first thing about this Uncle Sam."

"Now you sound like *my* mother. It's a chance to make history. Never mind actually helping eight hundred million Muslim women."

"A lot of those women are perfectly content, you know. I'll bet half of them *like* wearing the veil and being put on a pedestal."

"Some pedestal. How would you like it?"

"Living in a society that considered me a second-class citizen and restricted my rights? Let me get back to you on that."

" 'All that is required for evil to succeed is for good men to do nothing.' Edmund Burke."

" 'If you run away, you live to run away another day.' Mel Brooks."

"I can't do this without you, George. It's going to be fun."

"No. It's going to be a nightmare. And I'm going to be in it."

HANDS ON HER HIPS, Florence studied her dinner table. Uncle Sam had proposed the Alexandria safe house for the first group meeting, but she'd decided instead to cook them a good Italian meal at her little house in Foggy Bottom. She wasn't sure what the chemistry would be among them, but she did know there are few occasions in life that can't be improved by a delicious dinner of bresaola, risotto—crawfish and fava beans, her own recipe—chocolate-raspberry tiramisu, espresso and bottle after bottle of Barolo. She wore a black cashmere turtleneck, pearl stud earrings, toreador pants, heels and a flouncy apron that made her look even sexier, in a 1950s way.

The first one to arrive was Bobby Thibodeaux, the CIA guy. He rang the bell five minutes before eight. CIA people always show up early. They like to be in control of the situation. George arrived punctually at eight. Rick Renard arrived twenty minutes late, complaining of having been made so by a congressman "who wouldn't shut up."

Florence served flutes of iced Prosecco. The three men faced one another awkwardly. She found herself watching Bobby Thibodeaux's face as he took in his two new colleagues.

Bobby was in his late thirties, powerfully built, with short blond hair and hooded eyes that gave him a skeptical expression just shy of cool hostility. He moved economically, as if conserving his energy. His first word to her was "ma'am." She greeted him in Arabic and suppressed a smile when he returned her "Salaam" with an Alabama accent. He caught her look. He was not the sort of person on whom anything was lost. Florence found herself blushing.

"Well," she said, holding out her glass of Prosecco and clinking it against theirs in turn. "To Aqaba."

"Aqaba?" Renard said.

George and Bobby looked at him. Bobby said, "You'd be the PR guy?"

"Strategic communications," Rick said.

A mirthless grin crossed Bobby's face. He turned to George. "So, would you be with the *State* Department?" CIA people overseas tended to refer to State Department personnel as "embassy pukes."

Florence thought she'd better jump in. "I've been to Aqaba. It's quite lovely and cool. The king of Jordan maintains a small palace there."

"Where you been posted?" Bobby asked George.

"I've been here, actually."

Bobby's eyes drooped. "How long you been with State?"

"Sixteen years."

"You been in Washington for sixteen years?"

"Sixteen and a half."

Bobby turned to Renard. "How long you been strategically communicatin'?"

"I've had my own firm for four years," Rick said.

"You spent much time in the Middle East?"

"I get to Dubai pretty regularly."

"What d'ya think of the new airport?"

George tried to catch Rick's eye.

"It's . . . nice. Fine."

Bobby grinned.

"What's so funny?"

"There is no new airport in Dubai," George said.

"Shall we eat?" Florence said.

The Barolo and risotto with crawfish and fava beans took some of the edge off. George helped Florence clear the main course and, in the kitchen, whispered to her, "Where did you find him? Killers R Us? His knuckles touch the floor."

"We need him."

"You know he's the one who called in that cruise missile strike in Dar?"

"It was a good target."

"I'm all for bombing foreign ambassadors, but just because some redneck thinks he smells paint thinner . . ."

"George, it was a Qaeda chem-weap factory."

"Whatever. I think we'd better have another bottle of wine."

"Get back in there and protect Renard."

"He walked right into that one. A hit man from Dogpatch, a PR hack and a queer Foreign Service officer. Quite the A-Team you've assembled, Firenze. They'll be writing ballads about us, and thank God I'll be dead."

Florence came in with another bottle of Barolo.

Bobby was telling Rick, "In Vietnam, Navy SEALs, when they'd killed a VC cadre, they'd cut out the liver, take a bite out of it and throw it down by the body. According to Buddhist theology, you can't enter heaven unless you're whole. Put a major freak on 'em."

Rick paled and put down his knife and fork.

"You gonna finish that?" Bobby said.

"Uh, no."

"Mind?" Bobby took Rick's plate. He said to Florence, "This is quite excellent, ma'am. I never had bugs with risotto before."

"Bugs?"

"Crawfish, where I come from."

"Why don't you call me Florence?"

"Florence. Okay. Florence of Arabia."

"Just Florence will do." She raised her glass. "So, to Aqaba, then?"

Bobby raised his glass. "What the hell. To Aqaba."

"It's a metaphor," George said to Rick. "It means we're going to die before we get there."

" 'If the camels die, we die,' " Bobby quoted. "And the camels will start to die in twenty days."

CHAPTER SIX

The emirate of Matar (pronounced, for reasons unclear, "Mutter") consists of a ten-mile-wide, 350-mile-long strip of sand that runs along the western coast of the Gulf of Darius. Its northern boundary begins in the mosquito marshes of the Um-Katush. From there it runs on a generally southeastern course for several hundred miles, to the Straits of Xerxes, where it curves gently westward until it terminates at Alfatoosh, on the sparkling shore of the Indian Ocean.

Viewed on a large-scale map, Matar seems an illogical political entity, like so many American congressional districts, whose contorted outlines are the result of successive attempts to maximize incumbencies and to inconvenience challengers. One might suspect, contemplating Matar's bizarre physical configuration, that its borders had been drawn so as to deprive its much larger neighbor to the west, the Royal Kingdom of Wasabia, of access to the sea. One would be correct.

The account of Matar's creation is described in David Vremkin's magisterial history of the creation of the modern Middle East, *Let's Put Iraq Here, and Lebanon Over Here: The Making of the Modern Middle East:*

> Churchill was furious with the French, in this case with reason, as they had been carrying on separate negotiations with [Wasabi king] Tallulah over the matter of saltwater ports. By the time the conference convened,

he was in no mood to dither with the French foreign minister, Delavall-Pootriere. He had stayed up until five in the morning with Colonel Lawrence, Glandsbury and Tuff-Blidget, as well as Jeremy Pitt, miserable from the heat and another attack of gout. The next morning, as everyone filed in, Bosquet and Gaston Tazie both noticed that Tuff-Blidget's fingers were green, blue, yellow and magenta and signaled frantically to the French delegates. Too late. By the time the fifty participants had taken their places around the green felt table in the Great Hall of Sala-al-din at Majma Palace, the British had their maps drawn and ready. The ink, Chomondeley observed, was "quite dry."

Siggot, Sykes's majordomo (who, two years later, would be killed during a freak tea-pouring accident at Kensington Palace with Queen Alexandra), described the sound of "Winnie unrolling his map over the conference table" as "like a suddenly unfurled topgallant sail snapping in a twenty-knot freshet off Cowes." Vivid indeed. Realizing what was happening, Delavall-Pootriere tried to object on procedural grounds, but Churchill, pointing his cigar at the Frenchman "like a half-eaten breakfast banger," threatened to extend the Balfour Declaration, which provided for the establishment of a Jewish homeland in Palestine, into Lebanon and Syria—that is, well into the French sphere of influence.

The last thing the French wanted, Fleg-Wright noted in his cable that morning to Arthur Glenwoodie, was "wave after wave of irrendentist kibbutzim mucking about the Levant." Such a move would also have the effect of pitting the British branch of the Rothschild family against the French branch, which for some time had been eyeing the western slopes of the Bekáa and Noosh valleys as potential vineyards for experimental sauvignon noir grapes. Delavall-Pootriere could do nothing. He had been outmaneuvered.

King Tallulah, livid over seeing his promised coastline vanish with several strokes of the British cartographical pen, denounced the conference as a "gathering of jackals and toads" ("*jamaa min etheeab w eddafadeah*"), stormed out of the hall and left Damascus with his bodyguard of two hundred Bedou and Hejazi. Picot observed to Gastin-Piquet, "*Sa majeste est bien fromagee*" ("The king is well cheesed").

For his part, Gazir Bin Haz, the plump, pleasure-loving minor sharif of the Wazi-had—traders and fishermen along the Darian littoral since the time of Alexander—now found himself emir of a territory that effectively blocked Wasabia from getting its oil to the sea. This had, of course, been Churchill's plan all along. What better way to repay King Tallulah for his obduracy over the proposed tariff on unpitted dates, to say nothing of the endless arguments over who should enter Damascus first, and wearing what?

That night over brandy and cigars in the billiard room at the British Legation, Churchill told Glandsbury that he could not decide which had given him more pleasure, thwarting Delavall-Pootriere or "forcing that royal ass Tallulah to drink his own oil."

KING TALLULAH WAS LEFT with no choice but to cut a deal with the emir of Matar. Wasabia built its first pipeline through Matar to the Gulf shortly after the signing of the treaty. Over the years, a dozen more pipelines followed. Wasabia simply had no other means of getting its oil to market.

The Emirate of Matar prospered magnificently from this steady black income stream through its territory. The emirs never released official figures, but annual revenues from the so-called courtesy fees paid by Wasabia into successive Bin Haz exchequers were, by the end of the century, estimated to run annually to the tens of billions of dollars. The Bin Haz dynasty continued to maintain the official face-saving fiction that the country's extraordinary wealth derived from fig oil, dates, fishing and tourism.

This last assertion was in some ways the boldest, given Matar's fierce sandstorms and average summer temperature of 115 degrees Fahrenheit. Matar could, however, legitimately boast that part of its abundant gross domestic product came from gambling. The present emir had developed Infidel Land, a complex of hotels, casinos and theme parks on an offshore archipelago accessible by a ten-mile-long causeway. Matari residents were (officially) not allowed to cross the causeway and take part in the gaming—and collateral activities—but this law was rarely observed and never enforced. The emir had decreed it as a bit of window dressing for the local mullahs.

His handling of Matar's religious authorities had been, by unanimous consent, masterful. Matari mullahs were the best fed in the Muslim world. Indeed, they were so prosperous that they had acquired the local nickname of "moolahs." They received a generous salary from the state, luxury apartments, a new Mercedes-Benz every three years and an annual six-week paid sabbatical, which most of them chose to take in the South of France, one of Islam's holiest sites.

As a result of the emir's attentions in this area, Matar was a veritable oasis of tolerance. Its mullahs were among the most contented and laissez-faire of their faith. As one scholar put it, "Here, truly, is Islam with a happy face." Clerical careers were avidly sought in Matar, and strictly regulated.

This approach to matters religious stood in starkest contrast with that across the border in Wasabia. After Sheik Abdulabdullah "The Wise" came into power in 1740 (or 1742), he struck a deal with Mustafa Q'um, imam of the Nejaz, to consolidate his power throughout the territory. Mustafa preached an extremely austere version of Islam called *mukfellah*. Abdulabdullah agreed to make *mukfellah* the official religion of all Wasabia, if Mustafa would pledge his allegiance to the Hamooj dynasty. Thus Wasabia united under one rule.

Alas, this doomed Wasabia to becoming—as one historian put it—the Middle East's preeminent "no-fun zone." Unless, as he dryly noted, "one's idea of fun includes beheading, amputation, flogging, blinding and having your tongue cut out for offenses that in other religions would earn you a lecture from the rabbi, five Hail Marys from a priest and, for Episcopalians, a plastic pink flamingo on your front lawn." A Google search using the key phrases "Wasabia" and "La Dolce Vita" results in no matches.

This disparity in religious temperament, added to the matter of the national border, made relations between the two countries predictably strained. King Tallulah's successors chafed over having to pay Matari emirs the so-called Churchill tax.

In 1957, King Talubadullah, Tallulah's grandson, threatened to seize a twenty-mile-long strip of Matar on the almost ostentatiously flimsy grounds that Caliph Ibn Izzir (1034–1078 C.E.), a very remote Hamooj ancestor, had established a summer fishing camp there. He went so far as to move a tank division up to the Wasabi-Matar border, and to dispatch Royal Wasabi Air Force

Mirage fighter jets (supplied by Wasabia's great friend France) to fly "maneuvers" along the disputed area. This caused a few days of anxious hand-wringing at the United Nations, until the U.S. ambassador in Kaffa quietly told the Wasabi foreign minister to "cut it out."

The United States maintained good relations with Wasabia—the unthinkable alternative being to use less oil—but it had always supported Matar's sovereignty as a means of containing Wasabian power in the region. The old lion Churchill might have been drunk, but he was shrewd. The U.S. tilt toward Matar also had the advantage, as Henry Kissinger noted in *Years of Genius,* Volume XXI of his memoirs, "of driving the Wasabis nuts."

Wasabia periodically rattled its scimitar at Matar and threatened to push through to the sea, but these episodes were not taken seriously by the emirati. Protected by America, its economy guaranteed by Wasabi oil, the local religious fat, happy and uncensorious, Matar was the Switzerland of the Gulf. The only things it lacked were a Matterhorn and a chocolate-bar industry.

All in all, it was the ideal platform for Florence and her team. And there was this advantage: You could even order a drink at the bar.

CHAPTER SEVEN

F*lorence had given a great deal of thought to the emir's present.* It had to be expensive enough to get his attention, but she wanted it to be distinctive and conversation-starting, not just another gaudy bauble of gold to keep a drowsy emperor awake.

The emir was fond of hunting gazelle while sitting in a special seat mounted on the front of his Hummer. Bobby proposed a matched pair of gold-plated, engraved .30-06 rifles from Holland and Holland. George, who found the slaughter of gazelles grotesque, noted that the emir's gun collection already consisted of more than two hundred rifles. He counterproposed a twelfth-century edition of the Holy Koran that had been owned by the last sultan of Moorish Spain, bound in ivory and inlaid with Arabian sea pearls and Ceylonese emeralds—a steal at $3.4 million. Rick, ever with his eye on the PR aspect, said the fact that it had belonged to the *last* sultan of Spain could only prove awkward. Why not, he said, a private submarine that he had seen in the Sharper Image catalog? "Arabs like water, right? Bet they'd love the idea of being completely submerged in it." George complained that at $750,000, the sub wasn't nearly expensive enough for a man whose wealth ran to the tens of billions. There was some discussion about equipping the submarine with U.S. Navy torpedoes and missiles, to make it more exciting. Uncle Sam nixed that on the grounds that there were U.S. warships operating in the Gulf of Darius, and it wouldn't help matters if one of them accidentally identified the emir's sub as an enemy and destroyed it.

In the end, Florence decided on a helicopter. It was a civilian version of the U.S. Army Blackhawk, specially fitted out so the emir could sit in a 270-degree plexiglas turret in front of the pilots and shoot gazelles through an ingenious Mylar port. You can't be too thin, too rich, or own too many helicopters. The emir was delighted with his present, and Florence shortly received a summons to the royal palace in the capital city of Amo-Amas.

The four of them were registered at the Opulent, the city's nicest hotel, overlooking the harbor. The lights of the tankers lying at anchor twinkled in the distance. In Churchill Square, the large marble statue of Matar's patron glowed in the spotlights. The present emir's grandfather had erected it in the 1920s. The face bore an unmistakable smirk. The statue faced west, toward Wasabia.

They met in Florence's suite. George had managed to contract a stomach bug, no small feat, since most of the Opulent's room-service food was flown in daily from Paris. He sat clutching his bottle of Pepto-Bismol.

"Enjoyin' the Middle East so far, are you?" Bobby said.

"Why don't we start?" Florence said. "Are we all right having this conversation here?"

Bobby nodded. "Only bugs in here are the crawly kind."

George shuddered.

Bobby tapped at his laptop. A photograph of the emir projected onto the wall. He tapped another button, and up came a photograph of the emir's wife. Florence studied the image. The sheika was lovely, in her late thirties, fair-skinned, with intelligent eyes and a slightly disappointed expression.

Bobby tapped more buttons. Up on the wall came photograph after photograph of stunning women, which perhaps explained the sheika's look of disappointment.

"What's this, the Victoria's Secret catalog?" Rick said.

"A few of emir's special friends," Bobby said. "Mainly French and Italian. Lately, he seems to be inclinin' toward Russians. But he'll screw anythin', includin' the dog, if there's nothing else handy."

"Shall we try to keep it respectful?" Florence said. "Just in case the room is bugged?"

Bobby continued his brief. "His wife, the sheika Laila. Matari mother, English father. He was an engineer, worked on the pipelines. Made a ton of money. Married up, daughter of a well-to-do sharif. Laila, she was educated at Swiss schools, Lausanne. Went to Oxford. Bright girl. She had a nice TV career goin' in London, anchorin'—they call it presenting. Hung out with all the right people, includin' the royals. She and Prince Charles dated once or twice, but nothin' happened sackwise."

Rick said, "How do you know that?"

"I can't go into sources and methods. But hell, MI5, they got a whole section, all they do is analyze who the prince is bangin'. Movin' along—Laila, she fell in love with the then future emir, Gazzir Bin Haz, when he was on a visit to Royal Ascot. That's their big horse race."

"We know," George said.

"Never been, myself. Anyhow, he sort of swept her off her feet, literally. Dashing sort, scrubs up good when you put him in a top hat and tails. She had the right credentials, and he brought her back to Xanadu-on-the-Gulf and made her an Arab wife." Bobby looked over at Florence. "Happens."

"Go on, Bobby."

"Well, everythin' was jake connubial bliss–wise, for a while. They had a son together, Hamdul. Then, well, you know how it is, a man doesn't wanna eat at the same restaurant night after night. So he built himself a fuck palace—pardon, ma'am—a place down the coast, on the beach in Um-beseir. Got pretty much everything a man could ask for. Hell, we thought we were livin' high if we had some outdoor carpeting in the back of the pickup."

"Thank you for the cross-cultural reference," Florence said.

"Got a helipad and a three-thousand-foot runway, in case he's in such a hurry for the ladies that a helicopter isn't fast enough." Bobby chuckled. "Man, it's good to be the emir.

"Anyhow, the sheika, she's no idiot. She knows all about Um-beseir. In the past, she's been willing to do the thing a lot of wives do, look the other way, boys-will-be-boys. Part of it was that when she married Gazzir, knowin' he was gonna be emir once his old man croaked, she made him agree—in writing—

that he wouldn't take any more wives. This didn't play well with the local emirati and the moolahs. In this part of the world, you haven't amounted to much if you haven't left behind at least a hundred or so sons. That explains why they got forty thousand princes across the border in Wasabia. Hell, you can't spit in Wasabia without hittin' a crown prince. Not that they encourage spittin' on the royals. But he musta been in love, 'cause he went along with Laila's demand. Even got the head moolah to issue a theological ruling on it, which concluded—surprise—that it was *wargat.*"

"What does that mean?" Renard asked.

"Kosher."

"Why did she insist on monogamy?"

"Because she wanted her son to sit on the throne. A harem full of wives doesn't make for a real relaxed atmosphere. Historically, Arab wives were always lookin' over each other's shoulder, poisoning each other, poisoning each other's kid so that their own would succeed. Their son, Hamdul, he's now ten years old. But the recent development that's of particular interest to us is that Laila has put her foot down, finally, about all the bangin' and screwin' down at Um-beseir. She wants it to stop. Our information is that she's been makin' life quite difficult for Gazzir lately."

"Why?" Florence asked.

"This is sensitive information."

"We can handle it."

"There appear to be two factors. One, she's worried about gettin' a sexual disease from him. She's a very attractive woman, and every now and then the emir does get amorous with her. The second factor is that young Hamdul's gettin' to the age when he might pick up palace gossip. She doesn't want him to hear from some flunky that his dad can't keep his scimitar in his pants. So there it is."

"Thank you, Bobby," Florence said. "Extremely useful."

"Shouldn't we study this further before we proceed?" George said. His lower lip was crusted pink from dried Pepto-Bismol.

Bobby stared at him. "You mean spend six, seven months drawin' up a feasibility study? With lots of *tabs*?"

"Well, if you'd rather just rush in pell-mell . . ."

—

MATAR WAS LIBERAL in the matter of women's dress; nonetheless, Florence took care to observe the formalities. She wore a matching pantsuit of turquoise and purple shantung silk, and over her hair an Hermès scarf. According to Bobby, the emir liked to give these scarves to his mistresses. "If they've been good—really good—there'll be a diamond bracelet inside. And if they've been really, really good, a red Ferrari outside."

Florence was ushered into the audience room. The door was flanked by two bodyguards in ceremonial dress and swords.

"*Salaam alaikum,*" Florence said without accent. "*Sherefna, somow 'kum.*"

The emir's eyes brightened, and not just at his guest's flawless Arabic. He took her hand and bent and chastely kissed it. Florence blushed at the attention. She continued in Arabic, remembering that in Matar, conversation with the emir required use of the third-person address, not altogether easy for Americans, who want to call everyone "pal" or "bub" or "honey" after five minutes.

They sat. Florence noted that the Louis XVI chairs were a few inches lower than the emir's Louis XIV chair. At not quite five foot six, Emir Gazzir Bin Haz—"Gazzy" to his family and intimates—was not a tall man. Exactly the height, it occurred to Florence, of T. E. Lawrence. What large things small men have accomplished.

He was impeccably accoutred, in an immaculate white *thobe* garment, his head covered with a *gutra,* the triangular folded cloth tied with the traditional gold-rope *agal.* Four of his plump fingers, she observed, were adorned with rings. His goatee was perfectly trimmed, his lips oyster-moist from a lifetime's contact with the greatest delicacies the world had to offer, from caviar to Dom Perignon to foie gras. His face radiated contentedness; and why not? The Emir might just be the happiest camper on earth.

"Your Majesty is most welcoming," Florence said with a slight bow.

"It is a trait with us," he said, switching to English. He was, like most high-born Mataris, an Anglophile—they sent their future emirs to Sandhurst—and enjoyed displaying his excellent command of the language. "Even the humblest Matari will open his door to a stranger and share what he has." He smiled. "Not that you will *find* many humble Mataris, mind you. This, too, is a trait with us, I fear."

"Your country is truly blessed to have such abundance."

"Our fig oil is second to none."

"Justly famous throughout the world."

"It has many, many applications. Perfume, industrial—do you know that it is used as a lubricant on Chinese rockets?"

"I was not aware of this fact. But how marvelous."

The emir leaned forward intently. "It lowers cholesterol. Rather, it increases the *good* cholesterol. In time, the medical studies will establish this beyond question, God be praised."

"Matar is a river to the world."

They looked at each other.

"Shall we cease with the bullshitting?" He smiled.

"His Majesty is too gracious. I was about to run out of conversation about fig oil."

"I've never used it myself," the emir said, taking a cigarette from a gold box in front of him. A servant dressed to match the drapery appeared like a swift ghost. He lit the emir's cigarette and disappeared back into the folds with a soft rustle of silk. "Ghastly stuff. I prefer walnut oil, ground by four-hundred-year-old millstones in the Dordogne. I have it flown in. Anyway, who cares about cholesterol. I have my blood changed every month by Swiss doctors. I donate the old blood to the hospital. It is quite sought after, apparently. Now, Florence—and why don't I just call you that, since I am unable to wrap my tongue around all those pretty Tuscan vowels—you have given me a nice and, I must say, original present. I could show you an entire room filled with gifts I have received of the most *appalling* taste. The worst was a Monopoly game board done in twenty-four-karat gold, inlaid with rubies and diamonds and all manner of precious stones, with the little hotels and houses made of platinum, if you please. What did they expect me to do, melt it down? I know Arabs enjoy a reputation for vulgarity, but really. By the way, your Arabic is excellent. You are, I take it, with the government? Surely. In some capacity? CIA? It would be audacious of them to send a woman. Would they have such imagination? I think not. In the past, when your country has wanted something—and my dear, they *always* want something—the gifts have been . . . I don't mean to sound ungrateful, but dear, dear, dear. The sort of thing that God—praise be upon His name—would buy if he shopped at Wal-Mart. We are about to have a Wal-Mart here. *Such* excitement. Once I was offered a briefcase full of cash. Cash!" He giggled, waving a hand about the room, which looked as though everything in it had been dipped in gold, twice. "Do I look as though I need *cash*? So"—his eyes narrowed a bit, showing Florence a glimpse of the hard-eyed coastal trader of yore—"who are you, lovely lady? And without seeming rude, what do you want?"

This bluntness was un-Arabic. Had she put a foot wrong?

"Your Majesty favors me with his directness. I have come to ask your permission to approach the sheika Laila with a business proposition."

The emir grimaced. His face, a caramel pudding in repose, suddenly looked quite fierce. "Business proposal? The *sheika*? You've not come to ask her to endorse some product?"

"No, *soomoow el-amir.*"

"A cause? A children's disease? Let me guess. Land mines. All the beautiful women, they are against *land mines*. We don't have any here, I am happy to say. Though there have been times when I confess I would gladly plant them like flowers along my borders. But the gazelles might step on them. And we would rather shoot the gazelles, would we not? From our lovely new helicopter. *So* generous. Indeed, I wonder, what have we done to merit such . . . generosity?"

"I am pleased that His Majesty is pleased. But no, I do not seek the sheika's endorsement on behalf of any skin cream or disease or against land mines. We would like to start a satellite television station here in Matar, and have her be in charge of it."

The emir stared. "You do take us by surprise. I thought this was going to be about oil. It usually is, one way or the other. Last week some Americans were here from Texas. So often they are from Texas, or Okla-*ho*-ma. One yearns to meet Americans from other parts of the country. Where are you from?"

"A part with trees, Majesty."

"How very lucky for you. Television, you say. The sheika. I hardly think—"

"With His Majesty's permission, I would show him some numbers."

"No, no. The emir does not deal with numbers. There are ministers for that, for every kind of number."

"They are interesting numbers, lord. They suggest that there are vast sums to be made. But I will take them to the ministers, as His Majesty commands."

"How do you mean, 'vast'? The desert is vast. The ocean is vast."

"In the neighborhood of two billion dollars per year, my lord."

"That's not half vast."

Florence handed the emir the single sheet of paper she had prepared.

"What sort of programming?" he asked.

"The figures are based on targeting a female audience, my lord."

The emir screwed up his face. "*Female?*"

"They are the ones who do the shopping. Who make the purchases."

"I suppose. Who has the time but the women. But there are already two Arabic channels, Al Jazeera and Al Arabiya. I will say, in case you *are* with the CIA, that I am not in sympathy with either of their political points of view. Every time I turn them on, there is Osama sitting in front of his cave looking in dire need of a new kidney. But then one can always"—he pressed the button on an imaginary remote control—"see what is on the History Channel. There is always another documentary on Hitler. They really ought to call it the Hitler Channel. But why the sheika?"

"Many reasons, lord. First, she is the sheika, the first lady of Matar, a respected personage of reputation and authority. Second, she has experience in television."

"Yes," the emir said, as if warming to the concept, "she was *very* successful in London. Until she gave it up to marry a raghead!"

Florence smiled noncommittally.

"But a very nice rag. Go on. You have our attention."

"Third, we of course require a Matari partner in this enterprise, since by law, Mataris must own fifty-one percent of any business operating here. These three factors make the sheika a natural person to lead our venture."

"Who is 'we'? Who are *you?*"

"I am merely a television producer. This project is my concept. With an enterprise of this size, one has backers, investors. But we are prepared to give to you—"

"To the people of Matar, you mean."

"Fifty-one percent ownership."

"Um."

"Shall we say fifty-five percent?"

"My hearing is not what it used to be. The years of shooting gazelle . . ."

"Sixty percent?"

"I think I heard you say seventy."

"Sixty-five."

"Let us say two thirds, sixty-six. So much easier on the accountants."

"So it is done."

"And the sheika's role, she would be, what, ornamental?"

"On the contrary. It is our hope that she would become very much involved. It was this part that worried me in presenting the plan to His Majesty."

"How so?"

"I fear that we might be, well, taking her away from you. Starting a television station can be a very consuming enterprise. But very fulfilling."

"Ah. Well, that is for her to decide."

"His Majesty's reputation as an enlightened man and husband does not do him justice."

"We are not a backward people, Ms. Farfaletti. Unlike some in the region. I shall present your proposal to the sheika. I must say, I have mixed feelings, for is it not written that a man who makes his wife queen ends up washing the dishes himself?"

"But is it not also written, sire, that a man who gives his wife an occupation creates for himself an oasis?"

"I'm not sure what part of scripture we're both quoting, but you may have something there, Ms. Farfa—Florence. Now, if you will excuse me, my next audience is upon me. You see that an emir's life is not all fig oil."

"I hardly see how His Majesty manages at all."

CHAPTER EIGHT

Word arrived the next morning at the Opulent that the sheika Laila would receive Florence that same day for tea.

Florence felt oddly more nervous about this meeting than she had about the interview with Emir Gazzir. Perhaps it was because she had spent so much time going over Bobby's file. She felt she'd been prying indecently into the woman's life. She felt—yes, that was it—guilty. It was one thing to try to pull the wool over the eyes of a plump born-lucky potentate with the nickname of Gazzy, and another to deceive his long-suffering wife. All for a good cause, but still, Florence felt a kinship with the woman. They were both bright women who been swept away by princes to go live in sand castles. Florence's had simply crumbled first.

Bobby's briefing on Laila was appalling in its detail. It spoke well of the CIA's detail-gathering, but—really.

"No, no, I don't want to know that," she said after Bobby began to explain the circumstances under which Laila, at age seventeen, had lost her virginity: on a school trip, in Paris, to a guide at the Louvre. "It's just not relevant, and it's none of my or anyone's business."

"It's all business," Bobby said. "You never know what detail's gonna be the one saves you." He put the dossier down on her desk. "I'd seriously suggest you read this file in its entirety. Ma'am." And with that, he walked out.

She sought out George, who had recovered somewhat from his stomach distress. "Why do I feel like such a shit reading this?" she asked.

"I guarantee you feel better than I do. I don't want to agree with Attila the Hun, but he's probably got a point. Plus, I'm dying to find out if she lost her virginity in the Louvre."

"I'll let you read it yourself."

THAT AFTERNOON FLORENCE was ushered into the cool terrace of the sheika's apartment at the palace, overlooking an aqua stretch of beach. A hundred yards offshore, fountains shot seawater into the air in a pattern roughly approximating the Bin Haz royal crest. It had the practical advantage of cooling the air on the seaward side of the palace, though it left one's skin a bit salty.

Laila rose to greet her guest. The chairs in this room of the palace, Florence noted, were all of the same height. The sheika was quite beautiful, though this is not an especially rare quality among wives of princes. She was thirty-seven, one of the more innocent facts Florence knew about her from Bobby's briefing. She was taller than her husband, a fact accentuated by the three-inch heels she wore, in contrast to the normally slippered feet of Arab women. She had superb cheekbones, a fine nose and peregrine-falcon eyes. She could have been a model—in fact, she had been during a college summer, more to annoy her parents than for the money. She wore a silk pantsuit from Paris and the merest white chiffon scarf that set off her abundant dark hair. Around her neck was the simplest gold necklace. On her finger was an engagement diamond, admittedly a rock at eight carats, along with her wedding band. On a table behind her were two silver-framed photographs. One was of her and Prince Hamdul; the other showed her husband in full tribal regalia. Florence took in the separation of the two photographs.

"Welcome." The sheika gestured to a chair. Her manner was pleasant and hospitable, with just enough formality to prompt Florence to come to the point without dwelling too long on Matar's climate, natural beauty or the marvel of the sea fountains beyond the terrace.

"The emir has discussed with the sheika the matter on which I have come to Matar?" Florence said.

A smile played across Laila's face, softening it like a shaft of late-afternoon sunlight in a formal drawing room.

Florence blushed.

"The matter on which you have come to Matar? Yes, he told me all about it. Would you care for something other than tea? I sometimes have a glass of something around this time."

A servant materialized out of nowhere, just as the emir's had. The sheika nodded, and the servant disappeared, reappearing shortly with phantomlike efficiency, bearing a tray of beaten silver on which were two cut-crystal flutes filled with a bubbly crimson-and-gold liquid.

"Pomegranate juice and champagne," Laila said, handing one to Florence. "A Matari Kir, if you will. *Sahteyn.* Thank God we have a word for 'Santé' in Arabic. One would have thought otherwise."

The cool, tangy-sweet bubbles went down Florence's throat and filled her with a relaxing warmth.

"The custom was to offer our guests fig cordials," Laila said. "Promoting our national industry. But it was so truly disgusting that I discontinued the practice."

"The sheika seems to share the emir's views on figs."

"Why don't we dispense with the third-person nonsense? I've never gotten used to it. I keep looking about the room to see where this person is people are referring to, and it's me. Call me Laila. If we do this thing you propose, you'll be calling me that soon enough, I suppose. Do you prefer 'Ms. Farfaletti'?"

"Florence, please."

"As in Firenze?"

"Yes," Florence said, impressed. "My father was a proud Italian. Most are, one way or another."

"And what are you doing here, so far from Florence?"

"The emir did not explain?"

"He said you wanted me to run some kind of Pan-Arab television station aimed at women." Laila leaned back in the armchair. "What a proposition. Such offers hardly come along every day. Almost, one might say, too good to be true?"

"We think you're just the person to do it. Really, the only person. It could be very exciting."

"Do we?"

The two women stared at each other. There was no hostility in Laila's gaze, but it was as cool as the Kir in Florence's hand.

"This project—it is of your own devising?"

"Yes. Of course, one needs backers." The word lay on Florence's tongue like aluminum foil, harsh and unnatural.

"And in the interests of due diligence, who exactly are these backers?"

"They're all described here." Florence reached for her briefcase and took out a folder and handed it to Laila. Laila studied the pages listing the names of the backers, all of whom were fictitious, though actual human beings were standing by to play their parts, should Laila pick up the phone. As Laila studied the list, Florence studied her.

"They are in it for the money, one supposes?"

"In an impure world, money is a pure enough motive."

Laila smiled. "And your associates at the hotel—they are your *staff*?"

"Yes. I thought to bring them in the event that the project met with your approval, so we could get started. They were eager to see Matar. In all honesty, their enthusiasm might have had a bit to do with the duty-free shopping and the pleasures of Infidel Land."

"Duty-free shopping and slot machines," Laila said. "Ah, the richness of Matari culture. Your associate, Mr. Robert Thibodeaux—Farfaletti and Thibodeaux; it sounds like an expensive law firm. Now tell me about him."

Florence glanced out at the fountain. She had never been a very adept liar. "He's an executive producer. He makes things happen."

"And Mr. George—he is feeling better?"

Florence felt her mouth going dry. "Yes, thank you. You're very well informed."

"I own the hotel. My little project. The emir thought it might give me something to do. To occupy me. And now along comes your television project to occupy me even more. This will certainly keep me busy, wouldn't it? Or perhaps that is the . . . idea?"

Florence felt like a pane of glass.

"And Mr. Renard," Laila continued. "Renard. He would be the fox of the team?"

"Programming," Florence squeaked.

"It's this desert air. It can be quite brutal. Drink some water."

"You have me at a disadvantage."

"Yes, I rather do, don't I?" The sheika smiled. "So what part of the United States government are you with? CIA? It's rather . . . out of the box for them, isn't it?"

"To be honest," Florence said, "I'm not quite sure myself, disingenuous as that may sound."

"You look as though you could use another drink. You needn't worry. I'm not going to say anything. As long as I'm satisfied this isn't something my husband cooked up to keep me from objecting to that whorehouse he's got in Umbeseir. Actually, I'm rather intrigued. I think we'd both better have another drink."

CHAPTER NINE

Maliq bin-Kash al-Haz was the younger brother of Emir Gazzir. Maliq and Gazzy had different mothers, as is generally the case when a father has sired more than thirty offspring.

The two were quite different in temperament: Gazzir plump, hedonistic and deliberate; Maliq lean, intense and headstrong. The one quality they shared was a deep venality. Maliq's brand was in some ways the more understandable, given the disadvantages of his birth. His mother had been one of the maids in the palace, a comely Yemeni whom the emir simply could not resist. (Not that the emir ever really resisted anything.) As soon as the child was born, she was packed off to Sanaa with a sackful of Matari gold sovereigns. The child would have accompanied her, only the emir took a fancy to him upon seeing him for the first time, declaring, "What a fine-looking devil is this!" He promptly named him Maliq (Matari for "fine-looking little bastard") and added him to his already abundant spawn, to be raised in the royal household.

Early on, Maliq displayed a precocious talent for leveling whatever playing field he was engaged upon. When a camel race was arranged on his eighth birthday, he sneaked into the stables the night before and fed all the other princelings' camels barley mixed with charcoal, which, as anyone knows who has ridden a camel that has gorged on barley and charcoal, makes a camel particularly cranky and unsubmissive. Maliq won the race and the prize. Thus began a lifetime's fascination with racing.

As Matar's minister for sport, morality and youth endeavor, Maliq had, over the years, established the annual Matari 500 auto rally as the high point of the social season. He was not only the event's chairman and chief patron, he always participated in it and, God be praised, always won. Among the aficionados of the Matari track, the question asked was not "Who won?" but "Who came in second?"

There had been spectacular upsets. Gentile Fabriani, the Italian, had thrown a rod in the 389th lap and gone through the wall. Uldo Pantz, the dashing Bavarian, so tantalizingly close to the finish line, had mysteriously blown all four tires and come to smoky grief in the midfield. And when, in '99, the American Buddy Banfield hit an oil puddle that inexplicably materialized in front of his car as he sped toward certain victory—did not the whole racing world mourn? It had gotten harder to attract top-ranked drivers to compete in the Matari 500. Maliq had to keep raising the second-place purse to the point that it had reached rather extravagant levels.

But the race had done much over the years to raise Matar's profile in the world. Matar was now synonymous throughout the world with fig oil, duty-free shopping, gambling and corrupt auto racing. The emir's decision to go along with Florence's TVMatar idea was motivated not just by the prospect of another pipeline of cash into his exchequer, but also by a desire to show the world that Matar could take its rightful place at the global table of diversified industry.

But now, in his early forties, Maliq had begun to weary of auto races. Perhaps the novelty of winning every Matari 500 had worn off. The trophy room in his palace was so crowded with gold cups that it had begun to stir in him not pride but a certain ennui. Inspired in part by his exiled mother, who had taken to e-mailing him from Sanaa, he had set his sights on a higher trophy: his brother's throne.

His brother Gazzy, the emir, was not unaware of this fact. He had kept a close eye on his half brother ever the since the day of his twelfth birthday, when the camel he was riding violently pitched him into a nettle patch.

It was by Gazzy's assent that Maliq was allowed to win every Matar 500.

He knew it would keep the young prince content and fulfilled. But it is written that a well-fed scorpion does not lose his appetite; he only grows a larger stomach. Such was the state of affairs at the time of Florence's arrival in Amo-Amas.

Complicating the situation were the French, who tend to complicate every situation. They knew about Maliq's ennui and designs on the throne, and had cannily been maneuvering to exploit it. They maintained an embassy in Amo-Amas, and its staff had not been whiling away the lazy hot afternoons in coffeehouses along the quays. On the contrary, they were well aware that, in the terminology of the intelligence community, Maliq presented a target of the most delicious opportunity.

France had never really gotten over its humiliation at the hands of Churchill and his cartographers in 1922. "Revenge is a dish best served cold" may be a Spanish proverb, but as La Rochefoucauld put it, "How pleasant it is to cram cold dead snails down the throat of an Englishman." Here was France's chance to even an ancient insult and, with any luck, inflict a little collateral damage on America.

Over the years, France had missed no opportunity to exploit strains in the U.S.-Wasabi relationship. When America declined to sell its latest fighter jet or other frightful technology to the Wasabis on the grounds that they might use it against Israel, France would step in and shrug by way of showing how profoundly reasonable it was, and say, "But of *course* you may have some of ours!" American congressmen representing the districts in which the American fighter jets were made would then go and clamor to the White House that "those fucking Frogs" were making a killing while they were "sucking hind tit." (Such an elegant idiom, the lobbyist's.) Invariably, the president would need the congressmen's votes on some upcoming bill and would relent. The Wasabis would get their new jets, stripped of a few high-tech features so as to make the transaction more palatable to the Israelis. No matter. A single Israeli fighter pilot could shoot down the entire Royal Wasabi Air Force and still have one hand free to hold his bagel.

Sensing that history was handing them a golden opportunity, the French intelligence service contrived to lure Prince Maliq to Paris.

The invitation came from the president of Auto-Vitesse SA, makers of the world-class racing cars as well as the distinctive Allez-Oop mini-coupes so popular in America. Founded in 1912 by Emil Lagasse-Ponti, the firm had made dozens of winners of Grand Prix auto races. The company expressed its desire to have Maliq drive a Vitesse in the upcoming Matar 500. Maliq was not immune to such blandishments.

What a fete his French hosts put on for him when he came! Dinner at the Élysée Palace in Paris with President Villepin, a night at the opera, featuring an especially commissioned one-act entitled *The Thousand and One Laps*, with the outstanding French tenor Otmar Blovard in the starring role as Malpique, the dashing thirteenth-century Moorish camel racer who saves Islam by beating the evil English crusader, Bertram the Unwashed, to the finish line. The allusion to current events was not lost on the man sitting in the presidential box, surrounded by an adoring French female entourage. The next day Maliq's royal progress continued with a visit to the Vitesse plant outside Lyon for two days of celebrations and lunches and dinners. By the time he departed France in a government Airbus, with six gleaming new Vitesse Formule Un cars in the cargo hold, Maliq was firmly and permanently a Francophile. Who can resist the French when they deign to play the seducer?

Meanwhile, the announcement in *Al Matar*—the country's leading (and only) newspaper—that the sheika Laila had been appointed CEO of the new satellite television network, TVMatar, had not gone unnoticed in Paris.

A LARGE COMPLEX in a western suburb of Amo-Amas was made available to Florence and her team. During the first gulf war, it had housed a detachment of U.S. Special Forces commandos. Florence found a leftover graffito in her office, scribbled there by some Ranger or Navy SEAL: "Give War a Chance." The casual visitor would find mostly native Matari employees. But the heart of the operation beat in quiet obscurity in a distant wing of the complex. The sheika's own office was physically separate—it was thought more prudent this way—in a black-glass skyscraper in downtown Amo-Amas, designed by the Finnish architect Po Skaälmo, who had also executed the Grand Foyer at Infidel Land.

The work was proceeding at fever pace, twenty hours a day. What sleep was to be had was on cots in the office. But no one complained. Excitement and purpose coursed through their shop. Even Bobby and George were sniping less at each other. Uncle Sam flew in for a visit and pronounced himself delighted with their progress. He didn't whimper when George showed him the invoices, though he did remark that for this kind of money, they could start a TV network back in the States. Meanwhile, he had arranged for the necessary satellites.

"Got a great deal from the NSA on some used birds." He grinned in his wire-rimmed eyeglasses and slicked-back graying hair, the very picture of a 1950s General Motors executive. Was there anything they needed? Anything at all? He seemed to have an all-access backstage pass to the entire United States government. Florence no longer probed about his precise role within it. She was too busy, and why question a gift horse? She assumed that he was with the CIA, though Bobby said he'd never seen him before. Perhaps he belonged to some directorate within a directorate, one of those star chambers set up for a specific mission years ago, which someone forgot to shut down—still operating like a probe launched at a distant planet decades before, proceeding deeper and deeper into the frosty night of space, autonomous, serene, oblivious.

As TVMatar's chief of programming, Renard was in absolute paradise. What PR man hasn't dreamed of having his own television station with no client breathing over his shoulder? This morning Rick was doubly excited, since he was previewing for Florence and Laila the show that would be at the centerpiece of TVM's morning schedule.

"You're going to love this," he said. They were assembled in the screening room. Laila was wearing glasses and chain-smoking cigarettes, looking every centimeter the TV executive.

"This is our flagship. The tone-setter. The anchor, if you will."

"Weigh anchor, Rick," Florence said. "I've got to meet with the fragrance people in half an hour."

Florence felt more like an advertising director these days than the godmother of Arab feminism. When not attending to technical details at the station, she would be furiously courting advertisers. Strictly speaking, it wasn't necessary, but the more ads they had, the more legitimate the whole enterprise would look, and the more money would flow into Gazzy's coffers. Laila had been indispensable, attracting the manufacturers of the luxury goods sold in Matar's duty-free shops. She hinted to recalcitrants that if they *didn't* advertise on her new television network, they would lose their franchises at Amo-Amas

International Airport, the most lucrative duty-free environ in the entire Gulf region.

"Her actual name is Fatima," Rick said as the film rolled. The hostess of the show walked out onstage fully veiled, to the applause of the studio audience.

"They're all named Fatima," Laila said, exhaling smoke. "And the rest are named Laila."

"The focus group lapped it up with spoons," Rick said. "I've never seen a Q factor like we got."

The veiled figure walked onto the set, which was arranged in the manner typical of a morning talk show. She walked right into the coffee table, pitching head over heels, in the process revealing beautiful legs in sheer stockings as well as a flash of lovely thigh and garter belt. The soundtrack exploded in female laughter.

"We had to add that after the fact," Rick said. "The actual audience didn't know what to make of it. But once they got it, oh did they get it. It was like this release of a thousand years of repression and—"

"Shall we just watch, Rick?"

The name of the show came up in letters: *Cher Azade.*

"We tested," Rick said. "Most of them got it right away that it's French, that it means 'Dear Azade,' a play on Scheherazade, the chick from the *Arabian Nights* story."

"Chick, Rick?"

"Whatever."

The line below the title came up in Arabic: *The Thousand and One Mornings.*

The hostess picked herself up off the floor and bumped into one of the chairs. The audience roared. She groped her way to her seat and sat down. "This new veil," she said, "I can't see a thing . . ."

The audience howled with laughter.

Rick said, "*I Love Lucy* meets *The Arabian Nights.*"

"Don't tell the religious police," Azade the hostess said, "or it will be thirty lashes. And that's just for showing an inch of ankle!"

The audience laughed.

"Well," Florence said, "that'll get their attention. Laila?"

"Oh, yes."

Rick said, "Now here's the beautiful part. They can't touch her, technically. George found this loophole in the *Book of Hamooj,* where they get all these bullshit rules from."

"Rick, please don't use that language in front of the sheika."

"I can handle it, Florence," Laila said.

Rick went on, "The *Book of Hamooj* is where all the religious rules are, about what women can and can't do. Which basically includes everything, including having an orgasm, assuming they didn't cut out the . . . uh . . ."

"It's called a clitoridectomy," Laila said. "The genital mutilation of young women, to encourage chastity by depriving them of sensual gratification. One of Islam's prouder achievements."

"Right. The *mukfelleen,* the Wasabi religious police—the ones who go around with whips beating women on the spot if so much as an inch of flesh is exposed—are the ones who shoved the young girls back into the school that was on fire because they weren't covered. What a fucking country. But theoretically, they can't complain here because it was technically an accident that she tripped. George—he knows all this shit—he found this clause in that book where, if you reveal your flesh accidentally, you get a free pass. It goes back to like the fourteenth century. Some Hamooji princess fell off her camel and went ass over teakettle. Everyone saw her legs. It was this huge scandal. The whole caravan had to stop while they debated whether to stone her or cut off her head. Someone finally said, 'Wait a minute, this is the caliph's favorite squeeze we're talking about here. He's waiting for her in Kaffa, and we're going to bring him her head in a basket? Fuck that.' But the religious cops had to save face. So they wrote it into the law that you can't be punished if the flesh was revealed accidentally. From a religious point of view, they can't lay a hand on us."

"They're going to go absolutely ballistic," Laila said.

Rick smiled. "Isn't that the whole point?"

They watched the rest of *Cher Azade*'s debut.

Laila said to Florence, "It would seem Matar now possesses the atomic bomb. I can hardly wait to set it off."

"Should we preview it for the emir?" Florence asked.

"Why don't we not bother him with it? He's so busy these days with his affairs of state."

CHAPTER TEN

TVMatar went on-air at sunrise on the day of the new spring moon. Advertisements had been taken out in the Wasabi newspapers and magazines, alerting women to a new station: "Just for you!" and full of "delicious recipes" and "advice on everything from raising a family to being a good wife in today's society." The ads flew under the radar of the Wasabi censors, who assumed it was just another of those shows where you learn how to make zesty hummus and to properly starch your husband's *thobe*. How surprised, then, were the ruling males of Wasabia to hear the shrieking peals of delighted female laughter as *Cher Azade* was beamed into homes from Wanbo to Kaffa to Akbukir.

"My next guest—not that I can see her—are you there, Farah?"

"Over here, Azad!"

"God be praised. Now, Farah, I understand you have actually driven a car?"

"Yes! A Mercedes."

"It's too exciting. What's it like, driving an automobile?"

"Thrilling—thrilling beyond words."

"Did you hit anything?"

"Just some *mukfelleen* religious police who were chasing me. So I backed up and ran them over again."

"Oh, dear," Azade scolded. "*That* will earn you a good beating. What did you do then?"

"I kept on going till I got to the border. The car is outside. I left the motor running. Would you like to go for a drive?"

"Only if we can run over religious police. Now, don't go away, even if you do have a car, because we're going to have a commercial for some lovely perfume. And don't *you* go away—we have a wonderful program for you, including a self-defense instructor who's going to give us tips on how to cope with cranky violent husbands and boyfriends during Ramadan."

THE PHONES RANG at the Ministry of the Enforcement of Religion in Kaffa, headquarters of the *mukfelleen*. There wasn't much they could do immediately, other than go about smashing and confiscating television sets. Their trademark purple sedans careened through the streets, screeching to a halt at the sight of a television in a café or store, disgorging enraged, whip-wielding *mukfelleen* in their distinctive black and blue *thobes*.

"We're back, praise God. That was very useful, what the self-defense instructor showed us, wasn't it?"

"Most helpful," said Azade's co-hostess. "Now I might actually look forward to Ramadan."

"I'm going to get a big brass tray with handles so I can use it as a shield. Now, our next guest has written a book."

"How exciting."

"Needless to say, you won't find it in the stores. But we'll put a number on the screen, and if you call, you can buy it over the phone, and they'll mail it to you in an undetectable wrapper."

"What's the book called, Azade? You make me eager to read it already."

"It's called *Stop, You're Killing Me: The Repression of Women in Arab Societies and What You Can Do About It.*"

"God be praised. What's it about?"

The studio audience laughed.

"It's not a cookbook, I can tell you."

—

THE WASABI FOREIGN MINISTER telephoned Matar's ambassador to Kaffa. It vexed him to hear the program playing in the background of the ambassador's house as he excoriated him.

"This is a hostile act," he growled.

"I shall inform my emir, Your Augustness," the ambassador said, eager to get off the phone so he could return to watching.

"WHAT INSPIRED YOU to write this book?"

"It's hard to put my finger on it, Azade, but probably when the religious police pushed those girls back into the burning school because their heads weren't covered. I thought, *What kind of barbaric society do we live in that such abominations go on—every day?*"

The studio audience applauded.

"Thank you for sharing that. The book is *Stop, You're Killing Me.* By Yasmeen Khamza. I want everyone listening to buy two copies. Plus one copy for each of your husband's other wives. We'll make their heads spin, sisters. Thank you, Yasmeen, for being with us this morning. Now we're going to have another commercial, and then we're going to have a fashion show. Just because we have to wear these ghastly sheets over our heads doesn't mean we can't look our best."

A PHONE RANG in Paris.

"It's time," said the voice. "The moment has arrived."

"I think so, too."

IN UM-BESEIR, the emir's Xanadu-on-the-Gulf, his chief of staff, Fetish, was reluctant to disturb his master, inasmuch as the emir was ensconced in his satiny bower with three ladies. Two of the women were spectacular new talents from Kiev and St. Petersburg. The third was a Parisian, also talented. She had been introduced to Gazzy's harem by his brother Maliq, of all people. What a devil. He'd met the girl, Annabelle, on one of his trips to France to get new racing cars. The emir was most grateful to his brother, and was coming back to thinking that in matters of love, as in food, the French ruled supreme.

The sheika's new television project had so preoccupied her time that Gazzy was once again free—God be praised—to refresh himself, undisturbed, in the loamy fields of Eros, to take his pleasure without distraction by the crystalline shores and turquoise waters.

"My lord?"

"Really, Fetish—this is no time—"

Fetish proferred the phone and whispered, "It is King Tallulah himself."

It wasn't every day that the king of Wasabia called Gazzy.

"What's he want?"

"Lord, he did not tell me. His manner is not pleased. Indeed, he sounds wroth."

"Give me the phone, then. Honestly. Darlings," Gazzy said to the three women, "go and have a swim, eh? Hello?" The emir struggled to clear his head of the champagne. "Majesty? You honor me greatly with this call. May you be in good health and have the strength of ten men half your age. What is the nature of this urgency that I am summoned in the midst of prayer? Television? No, no, no, it's Laila's—the sheika's—enterprise. Women's business—recipes, clothes, child rearing, baking pastries, that sort of— Ah? Eh? Oh. Um. Well, I'm sure there's some explanation. Of course I will look into it. Yes, yes. Um-hum. And the prince, your brother, he is well, God be praised? And the forty thousand crown princes? God is truly abundant and merciful. Absolutely. You have my word upon it. Before the sun has kissed thy western borders, thou shall hear from me. Be assured of my word. My best to your good wives. And the little princes. *Salaam.*"

He clicked off and tossed the phone at Fetish, who, from experience, was adept at catching phones tossed in disgust.

"Shall I alert the pilot royal that we will be returning to Amo-Amas, lord?"

"Certainly not. The old son of an Egyptian whore acting the king with me. Matar is not a province of Wasabia, last I looked at a map. It seems that the sheika's new television program does not meet with his royal approval." Gazzy considered. A pleased look came over his face. He grunted, "Hah—good. Well, tell Azzim to look into it and make a report. But Fetish?"

"My lord?"

"Tell Azzim—no hurry, eh?"

The emir chuckled to himself. He looked out past the silk tent folds toward the palm-fringed lagoon, where the women loitered bare-breasted in the waist-deep shallows, like the three ladies of Baghdad, braiding one another's hair.

"Will my lord be taking a swim before lunch?"

"Well, if you're going to chase after me with telephones, Fetish, there would be no *point.* I mean, would there?"

Fetish smiled and bowed. "I am confident that my lord will receive no further interruptions."

"In that case"—the emir sniffed—"I will take my refreshment in the lagoon. Then I will take my lunch. We'll have the lobsters and the caviar with the crème fraîche. To make our Russian guests feel at home. And then the Sultani orange and myrtleberry sherbets."

"Excellent, lord."

So picturesque, the girls, the way they arrayed themselves in the lagoon like natives in the Gauguin painting, their skins glistening with oils in the sunlight shafts that pierced the palm canopy.

"Fetish, when you present the sherbets, place a large pearl atop each mound."

"The cultured pearls, or the natural Gulf pearls?"

The emir considered. "The Gulf. It's a special occasion, Fetish. Really, what a terrible miser you can be."

"As my lord commands."

UNCLE SAM CALLED Florence, sounding delighted. "Goodness, goodness, goodness, did *you* ever kick up a sandstorm. They're having meetings about it at the UN. The Wasabi delegate demanded an apology from the Matari delegate."

"Wait till you see next week's prime-time lineup."

"I'll be watching. Now, you watch out for yourself, young lady. There are snakes in that desert. Keep a low profile. Pay attention to your man Thibodeaux."

It was tricky, conducting polls in a country like Wasabia. This fell to George, who was naturally inclined, inasmuch as the State Department's standard approach to any problem was to study it until it organically expired. He hired a Dutch firm in The Hague (a veritable geographical synonym for inoffensiveness) to conduct a Trojan-horse phone survey of Wasabi households. Most of the questions had to do with imported vegetables.

George presented the results to Florence and Rick and Laila. Bobby was not there, occupied as he was of late with security matters, or what he called "proactive preemption."

"They seem to be eating it up," George said. "We're basically number one in Wasabia."

"If there's such a thing as 'must-see TV,' this is it."

"Good job programming, Renard," Florence said.

Rick nodded.

"How are we doing with the men?" Florence asked.

"Not great among the conservatives. A lot of TV sets are being turned off or tossed out into the street. Good news for Sony. The younger men seem to be rather fascinated." George looked up from his papers and sighed. "This isn't terribly scientific. I'd have preferred a more longitudinal study over—"

"We don't have time. What else?"

"Four fifths of women said they want her to take off her *abaaya* on-screen."

"I don't think we're there quite yet," Laila said. "Azade is a blossom that we ought to let bloom gradually."

"Two thirds want fewer recipes," George continued, "and more sex, and an overwhelming majority want Britney Spears on to talk about her navel piercings. I don't know how that question got in there. I didn't put it in. I've never really gotten the point of Britney Spears."

"How's Yasmeen's book doing?"

"Gangbusters. We're giving it away, of course, since women can't have credit cards. Sending it from Holland and France. The Wasabi customs agents have been confiscating about half of them. We're having to get creative in the packaging and mailing origins. We've been labeling the boxes 'Tulips' or 'Chocolate' and marking them 'Perishable.' But we'll have to shift strategy, probably. FedEx is being difficult."

"Thank you, George. Good work."

"We'll do another survey next week, after the new show."

THE NEW SHOW was *Chop-Chop Square,* a prime-time soap opera about a royal family living in an unnamed country that looked uncannily similar to Wasabia. It debuted in the eight P.M. prime-time slot and was being denounced from five hundred mosques by dawn the next day. The Wasabi Information Ministry called it "an abomination before God."

Bobby, looking more sleepless than usual, reported that the grand mullah of Muk, Wasabia's leading religious authority—and certainly no cream puff, he—was preparing to issue "the mama of all fatwas."

"Well," Laila said, drawing on another cigarette, "that'll melt the wax in Gazzy's ears."

Florence noted that Laila seemed to be reveling in it all. She ascribed this not so much to the fury TVMatar had unleashed among the Wasabis as to the predicament into which it had thrust her husband, the emir. Laila confided to her that there had been a rather royal scene the night before.

The emir had said, "What are you and that American woman doing, in the name of God the most merciful? Tallulah himself has called me—*thrice.*"

"He called here first, darling. I told him you were at Um-beseir. Unwinding from the rigors of your duties here."

"There's no need for that, madame. You might have informed me about the content of this—this television station of yours. By the prophet's holy beard, Laila. What are you and this American woman doing? I *hear* things about her."

"She's a very shrewd businesswoman. Would you like to see how much money you made last week? I have the figures. Here."

"Um. Are these . . . true?"

"These, darling, are only the beginning. Has it not escaped my lord's notice—"

"Will you *please* not call me that? What has gotten *into* you?"

"Perhaps it's what *you* have gotten into."

"Have I taken more wives? No."

"Is that your definition of fidelity?"

"Laila, you are giving me pains in the chest. You must stop. Do you want

Hamdul to be fatherless?" It was the emir's practice to fake chest pains whenever he found himself cornered.

"Shall I summon the royal cardiologist?" Laila said.

"It's passed. Not that you'd *care.*" He studied the sheet of paper with the figures. "I must say, these *are* impressive."

"So is this." Laila handed him a clipping from *Al-Ahram,* the Pan-Arabic newspaper. The headline said, IS THE "PUDDING OF MATAR" THE NEW SALADIN?

The story had been written by George and placed by Renard and paid for by Bobby.

> TVMatar, the new satellite television station based in Amo-Amas, comes with a bold agenda and is causing speculation throughout the region that Emir Bin Haz, until now thought to be merely content to rake in his Churchillian riches and disport himself at his "winter palace," has a heart that, contrary to reports of faintness, appears to beat strongly indeed.

"Hmm," said Gazzy, frowning.

"My lord is not pleased?"

" 'Pudding of Matar'?"

"Darling, they're calling you the new Saladin, for heaven's sake. Accept the compliment."

"Well," Gazzy said, tossing the clipping to the floor, "this is your thing, not mine."

"By all means, come aboard, dear husband. Join me." She stroked his cheek tenderly. "It has been a very long time . . ."

"Hmm . . ."

"Darling?"

"Yes, darling?"

"You have been busy, and I don't want to catch something."

"Really, Laila!"

"*You* are not the offended one, Gazzir. Don't have a Potemkin tantrum with me. I am making a hygienic point."

"You certainly know how to spoil the mood."

"Oh, for heaven's sake. Hamdul is more mature. And he's ten years old. All I'm asking for is a blood test. Hardly unreasonable. You have your blood changed every month as it is."

"Never mind. Now, what about this television?"

"What about it?"

"It's got Tallulah in a temper."

"Darling, you detest Tallulah and the Wasabis. And 'this television' is going to make you one of the richest men in the gulf, not to mention 'a new Saladin.' If there's a problem, I'm not getting what it is."

"I'll have to discuss it with my ministers."

"I'm sure they'll be full of wisdom, and you will emerge wiser than ever."

"God be praised," the emir said, "there are times when I wonder if I mated with a she-devil!"

"You used to say that to me in bed. Our first night at the Connaught. Oh, what a *lion* was my lord," she teased tenderly, stroking his cheek.

He wanted her badly, but he was not about to lower himself to having a blood test. He stomped off to continue his growling in private. Yet he was also tempted to smile, for this projected advertising revenue stream was indeed like a gush of sweet water in the baking sand of the desert. And it was pleasant enough to be called the new Saladin, even if he was not quite clear who the infidels were.

CHAPTER ELEVEN

The gist of what Delame-Noir was explaining to Maliq, as they sat drinking coffee in the grand salon of the Palais Framboise outside Paris—headquarters of Delame's corner of the French government—was that the moolahs were key to the whole business. Maliq was impatient and uncomfortable. He did not enjoy being condescended to by the tall, elegant, exquisitely tailored man, who kept dropping knowing references to Wasabi and Matari history.

Dominique Delame-Noir was head of the Onzième Bureau, which undertook France's more sensitive foreign operations. He was also the author of a monumental account of the 1922 Middle East peace settlement, written from the French point of view, entitled *We Will Take the Lebanon and Syria, and You Can Keep the Jews and the Palestinians.* He spoke three dialects of Arabic, also Pashtun and Kurdish; he would apologize—perhaps overdramatically—for his Farsi. He also published poetry in Arabic. *Le Soir*'s critic called it "an attempt to fuse the obtuse mysticism of Gibran with the hypercaffeinated, wall-eyed nihilism of Sartre." Whatever.

"Of course," Delame-Noir said to Maliq with the air of a rising soufflé, "the dialectic that was in place in the early eighteenth century, between Rafiq and the imam of Muk, this is not something we would want to see in the new Matar?"

Maliq countered with an opacity of expression intended to signal that his brain was so occupied weighing the nuances and permutations that he had no neurons to waste on trivial facial muscles. In truth, he didn't know what the hell Delame-Noir was talking about. *Just get to the part where I become emir.*

"Nor," Delame-Noir droned, "would anyone welcome a return to the period of 1825 to '34! The discordant interregnum of Ali bin Hawalli, and the consequent retrenchment of the Mohab, followed by the *nouvelle hejira* of the Bahim Habb?"

Delame-Noir smiled serenely and arched an eyebrow by way of highlighting the Cartesian brilliance of this historical perspective. Maliq yearned to be in one of his Formula One cars, vibrating with speed down the hot asphalt straightaway at one quarter the speed of sound, past adulatory crowds screaming with all their might, "Maliq! Maliq the Magnificent!" Enough of this—*enough.*

"I am aware of all this you say," he said, putting down his Sevres china coffee cup on a table that had been made for one of Louis XV's mistresses. "But I have come to discuss the *future* of Matar, not the past."

Delame-Noir touched him on the sleeve with the tip of his fingers. "But exactly!"

Maliq stared.

"How well you appreciate the historicity of the situation, perhaps alone among the contemporary *umara.* And how interesting to contemplate the parallel facing the present emir—your brother—and his and your great-great-great-uncle, Mustafa bin—"

"Yes, yes, *yes,* Mustafa," Maliq groaned. "The parallel leaps out at one like a Sirhan adder. *But what about the bank accounts?*"

"Ah," Delame-Noir purred, aiming a long finger toward the twenty-two-foot ceiling, where fresco putti flitted. "Your apprehension is total. For you, Maliq bin-Kash al-Haz, this is not a matter of mere political opportunity—no, no—but of *duty.* Consanguinity in perfect harmony with duty, within the gyrodynamic of historicity."

What was this old fool talking about? At least he seemed to be concluding this stream of elegant drivel.

"No, no, this we do not see every day. Bravo, *mon prince.* I salute you."

"The bank accounts," Maliq tried again.

"Yemeni," Delame-Noir said. "It's all fixed."

"What about the American woman, Farfaf—however you pronounce it—Flor-ents."

Delame-Noir was keenly interested in the American woman but for the time being was resolved, wise old spymaster that he was, to keep certain details to himself, such as the fact that he had inserted one of his people, the talented Annabelle, into Gazzy's Um-beseir harem.

"We are of course keeping a close eye on her," Delame-Noir said, his speech now plain and to the point, stripped of rococo curlicues and acanthus leaves. "She is making a big success with her television station. Your brother is making very much money. He seems very content, I must say."

"My brother is a debauched toad."

"The question is *how* to restore Matar to its true greatness. Now, I think it would be a very good idea for you to begin the cultivating of the mullahs. I think you should start spending more time in the mosques."

"The *mosques*?" Maliq snorted. "I'm a race-car driver."

"And a brilliant one. Twenty *times* the champion!"

"Twenty-one."

"Exactly. But is this any reason not to have a religious conviction? Surely this—along with the Yemeni bank accounts—would make them see you in a new light?"

Maliq sighed. "My reputation isn't very religious."

Delame-Noir pretended to be thinking it over, when he had actually planned every word of this conversation, every comma. He looked up at the ceiling as if searching for the answer. "You know the saying—it's originally French, but the English stole it, along with everything else—'There are no atheists in foxholes'?"

"Yes?" Maliq lied.

"Is it not also true that there are no atheists in the cockpit of a Formula One in flames, going four hundred kilometers per hour?" Delame-Noir smiled.

"What are you proposing?" Maliq said with the annoyance of the slow learner. "That I burst into flames and crash?"

A look of pain played across Delame-Noir's face. "Not at all, *mon prince*!" The smile returned with a sly upturn at the corner of the mouth. "I was thinking that we could assist with certain technical details. Or perhaps your own technical crew is already proficient with certain, shall we say, special effects?"

Maliq didn't like the insinuation, but Delame-Noir's scheme was now apparent, and he rather liked it.

"THE PRINCE MALIQ is safe!" TVMatar's news announcer Fatima Sham told viewers. "He is alive and safe! God be praised!"

Florence was watching the broadcast from the control booth with George and Bobby and Rick. She still hadn't gotten accustomed to hearing "God be praised" from the mouths of TV news announcers. It didn't ring right to the American ear. *The chairman of the Federal Reserve today said that he was cutting the prime rate by a half point. God be praised!*

Renard winced, too. PR types tend as a rule to be godless, unless there's money to be made, in which case they can become very pious indeed. But George had been adamant about having the anchors and reporters drop in the occasional "*Allahu akbar*" on the grounds that it "gives us Arab Street cred." A little street cred was probably a good idea, given the babe quotient in TVMatar's announcers. They were all women, and dazzlingly good-looking, and utterly Westernized.

In this particular instance, Florence thought "God be praised" might be appropriate. This year the Matar 500 had its most dramatic finish ever. Prince Maliq's car—in the lead, as usual—had suddenly begun spewing black smoke. But rather than pull over, the prince had bravely kept going the two remaining laps. After he finished first, his car's rear end burst into flames. He slowed to a stop and leaped out, blackened with soot. The fire-rescue team hosed him down with chemical foam. Standing there, black and foamy, he was a strange but triumphant sight. George declared that he looked like "a blackamoor Pillsbury doughboy."

Fatima, the news announcer, was reporting that Prince Maliq had gone straight from the racetrack to the mosque, "where he gave thanks for his miraculous escape."

"I suppose I'd do the same," George said, "though you wouldn't find me driving one of those things in the first place."

Bobby was intently watching the interview with Maliq on the monitor. It had been taped before the start of the race. Maliq was telling the reporter how "really great God is."

"He's awful religious all of a sudden," Bobby said.

"Maybe he found God," George said. "It happens. People are always finding God in the desert. He doesn't have much competition out here. No one finds God on Madison Avenue."

"I found God on K Street," Rick said.

"What are you talking about?"

"The day I got the sultan of Brunei account. I walked out onto the street, and the whole heavenly choir was singing. My whole body was vibrating. It was a total religious experience. Fifty-thousand-dollar monthly retainer. I felt *exalted.*"

"You know, Rick," George said, "every time I think about going into the private sector, you open your mouth, and my drab, colorless existence and niggardly paycheck suddenly seem noble."

"That car he drives," Bobby said, still watching the monitors, now replaying in slow motion Maliq's accident, "it's French-built."

"The prince is a major Francophile," George said. "Spends a lot of time in Paris. He was just there. They all go there to shop. Everyone goes to Paris except poor old George, stuck in this *hole,* working for Queen Cruella for slave wages."

"Why doesn't poor old George go shop at the duty-free," Florence said, typing at her computer terminal. "Amazing bargains."

"I spent all my money on those slot machines at Infidel Land. They're rigged, I'm telling you. This entire region is corrupt."

"Why don't you write a long cable to Charlie Duckett about it?"

"Say what you will about him, he didn't chain me to a desk the way you do. At least in Washington, I had a life."

Bobby stood and put on his jacket.

"Where are you going?" Florence said.

"Gonna go see if I can find God."

"Give Him my regards," Renard said.

Florence watched him go. George watched Florence watching him go.

"Are we developing a crush?" George murmured.

Florence blushed.

"Rather a nice package, I admit, but really, Firenze, not your type. I'm sure the sex would be earthmoving and volcanic, but what would you talk about afterward? Alabama versus Auburn? How to crush someone's windpipe? Blowing up a car? Tapping telephones?"

"If you don't have anything to do, I'll find something for you to do."

"Why—why—did I let you drag me off to this macabre place?"

"Rick," Florence said, "can we run next week's episode of *Chop-Chop*?"

Rick dialed it up onto one of the monitors. The three of them watched. In last week's episode, Princess Mahnaz was unjustly accused of adultery by her husband, the evil prince Wakmal. She had found out that Wakmal was secretly supporting a terrorist cell aimed at deposing his good brother, the king of Ambalah. Wakmal had thrown her in jail and was planning to cut off her head. Mahnaz's first cousin, the dashing young Tafas, had smuggled a message of hope to her in prison inside a chocolate bar, telling her that he and his commandos were planning to rescue her. But Wakmal had gotten wind of the escape plan and, unbeknownst to Tafas, had laid a trap. *Chop-Chop Square* was TVMatar's number one show, getting huge ratings. The Wasabis were not amused.

FLORENCE PEERED THROUGH the fish-eye peephole on her apartment door. When she saw it was Bobby, she flipped the safety catch back on the pistol and opened the door. She was in her silk pajamas, as it was past two in the morning.

He looked sheepish, flushed. "Sorry to bother you, ma'am."

"Ma'am" at this hour? "Can I—would you like something to drink?" she said.

"It's not a social call." He seemed nervous.

"Are you all right, Bobby?"

"I screwed up, I'm afraid."

"Let's have a drink anyway." She poured bourbon into two glasses and gave one to him.

"I went to the racetrack," Bobby said. "I wanted to take a closer look at the prince's car. All that smoke, I don't know if you noticed, but it seemed kinda even on both sides. Anyhow, I found his car, and sure 'nuff, it was rigged with smoke makers."

"We knew he cheats, right? He's won every race."

"Wasn't that got my attention. It was all that yakety-yak about God being wonderful, runnin' off to the mosque. His car bein' French-made. You have to look at the whole picture. I did some checkin'. Two weeks ago, he went to Paris, and while he was there, he paid a visit to the Onzième Bureau."

Florence knew about the Onzième. "He did? You know this?"

"Yeah. So I thought it would be worth checkin' out the car." Bobby looked into his untouched glass of bourbon. "It didn't go so well."

"What happened?"

"Had a little accident. Someone got killed. I didn't honestly have a lot of choice in the matter. They opened up on me first." He looked at her, and there was innocence to it. "I'm not—I don't—" He fidgeted. "I'm not one to kill noncombatants, y'understand."

"Go on."

"I was lookin' inside the car, and suddenly, someone's shootin' at me. Like I say, there wasn't anything else I *could* do. I'm sorry about this, I truly am. I recognize that it complicates things. On the other hand, what I found out was probably worth findin' out."

They sat for a moment in silence.

"It could have been a burglary," Florence said.

"Not really."

"Industrial spying."

"I don't think so."

"It could have been a relative—of one of the race-car drivers over the years who was killed racing against Maliq. They were breaking into the garage in order to sabotage his car. Revenge. What better motive is there in this part of the world?"

Bobby looked at Florence. He nodded thoughtfully. "That's all plausible, but there's two problems. First, that wouldn't go very far in a Matari court; second, it's worth even less if the other guy was to identify me."

"The other guy?"

"There was another guy. He got away. My second screwup. I'm not doin' all that great tonight. Point is, I've got to go now."

"Go?"

"Well, yeah. I've gone from the asset to liability column. I feel bad about this."

"It couldn't be helped. But you can't just leave," she said. She realized that she had been leaning closer to him. He seemed aware of this fact as well and looked awkward.

"It wouldn't do your operation much good if they arrested me. This is a pretty liberal place by some Middle East standards, but he is the brother of the emir, and someone just killed one of his people while pokin' about his garage."

Florence considered, her mind racing. "But how's it going to look if you just disappear?"

"I think I can accomplish that part in such a way that it doesn't look suspicious."

"How?"

"Do you want to know or need to know?"

"Both."

Bobby looked at her. "I have someone at Immigration. He'll backdate my departure so that the record will show I left the country yesterday."

"Oh. Well. But how *are* you leaving, then?"

"Thought I might do some fishing. There's lot of fish in these waters, you know." He stood to leave. "Look, I'll be back as soon as I can, all right? You hang in there, Flo, hear?"

CHAPTER TWELVE

News of the killing in Maliq's garage ran on page one above the fold in Al Matar. It was also duly reported on TVMatar. Florence had no choice in the mutter. Matar was uniquely peaceful among the countries of the region, and this murder, of one of the servants of a crown prince—on the day of his miraculous escape from death!—smacked of mischief. The police were said to be pursuing leads.

Florence found out what she could while appearing not to take too great an interest. Meanwhile, she put off having to face Laila for as long as she could, faking a cold. She decided for the time being not to tell George and Rick what had happened, in the event that they were hauled in and questioned. She felt very alone.

There was another development: Maliq announced that he was giving up professional racing and was pursuing a new passion—religion. He declared that the killing of his servant Abu Tash was nothing less than "assassination" undertaken by "the enemies of Islam." This left a good many people in Matar, even among the more conservative religious element, scratching their heads. It was unclear why a shooting in a garage was religiously motivated, but whatever. Moreover, Maliq asserted, the real target had been he. An advertisement appeared in *Al Matar,* offering a reward of five hundred thousand baba

($100,000 U.S.) for information leading to the arrest and conviction of the "assassin."

"Where's Attila?" George asked a few days after Bobby had disappeared. "I haven't seen him. Is he out blowing up bridges?"

"He went back to Washington," Florence said as casually as she could. "You remember, he left the day before the race."

"No, he didn't."

"Yes, George, he did."

"Firenze, what are you talking about? He watched it with us right here in the control room."

"No, George, you're mistaken. He went home the day before."

Rick chimed in, "No, he was here. I remember."

Florence looked at the two of them. "George, Rick, listen to me. Bobby went home the day before the race. *Do you understand?*"

They stared at Florence. Finally, George whispered, "Oh, God."

"Keep smiling," Florence said. There were technicians present.

"I knew this was going to happen."

"We're not going to discuss it now, George."

"And we're left to clean up after him? Typical CIA—"

"It was an accident, George," Florence said. She was trying so hard to make her expression look normal that it felt like a bad face-lift.

"Accident my—"

"George, please shut up. We'll discuss it at the appropriate time. Meanwhile, in the event you're asked questions, all you know is that he went home on some family matter. The day *before* the race. Don't say any more about it."

"They'll know."

"No, they won't. It's all been taken care of. Just concentrate on your work."

"You might have told us," George said, sounding wounded.

"I was trying to protect you."

"Well, thank you. I feel so much safer." George stomped off.

"Sorry, Rick."

"It's the Middle East." He shrugged. "What can you expect. But look, if they start pulling out my fingernails, you might as well know right now: I'll tell them everything."

"I'll bear that in mind."

A moment later, he said, "Do they . . . *do* that sort of thing around here?"

"No. It's one of the most progressive countries in the region. The land where duty-free was born."

The doors to the control room opened. Laila entered, followed by four fierce-looking men. "Florence, where have you been hiding? Are you better? You look a bit peaked."

"Just a cold." Florence regarded Laila's entourage, who had taken up stations ten feet away.

Laila tracked her gaze and explained, "Gazzy's orders. Because of the killing in the garage. Everyone is acting completely gaga."

"Have they found out anything?"

"You must understand, the Matari police are known around the world—for incompetence. There isn't much crime to speak of. They're out of practice. They have a description of some kind, but it was dark."

"Do they know what the"—Florence forced the word out—"murderer was after?"

"Maliq's insisting it was some kind of assassination gone awry. I can't for the life of me think why anyone would bother assassinating him, unless"—Laila lowered her voice—"it was a relative of one of the drivers he beat."

"That had crossed my mind," Florence said, trying to give the theory a nudge. "But we can't say that on TV."

"No," Florence said. "Of course not. Maliq seems quite . . . changed since his accident."

"You have no idea. He came to see Gazzy yesterday at the palace and in front of people began lecturing him on the Koran. Can you believe—Maliq! Gazzy wasn't at all amused. He said, 'My *dear* brother, I think you must have bumped your head against the steering wheel.' Maliq became very demonstrative and began denouncing Gazzy for selling the country out to infidels. His exact words. Gazzy was *livid.* He ordered Maliq out of the palace. And now some of the moolahs are making an enormous to-do out of it all, encouraging pilgrimages to Maliq's garage. To touch the miraculous vehicle. It's straight out of a TVMatar soap opera. One of the moolahs has even issued a fatwa saying it's a religious duty! Do you believe? It has been a very long time since any fatwa was issued in Matar. Gazzy called in the moolah who issued it and gave him what-for."

"Laila," Florence said. "Is it possible that Maliq is up to something?"

"It's more likely that he's down to something. But what do you mean?"

"Is it possible that Maliq is trying to mount some kind of coup against the emir?"

Laila stared at Florence. "Do you know something?"

"No. But sudden religiosity always makes my antenna go *ping*. And why are the moolahs suddenly so exercised? They've been pretty quiet up till now."

"Gazzy thinks they just want new Mercedeses. He's instructed the imam to tell them to behave or they'll find themselves walking to Mecca on their next hajj. Do them good. As for Maliq, who knows, maybe he found God on the final lap. Who can fathom the mind of Maliq. Who would want to? So how's the new episode of *Chop-Chop Square*? I'm dying to see it."

"We were discussing whether to kill off Princess Mahnaz or have Tafas rescue her in time. What do you think?"

"I myself love a neat happy ending, lots of ribbons, but then Mummy brought me up on Dickens. Is Bobby here?"

"Bobby?"

"Mr. Thibodeaux."

"He had to go back to the States."

"Oh? When?"

"Earlier in the week," Florence said, trying to sound matter-of-fact.

"Pity."

"Why?"

"I wanted to ask him something."

"I'll probably be speaking to him. Anything I can pass on?"

Laila looked at Florence. "He's coming *back*?"

"Of course."

"When?"

"As soon as he can."

"Ah. It can . . . wait," Laila said, though her look had turned into a stare that was making Florence squirm.

—

FLORENCE PHONED UNCLE SAM on the secure satellite phone, the one Bobby had said to use only "once we start taking mortar fire."

"How's my girl? Hey, I love the new show. I'm betting on Tafas to swoop down at the last minute and rescue Fatima."

"Mahnaz."

"I thought they were all named Fatima. Hard to tell them apart with those veils."

"That's what we're trying to change. It may not be Mahnaz who needs rescuing. Have you spoken to our friend?"

"Oh yes, oh yes. He called in this morning. He's in—we're on the secure phone, I see—Paris."

"Paris?"

"He's finding out all sorts of interesting things. Have you been getting any knocks on your door in the middle of the night? They're notoriously incompetent, the cops there."

"No. I had to tell George and Rick. And Laila just dropped by and seemed kind of curious about our friend's absence."

"She's a sharp one, the sheika. It's that British education. Well, you're doing God's work over there, young lady, keep it up. Uncle is proud, darn proud. Don't speak to any strangers. And keep that phone handy; remember, it's your lifeline."

Florence hung up. She felt paranoid. She wished Bobby were here, but if he was on to something fruitful in Paris, good.

George was off pouting somewhere, so she sought out Renard, who always managed to cheer her up with his unabashed venality and outrageous schemes.

"Rick," she said, "what did you want to be when you were growing up?"

He looked up from his editing machine. "You mean, did I always want to be a sleazy PR hack?"

"I didn't say that."

"Gosh, Frenzy"—Frenzy was his nickname for Florence, a corruption of George's Firenze—"all I wanted to do was help people."

"Really?"

"I remember clearly as a young boy of seven or eight, dreaming of one day helping rich Florida citrus growers get sweeter tax breaks out of the Appropriations Committee at the expense of California melon growers."

"You're very cynical, you know."

"I'm not saying I don't have standards. I turned down Michael Jackson as a client."

"You did?"

"I wasn't sure he had the money. But look at me now, Renard of Arabia, helping to liberate nearly a billion veiled women, to create lasting peace in the Middle East, a region that has known nothing but strife and sectarian hatred for thousands of years. Look." He pointed to his forearm. "Goose bumps."

"That's sunburn."

"You step outside here for thirty seconds and—zap—skin cancer. It's like walking around inside a microwave oven. No wonder they dress like Casper the Ghost. It's a very strange place, this."

"Why are you here? The money?"

"Why not?"

"I'm not sure I believe that."

"There might be another reason."

"Oh?"

"I'm not sure you want to hear it. At least right now, what with everything going on."

Florence stared, mute, inarticulate. He was attractive, Rick, lean and wolfish, and had circumstances been different, who knows.

"No." He smiled. "Don't ruin the exquisite awkwardness of the moment by saying something nice. Anyway, at Renard Strategic Communications, we never get emotionally involved with the client. It almost always ends with them wanting a discount."

Rick turned back to his editing machine. "I've got a killer idea for a new show. I've been kicking myself in the ass that I didn't think of it sooner."

—

GEORGE'S REACTION WAS "You *can't* be serious." This persuaded Florence that it was exactly the way to go. George was still in many ways a creature of the State Department, and if it made him blanch, the idea was certifiably bold.

The three of them presented it to Laila, who kept saying as Rick laid out the plots of the first three episodes, "Oh my," "Oh my *my*" and "Jesus." When he was finished, she said, "This will go down like a pound of bacon in the middle of Ramadan."

"Do you want to give the emir a heads-up?" Florence asked.

"Good God, no." Laila laughed. "No, I think we'll make this a surprise for the emir. He's so busy these days. The hectic pace of Um-beseir. How he survives, I don't know."

Florence and Rick got up to leave. Laila said, "And how is Mr. Bobby?"

"Fine. Busy."

"Will he be rejoining us soon?"

"Yes," Florence said, "I'm sure."

"Oh, good." Laila smiled. "It's so very *dull* here without him."

CHAPTER THIRTEEN

The knock on the door came not quite in the middle of the night, but close enough for dramatic purposes: 11:35 by Florence's digital wall clock.

Looking out her peephole, Florence counted three men. Even in the ambiguous sterility of their white *thobes,* they looked like police—either police or members of a death squad. They identified themselves over the intercom as "Inspectors Muhammed, Rama and Azbekir from the Division of Internal Services, madame."

Florence pressed the redial button on the secure cell phone that Bobby had given her. This theoretically alerted the cavalry.

"Gentlemen," she said through the intercom, "it is late, and I was asleep." She spoke in English rather than her fluent Arabic.

"It is most urgent, madame."

"What does it concern?"

"Your colleague, Mr. Thee-thi-boo."

"He's not here."

"Yes, madame, this is the precise urgency."

"If it's urgent, you should speak to him directly."

"But he is not here."

"Then how can it be urgent?"

"But . . . madame, you must admit us. We are the police."

She wondered how long she could weave this conversational Möbius strip. Suddenly, her phone chirruped. When she answered it, a gruff American voice sounding like the personification of the 101st Airborne Division said, "You all right, ma'am?"

"There appear to be policemen outside my door."

"Did they say what they want?"

"Questions about our friend."

"We're nearby."

"What should I do if they take me with them?"

"Remain calm. Keep your head down."

"Who are you, anyway?"

"Not quite sure at this point, ma'am."

"I can handle them. I don't want any more shooting."

"Madame!" Inspector Muhammed said insistently over the intercom, sounding plaintive, "you must admit us! It is official business. Please be putting on decent clothing."

Florence opened her door and faced the three men with the appropriately furious air of a chaste and blameless Arab woman rousted from prayers at an uncomely hour. "What is the meaning of this?"

"We must speak to you about your colleague Mr. Tee-boo—Thee-bo—"

"Mr. Bobby. What about him?"

"He has departed the kingdom," Inspector Muhammed said with alarm.

"So do hundreds, thousands, of people every day."

"But there is an irregularity."

"*What* irregularity?"

"He was witnessed severally here in Amo-Amas, in this city, by many persons, on the fifteenth of this month."

"So?"

"But we are told by his office here that he departed on the fourteenth. This cannot be true."

"I don't remember when he left. I think, yes, it was the day before the big auto race."

"No, madame, this cannot be."

"What is the problem?"

"The problem is that he is desired for questioning."

"Why?"

"We are doing the questioning, madame. We have spoken with him by the cell telephone, and he is informing us that he departed Amo-Amas by Air France on the fourteenth, but there is no such record of his ticket with Air France."

"What does your Immigration Department say? He would have been checked out of the country by the proper authorities at the airport."

Inspector Muhammed frowned. "That is very correct. What you say is precisely the case, yes."

"So?"

"There is an irregularity. The information of the Immigration Department and Air France is not in accordance."

"Who are you going to believe?" Florence said with disdain. "Your own government or some French *airline*?"

"The problem is remaining, madame," Inspector Muhammed said.

"Not here and not at this hour. But I'll tell you what, I will personally bring it up with the emir, may Allah keep him safe for a thousand years."

"The emir?"

"Yes. I have an audience with His Majesty tomorrow at nine o'clock. Assuming I am allowed to have any sleep before then."

"*Thank* you, madame," Inspector Muhammed said unhappily.

THE NEXT MORNING, precisely at nine o'clock, Florence and Laila presented themselves before the emir. On the agenda were the latest (eye-popping) advertising revenue figures for TVMatar.

Florence managed to slip in a coy reference to the fact that Matar's answer to the secret police had banged on her door at a late hour. She watched the emir's and sheika's faces closely for a reaction. Laila appeared surprised and displeased.

"The Lions of Matar," she snorted. "That's their motto. Lions! An ostrich could defeat them in battle."

"Laila," the emir said, "you must not speak of them that way. They are thoroughly professional and vigilant."

"What about that assassination squad sent from Iraq three years ago to kill you? Who warned you of it? The CIA. Where was the vigilance of the 'Lions of Matar'?"

"Our people knew all about the Iraqi assassins. They work in concert with the CIA."

"Darling, they're imbeciles. Starting with their chief, your cousin Fahim." Laila turned to Florence. "The emir has, as you know, seventeen half brothers, all of them half-witted, for a total of eight and a half brains among them."

"Laila!"

"Praise God that my dear husband was endowed so well. In *all* respects."

"Why do you speak so disrespectfully, and in front of Florence? You embarrass her."

"No, darling, I embarrass *you.*"

The emir's face was a prune of displeasure. "Truly, I am out of patience. Show me the advertising figures." As he studied them, the prune was transformed into an apricot, tender and smooth. "Um . . . *hm* . . . God be praised . . . Well, well, I must say, this is *most* satisfactory."

"I am gratified that my lord finds our humble work so worthy," Laila said.

"My wife," the emir languidly said to Florence, "has developed what you in the West call an enormous 'attitude' since she started working with you. Some *might* call it a Western *infection.*"

"The only infection to be found around here," Laila said, "has not been brought to Matar by Florence."

"I will not be spoken to in this manner!" Gazzy exploded. "Is the emir of Matar to have no peace in his own tent?"

"You do push him," Florence said when they were alone.

"I might as well have some fun. I assure you, it's just an act on his part. It's so he can fly off in a swirl of self-justification to Um-beseir and his huge bed and his Russian hotsy-totsies. If he ever gets around to writing his autobiography, it should be titled 'The Seven Pillows of Wisdom.' "

"Maybe we should do a show called that." Florence smiled.

"I've seen it," Laila said.

—

MUKFELLAHS, TVMATAR'S NEW SITCOM about an inept, though ruthless, squad of Wasabi-type religious police, caused a immediate sensation throughout the region. A prominent Cairo television critic dubbed it *Friends from Hell.*

The opening episode showed the six regulars all relaxing at the office after a hard day of whipping women for a variety of offenses, complaining about how their arms hurt and passing around ibuprofen tablets.

"That last one put up a struggle. But that'll teach her to walk on the sidewalk without a male escort."

"We live in a shameful world, brothers. If it were not for us, hell would be full to bursting."

"My arm, how it aches! Five hundred lashes I dealt today. And three stonings tomorrow."

"Listen to Mansour! He whimpers like that woman at the mall today!"

"God's mercy upon us!" declared another. He was reading the label on the bottle of ibuprofen. "These pills are manufactured by a company named Phitzer!"

"So?"

"It's Jewish, you fool!"

"German. Surely."

"Do you want to take that chance?" The man thrust his finger down his throat and ran off-camera, making terrible sounds.

The others exchanged a glance and then plunged their fingers down their throats and ran off-camera.

"Clever," Florence said, "the way it deals so subtly with the issue of anti-Semitism."

"Yeah," Rick said, "I was sort of pleased with that, too."

THE GRAND IMAM of Muk, the highest religious authority in all Wasabia, issued a fatwa calling for the assassination—"the more bloody, the more pleasing in the eyes of God"—of the entire staff of TVMatar. The fatwa, published in

Al Kuk, Wasabia's leading newspaper, further stated that anyone who performed this holy deed would be guaranteed not only eternity in the nectar gardens of paradise but also twice the usual number of kohl-eyed virgins, for a total of—here religious scholars differed, but—more than 140, enough to keep most men, even the stoutest, busy for eternity.

The reaction to the show from the Wasabi Royal Ministry for Foreign Matters was equally furious. They denounced the broadcasts as "an act of gross interference in the internal affairs of Wasabia" and as "a severe provocation."

The Wasabi Ministry for the Enforcement of Chaste Technology was tasked with jamming TVMatar's satellite broadcasts into Wasabia. This they managed to accomplish, for a few hours. All at once their jamming was counter-jammed by an apparently superior technology, originating, as it turned out, in Tel Aviv, where the broadcasts of *Mukfellahs* had developed an early and enthusiastic following, even among the ultra-Orthodox, who did not even believe in television. The Wasabi Ministry for the General and Permanent Disapproval of Israel promptly took its case to the United Nations Security Council. For several days, soft clucking noises could be heard around the table as Wasabia's indignation was simultaneously translated into 196 languages, at which point the United States delegate pointed out that there were not that many countries in the world. The United States permanent representative to the Security Council, a bald pate set in a sea of frowns, raised his pen high in the air and vetoed whatever it was that needed to be vetoed, and everyone went off to the Henry Kissinger book party at the Four Seasons Grill Room. The situation in Amo-Amas, on the other hand, was more and more becoming less and less placid.

CHAPTER FOURTEEN

Explosions are not, alas, unusual events in the Middle East, but until now Matar ("Switzerland of the Gulf") had been spared the ambient blast of gelignite.

The last time there had been any explosion worth noting was in 1936, during an official visit by H.M.S. *Indubitable,* carrying the duke of York, filling in for his brother, Edward VIII, who had jumped ship in Cap d'Antibes when he learned that Mrs. Simpson was there attending Verbena Goughsborough-Pong's masked ball. He simply announced to his aide-de-camp that he had no intention of continuing on to Matar to "swat flies and be surrounded by a lot of frightful smelly wogs," leaving the Foreign Office to explain to a naturally disappointed emirate that His Majesty had been stricken with shingles.

The poor duke of York, who in a few years would be thrust unwillingly upon the throne of England after his older brother succumbed to the mysterious charms of the Baltimore divorcée—some said it had to do with ice cubes—was dragged twitching and stuttering down the *Indubitable*'s gangway to convey the crown's "d-d-deep f-f-f-feelings of f-f-f-f-f-friendship for the p-p-p-people of Muh-muh-muh . . ."

Not desiring to prolong the duke's distress, the *Indubitable*'s commanding officer, Admiral Sir Knatchbull Cavendish-Hump, ordered the commencement of the nineteen-gun salute. The gunner's mate mistakenly loaded a live round, which landed in the Dismalya Quarter, ever after nicknamed "Dismal Street."

The episode provoked a full-fledged nervous breakdown in the duke, who was taken below and not seen on deck until the ship reached Aden. A condolence fund was established for the family of the bereaved, and for the building of a vocational school, which still bears the plaque commemorating "the historic bond and comity between Great Britain and the Royal Emirate of Matar."

The old-timers on Randolph Churchill Street, along Amo's harbor front, sipping mint tea and smoking their noon pipes of *qoosh,* the mildly narcotic herb mixed with tobacco, remarked that this explosion had reminded them of that day back in 1936 when the future king visited.

No one was killed this time, God be praised. A miracle, it was said. The explosive was in an SUV parked at the intersection of Chartwell and Marlborough streets. It disintegrated into ten thousand pieces, but the blast acted as a propellant for a nearby car. Witnesses watched the vehicle loft hundreds of yards into the air and then make a graceful parabolic descent through the roof of St. Margaret-in-the-Marsh Anglican Church. Had Deacon Whitcomb been less ginger, the event might well have ended in tragedy.

Naturally, the incident caused intense speculation in the cafés of Amo-Amas, those hatcheries of Matari gossip. Had the blast been directed precisely at St. Margaret's? And if so, was this the opening salvo in a jihad? And if so, why the Anglicans? Could it be a reaction against the recent ordination of the transgendered bishop of Leeds? True enough, the event had not gone down well among the more conservative element in the far reaches of the Anglican communion. Taking no chances, Whitehall announced that it was dispatching a team of forensic experts to "assist" the Matari authorities in their investigation. *Al Matar* called the episode a "wake-up call," while acknowledging that it was unclear who exactly was supposed to wake up.

Meanwhile, Maliq, now preaching daily from the pulpit of his new madrassa, where students memorized the Holy Koran while learning how to service race cars, denounced the bombing as the work of "foreign blasphemers who have been allowed to defile Matar's holy soil." This was a clear shot at the palace. The emir was not pleased.

"There's never been anything holy about Matar's soil," Laila said to Florence. "But it is getting rather messy. I don't suppose you know anything about this?"

"Of course not." It had the advantage of being true.

"Only asking. You sound offended."

"Why would I know something about a bomb blast in downtown Amo?"

"Darling, I'm simply saying that things were rather more quiet in Matar until you and your entourage arrived. We used to be the Switzerland of the Gulf. It's starting to look more like Baghdad. Gazzy's in a stink. He's on his way back from Um-beseir, which always puts him in a foul mood. I overheard his man Fetish talking about a four o'clock appointment Gazzy has today with Valmar, the French ambassador."

"Oh?" Florence said, trying not to sound too interested.

"Maybe he has a question about what wine to serve with which mistress. Change of subject. Darling, they're starting to ask me rather pointed questions about your Mr. Thibodeaux. I do think it would make sense if he returned from this urgent family business that seems to be occupying his time. They want to ask him some questions."

"About the shooting? Why would he know anything about that?"

"Just mention it if you speak to him."

Florence shrugged. "Sure."

SHORTLY BEFORE SIX O'CLOCK that afternoon, Florence's office door opened to reveal an unhappy-looking Fetish, accompanied by two men of the royal household whom Florence recognized as members of the royal bodyguard.

Fetish dispensed with the usual bowing and scraping. He was in a bad mood for two reasons: the grouchiness of his emir, and having to depart Um-beseir. Fetish liked Um-beseir almost as much as the emir, for the reason that he was enjoying a little liaison on the side with the new talent from Paris, Annabelle. Dangerous, to be sure, but well worth it.

Florence was wanted by the emir. "Right now."

It was while she was sitting in the back of the sedan, the glum Fetish in the front passenger seat, that Florence's secure cell phone rang. She answered, and on the other end, she heard the welcome if problematic voice of Bobby.

"Why, Dad," she said, "how are you? I'm sitting here with Sharif Fetish.

We're on our way to see the emir. In the palace. Isn't it exciting? How's Mom? Is she feeling better?"

"The car bomb," Bobby said. "It was the Frogs."

"Really? Isn't that wonderful. Is she being nice to the nurses?"

"I'm on my way back there."

"No, no, I don't think it's a good idea to move her right now."

"I'll be in touch."

"Bo—" she caught herself. "Bye." She said to Fetish, "My mother. She's in the hospital. She's doing better." Fetish accepted this tiding without emotion. Florence added under her breath, "Thought you'd want to know."

LAILA WAS IN the emir's office when Florence arrived. The air in the room had the distinct aroma of a recent argument.

"Leave us," the emir said to Fetish and various attendants.

"Florence," Laila said, "the emir has just—"

"*I* will conduct this audience, thank you. Just because you two are broadcasting over my airwaves does not mean that I will be preempted in my own tent."

"Darling, no one is trying to 'preempt' you."

"Never mind, 'darling.' Now, Florence, certain allegations are being made. I shall pay you the courtesy of repeating them to you directly."

"Yes, my lord."

"And never mind 'my lord.' Don't think you two fool me with these flatteries. You may spin your spiderwebs, but I am no insect. Now, I'm going to ask you straightforwardly. Are you making love with my wife?"

"Gaz," Laila said, "really, this is too mortifying."

"Let her answer."

In the car on the way, Florence had rehearsed answers to "Are you with the CIA?" This question she had not anticipated.

"Well, no. Since you ask."

"There's talk. Talk about the two of you."

"Talk from who? Who has told you this nonsense?" Laila said.

"It is enough that it is *being* said."

"A fine standard!" Laila said.

"Never mind standards. A rumor is circulating that my wife—the sheika—is having a thing with another woman! It's demeaning. An affront to the manhood."

"Darling, I shouldn't think your manhood is in any question whatsoever, given the workout it's been getting."

"Woman, you vex me!"

Florence said, "May I show Your Majesty a news article that appeared yesterday in *Al Matar*? It concerns this mutter—matter—of your dignity."

She produced a folder from her briefcase and presented it to him.

He took it grumpily and read. The headline said:

EMIR IS GUIDING FORCE BEHIND TVMATAR

> According to those in the know in Amo-Amas, it is the emir Gazzir Bin Haz himself, and not the sheika Laila, who has guided TVMatar from its inception.
>
> "It is from his vision that the programs stem," says this person. "Gazzir brilliantly understands the power of the medium, and is using it to transform the Arab world and to bring it into harmony with modernity, while preserving what is fundamental in our rich religion and culture. To be sure, this will earn him enemies, but worthy ones, and no leader can be called great who does not have great enemies. In this sense, Gazzir can be called 'the New Nasser' or, what with the current crusades being mounted against Islam by the United States and England, 'the New Saladin.' "

The story had been written by Rick, translated into Arabic by George, and placed in *Al Matar* by Bobby.

"Hmm," the emir said.

"Keep reading," Florence said. "There's a paragraph about Laila."

> Though Sheika Laila is the nominal head of TVMatar, she gives full credit to her husband for conceiving and implementing the revolutionary broadcasts.

"The emir," she said in a telephone interview, "is a visionary. For him there is no present, only the future. As head of state, he is immersed in the thousand and one details of governing his country. It's true that I had some minor experience in broadcasting, so it was only natural that he would ask me to help him. But from beginning to end, TVMatar is the emir's achievement."

"You said this?" the emir asked.

"It's there in black and white."

"What are you two she-devils up to? I demand to know."

"Helping you become the New Saladin," said Laila. "But if you'd rather just go down in history as another rich Gulf emir, say the word. It's up to you."

The emir looked at Florence. "Is this true?"

"If greatness is being thrust upon you, sire, why fight it?"

The emir stroked his goatee. "I had a telephone call from Kamar ak-Zaman this morning. He's secretary of the Arab League."

"Oh?" Laila said.

"They want me to address the conference. In Bahrain. Next week."

"That's marvelous, darling! They've never asked you before."

"Sire," Florence said, "this is truly wonderful news. And yet I fear that your absence from the country at such a time might prove . . . irresistible to certain elements."

"What do you mean?"

"I mean, sire, that your brother Maliq might seize the opportunity of your absence to move against you."

The emir stared at Florence for a second and then laughed. "Maliq? Depose *me*? Please."

"Consider," Florence said. "Your brother goes from being a race-car driver to a raving ayatollah in less time that it takes to accelerate from zero to sixty miles an hour. Suddenly, all your moolahs are preaching that you are corrupt—I'm not saying they're right, mind you. Then the French ambassador tells you that your wife and I are having a lesbian affair."

The emir recoiled. "How did you know that?"

"Simple deduction, Your Majesty. You met with him and summoned me and confronted us with this canard. Which it is. Meanwhile, the Wasabis have put their military on alert and are flying fighter jets along the border. A car bomb goes off in downtown Amo. And now you're being lured—invited—out of the country. Call me paranoid, but it has all the elements of a coup in the offing. By the way, you might ask M. Valmar, the next time he comes in to relay rumors about your wife and me, whether any of his staff at the embassy here are explosives experts."

"What are you saying? The *French* set off the bomb?"

"Your brother and the French do get along very well."

The emir turned to his wife.

"It's all rather more interesting than presiding over the Switzerland of the Gulf, if you ask me," Laila said. "Florence may well be right. You don't have to go address the conference. You can be the New Saladin right here at home and go on getting richer off the advertising revenue. Saladin never had numbers like these. And there's this: Do you realize how long it has been since an Arab country put something on the table other than self-pity, denial, finger-pointing and suicide bombers? For the first time in centuries, an Arab country is generating income not from oil but from an idea. In this case, that women might just have something to contribute to civilization other than their vaginas. Don't you see what's happening? You could be the Arab leader to take the Middle East out of the Middle Ages! And you greet this opportunity that has landed in your lap like a plump fig by wringing your hands and accusing us of being a pair of Sapphos?"

"Clap, clap," said the emir. "What a pretty speech." He turned back to Florence. "You think King Tallulah is involved in this so-called plot against me? He is flying his fighter jets along my border. Back and forth, day and night. The desert roars with the sound of his engines. All because of your television station."

"I don't know, sire. But historically, Wasabia has yearned for a coastline."

"Would the Americans permit such a thing?"

"I can't speak for the U.S. government. It's true that there are more American and British warships off your coast than there are fish. But after the way things have been going, it's possible that they might not be so anxious to intervene militarily."

The emir considered. "Why then would the French ambassador come in and tell me that the Americans want to overthrow me?"

"I must say," Laila said, "M. Valmar had all *sorts* of things on his mind today, didn't he? He told you that?"

"He told me that Florence is a CIA spy who was sent here to undermine my regime."

"By making you rich and the New Saladin—the moral leader of the Arab world? That's some undermining."

"*Are* you a spy, Florence?" the emir asked.

"Don't you think you've accused Florence of enough for one day?" Laila interjected.

"No," Florence said. "I'm not a spy."

The emir didn't look especially convinced, though at this point, his head was spinning. "But why would Valmar have told me that he was concerned about the possibility of conflict between Matar and Wasabia?" he said.

"Who knows, darling? Maybe he wants you to buy some French fighter jets. Did that subject happen to come up?"

"He mentioned . . . something."

"So."

"Whatever the case, from now on, I don't want the two of you going about in public together. It would only cause talk."

"Ridiculous," Laila said.

"I'm the emir. I have to think about the dignity of Matar. Now you both may leave us. We have a headache."

" 'DIGNITY OF MATAR,' " Laila said to Florence outside the office. "The three most preposterous words in the English language. I'm sorry, darling. Looks like we won't be having any more mad, passionate sex. But if the dignity of Matar is at stake, what can one do? Honestly."

Florence was thinking about the concept of sexual abstinence. "Let me try something out on you," she said. "In case we want to take this to the next level."

CHAPTER FIFTEEN

The text message on Florence's secure BlackBerry said, "Blenheim Beach 2250 hours."

Blenheim Beach was an hour's drive south of Amo-Amas. A travel magazine had once named it one of the ten most beautiful beaches in the world. It had not gone on to become one of the world's most popular beaches, owing to the fact that it was the spawning ground for the banded sea krait, one of the world's prettiest and most deadly snakes. Before being renamed for Winston Churchill's illustrious ancestor, the area had been known as Noosh al Zhikh-ir, or Eve's Lagoon. Local legend said it was the site of the Garden of Eden.

Florence sat in her parked car looking out on the empty beach and the moonless night. She felt very exposed here. She'd taken pains to make sure she had not been followed. She was tired, her nerves jazzed from caffeine and adrenaline. The inside of her head felt like a ball of crumpled aluminum foil. She wanted to be home in Foggy Bottom, in a hot bubble bath, not on a stretch of sand wriggly with venomous snakes.

At a quarter to eleven, she got out of the car and walked to the water's edge, keeping an eye out for slithering things. Presently, she heard the sound of an outboard motor. She signaled with her flashlight. The signal was returned. She could not make it out until it was almost ashore: a swift inflatable boat, three men with blackened faces holding automatic weapons. A figure with an unblackened face jumped off the bow of the boat and approached.

"Bit dramatic, isn't it?" she said.

"All the flights were booked," Bobby said. He turned to the men in the boat. "Thank you, gentlemen. My compliments to the captain."

The boat backed into the surf, turned and buzzed off into the darkness.

"Man, the size of these submarines today. Had a whole room to myself. In the old days, they'd have you sleepin' inside a torpedo tube. How you been, Flo? Missed you."

Something about him seemed different. It wasn't until they were inside the car with the interior light on that she realized just how different he was. His short blond hair was now black, long and tied at the back in a ponytail. He also had a mustache. He grinned at her. "Say hello to Willie G. Underwood." The southern accent was gone, replaced with a western twang. "Reno, Nevada. Damn pleased to meet you. My card."

JACKPOTS INTERNATIONAL GAMING CONSULTANTS

"Our Dice Are Always Hot."

"And what fresh hell is this?" Florence said.

"Slot-machine repairman! We don't call ourselves that. We prefer the term 'reward adjustment specialist.' We service the big machines, your Trump 7600 or the Bugsy 1200—the monster slots that pay half or a million bucks. The ones with whistles and sirens—*Weeooooo! We have a winnerrrrrrr?* Why risk making some Dutch cigar salesman a millionaire, right? You with me?"

"Why, indeed."

"You mad at me or somethin'?" He lapsed back into his Alabama accent.

"I've been getting a lot of questions about you. Even Laila. Someone fingered you."

"Figured. That's why I'm here to fix slot machines. You got to blend in this business. It's all about blending."

"Where are you staying?"

"I'm booked into the Aladdin, on Infidel Land."

"You'll certainly blend there."

"If I really want to blend, maybe I should order up a couple Russian hookers. I'm startin' to like this assignment. You look beat, Flo."

"The reason I look 'beat' is that I've been getting visits in the middle of the night from police looking for you."

"Sorry 'bout that. But they're about to have bigger things to worry about than a little shootout in a garage."

"What are you planning to do?"

"Gonna refocus the energy around here. I see our friend Maliq has become quite the religious leader."

"Yes, and he's been doing a lot of preaching lately. Whipping up the moolahs."

"That happens when a man gets religion, puts aside his sinful past," Bobby mused. "Most of the founders of your major world religions were playboys of some kind before they found God. Then one day they hear this voice, and there's a flash of blindin' light, and the next thing you know, the hallelujah chorus is singin' and they've got a billion followers. When you think about it, Jesus was really the only one who founded a religion without first going through a young-'n'-crazy phase. He can't have had that much fun bein' a carpenter.

"I got a message for you from Uncle Sam. He's worried about you. He wants you out of here. I think he's right. Stuff's happenin' here, with more stuff about to happen."

"I'm not about to leave. This is my operation."

"I'm only the messenger. Ma'am."

"What's going on? What did you find out in Paris?"

"Since right around the time of Maliq's miraculous escape in the car, seventy-eight bank accounts at the Banque de Cannes got opened up. The names on the accounts match the seventy-eight leadin' moolahs and were funded to a hundred thousand dollars each. Between what these guys are gettin' from the French, on top of the baksheesh their own government here pays 'em, I'm contemplatin' taking up the religious life myself."

"So it's true—they're mounting a coup against Gazzy?"

"That would be my guess," Bobby said. "They've been cultivatin' Maliq for some time now, givin' him fast cars and pourin' enough Château Lafite in him to drown a cat. With Maliq in, they'd have what they've always wanted—shorefront. Naval bases, tanker terminals. Hell, by the time they're finished in Amo, it'll look like the Riviera. They'll probably even have film festivals. They'll say to King Tallulah and the Wasabis, 'Okay, we got rid of Emir Gazzir for you and installed the idiot brother. *Naturellement,* we'll be wantin' a discount on crude. But don't worry, you can make up for it chargin' the Americans double what they've been payin'.' " Bobby shook his head. "I really should've figured this out a lot sooner. If I had, I sure as heck wouldn'ta used Air France for my fake flight out of here. That was *truly* stupid of me. That's why they knew it was me killed that guy in the garage. They blew me to the Mataris. On the other hand, that's what led me to them. So in a way, we're even. But not for long, 'cause I'm about to open a can of industrial-strength whup-ass on our French friends."

"What are you going to do?"

"Flo—Florence, you really don't need to know that."

"You're still working for me," Florence said. "Aren't you?"

"I'm not sure this entire situation has a whole lot of coherence to it at this point. But listen, I think Uncle Sam's got a point about you gettin' out of here. TVMatar was a great idea, but instead of liberatin' women, it appears to be plungin' the region into considerable distress."

"It'll be a nightmare here, especially for women, if Maliq takes over and the Wasabis are calling the shots. You know what they'll do."

Bobby looked out the window. "Yeah," he said, "if I was a Matari, I'd definitely be inclined to invest in companies that manufacture *abaayas* and veils. Things could get quite ugly around here."

"The French ambassador told Gazzy there's a rumor going around that Laila and I are lesbians."

Bobby sighed. "Man, they are good. Gotta hand it to them. If word goes 'round here that you and the emir's wife are havin' a roll in the hammock, I'd better call that water taxi that just dropped me off and tell 'em to pick you up."

"I'm not leaving, and that's that."

"You're the boss." They rode in silence. "Uh . . ." Bobby said.

"What?"

"This rumor—that's all it is, just a rumor?"

"I—where do you—how can you ask me such a thing?"

"I'm only askin'. As the person in charge of security here, I might as well have all the information."

"Well, now you do."

"All right, then."

"Just because I haven't made a pass at you—"

"Flo"—Bobby sighed—"that has nothin' to do with it."

"Would you mind not calling me that?"

"All right. Ma'am."

"Don't call me that, either. Why do I have to sound like a cleaning woman or an old lady?"

"All right. Florence of Arabia. Is that what you want me to call you?"

"Don't call me anything." Florence looked over at Bobby. He was smiling. "What's so funny? I don't see anything funny."

"I was just thinkin'," Bobby said, "what great strides we're makin' toward peace 'n' stability in the Middle East."

CHAPTER SIXTEEN

Florence decided for the time being not to tell George and Rick that Bobby was back in town. In the event of an interrogation, the less they knew, the better.

"May I say something, Firenze?"

"Yes, George."

"You look awful."

"Thank you."

"Maybe I don't look so hot myself. May I say something else?"

"*Yes,* George."

"I'm getting the distinct feeling that you're not telling me something. Renard also feels this way."

"There's just, you know, lots going on."

"Do you mind if I ask you something?"

"*What,* George?"

"It's really none of my business. Don't ask, don't tell, I say, but are you and the sheika . . . There's this rumor going around."

"No, George, I am not having a fling with the sheika."

"Not that I'd mind—"

"That's hardly the point. Really, I wouldn't expect my own staff to be gossiping about this. It's disinformation put out by the French, among others."

"Ah. Rather clever of them. They tend to look down on those of the Sapphic persuasion around these parts."

Renard walked in. "Hey, Florence, you know anything about this rumor going around about you and the emir's wife?"

"We were just discussing it."

"Oh." Rick nodded tentatively.

"It's not true," Florence said.

"Hey, you know, whatever."

Florence sighed inwardly. Did she now have to explain to Rick that because she hadn't made a pass at him, that didn't mean she and the emir's wife were—how had Bobby put it—having a roll in the hammock?

"Never mind," she said. "Why don't you put it out on the six o'clock broadcast that I'm not having an affair with the wife of the ruler."

"We ought," George said, "to give *some* thought to this. You don't want something like that going around. They may be liberal in Matar, but they're still Arabs."

"I'm wide open to any ideas you have."

"I have an idea," Rick said. "I think you and I should be seen in public pawing each other."

Florence stared at Rick. "Thanks for the input."

"I'm serious. If you want to show them you're hetero, what better way?" He grinned. "We could sit at the Café Clementine and smooch."

George said, "They're not crazy for public displays of affection, hetero *or* homo."

"If it's a choice between having people think she's doing it with the emir's wife or with me . . ." Rick shrugged.

Florence's secure phone went off. It was Bobby, or Willie G. Underwood, or whatever he was calling himself these days. She heard the sound of slot machines in the background.

"You alone?" he said.

"I'm sitting here with George and Rick. What's up?"

"There's a situation developin' in Kaffa. No one knows about it, so don't tell anyone about it. We just received word that Princess Hamzin, King Tallulah's second wife, busted into the king's council meeting yesterday. That's bad enough. The last time somethin' like that happened in that country, dinosaurs were still walkin' the earth. As if that wasn't bad enough, she was wearing no veil, and pants. *Pants.* And if that wasn't bad enough, she started lecturin' the king and his council about improvin' the lot of women in the royal kingdom. Appears the princess is a real fan of TVMatar. The king was reportedly taken to the hospital with chest pains."

"It's begun, then," Florence said. "The revolt of the Arab women. This is great news, Bobby."

"I'd say that depends on your definition of 'great.' The Wasabis are madder'n adders. Our birds are picking up all *sorts* of chatter. And it's pretty clear who they blame for this. This is your revolution, Flo. My guess is someone's gonna walk into your office any minute now and take you to see the emir. That's why I'm calling—to put you in the picture."

"We need to get this out, put it on the news."

"Whoa, whoa. Negative. Who are you, Bob Woodward? This is all off the record. No one outside the palace knows about this. They don't want anyone to know about it, for obvious reasons. You go puttin' this on TV, all hell's gonna break loose."

"Then why did you tell me?"

"So you can keep your head down. I sure didn't tell you so's you could go wavin' red flags in their faces."

"Bobby, this is why we came here in the first place."

"Yo, Flo of Arabia, listen up for a second. We did not—let me say it again—*not* come here to start a war between Wasabia and Matar. Are we on the same page here? I'll bet you a million dollars—which I can access, now that I know how to fix a damn slot machine—that our Uncle Sam would agree with me on this."

"May I remind you that this isn't your operation? You're along here to provide security and intelligence. And all you've managed to do thus far is shoot up a garage and alert the French secret services to our presence here. Are *we* on the same page now?"

"If you don't want to listen to me, why don't you call Uncle Sam and ask him his opinion of the situation? Inasmuch as he's payin' our salaries."

"I'll do just that. But what about the princess?"

"I'd say it's not lookin' great for the princess."

"What do we know?"

"Is this off the record?"

"Who are you, Deep Throat? What do we know?"

"Sounds bad. We picked up some references in the chatter to lapidation."

"Lapidation? Stoning?"

"This wasn't exactly the brightest thing she could've done. Embarrass her husband, the king, in front of all his ministers? Hell, I wouldn't do that back in Alabama."

"What are you saying?"

"I'm saying that Princess Hamzin is in for a real rough ride."

"We can't just abandon her, Bobby."

"What do you mean? She's not working for us."

"But this is our fight. This is our revolution. We started it."

"Wait a minute. We didn't tell her to storm into her husband's meeting and give everyone the finger."

"Have you ever *seen* a lapidation?"

"Well, no, but what's that got to do with it?"

"I have. A video clip, anyway. She couldn't have been older than nineteen. Adultery. They use small stones so it takes longer. It was awful, Bobby."

"I don't doubt it for a second, but look, Flo, we got to keep our eye on the big picture here. You go public with somethin' like this, and they're gonna know exactly how you came by the information, and this whole thing is gonna come down on your head. And they won't be throwin' small stones, either. Giant big fuckin' rocks the size of—"

"Bobby, this is the moment. This is Aqaba. We can't back down now. We can't just leave her to die."

"Dammit, girl, what did you *think* was going to happen? That broadcastin' all this feminist crap into a kingdom that's still back in the fourteenth century was gonna result in some conference or somethin'? That there'd be panel discussions with everyone wearing name tags? And that they'd say, 'Oh, why, you're quite right, wise American lady, you're absolutely right, we shouldn't be persecutin' our women like this. How medieval of us! Okay, ladies, throw away your veils, this way to the driver's-license window. And just to demonstrate how liberal we're gonna be—we're not even gonna chop off your little heads anymore!' Is that how you thought this was going to play out? This is the Middle East! The cradle of destabilization, mother of all tar babies, the planet's longest-runnin' argument! Don't you understand that since the dawn of time, startin' with the Garden of Eden, *nothing has ever gone right here*? And nothing ever will go right here."

"Then what are we doing here?"

"From the looks of it, fuckin' things up even worse. But at least we're consistent. That ought to be our motto: 'U.S. Foreign Policy in the Middle East: Making Matters Worse.' Flo? You there? Talk to me, Florence. Flo! Dammit, girl . . ."

Florence called Laila. "I have to see you. It's urgent."

"It's not the best time," Laila said. "Gazzy's in a foul temper. He's had all sorts of calls. Something's going on, and he won't tell me."

"I think I know what it is, but I don't want to explain over the phone."

"I don't think it's wise to annoy him right now by being seen together. I know it's all absurd, but we oughtn't feed this ridiculous rumor."

"It's important," Florence said. "I wouldn't otherwise. Chartwell Mall, by the Starbucks. I'll be outside by the ficus tree."

"Is this wise, darling, to be hitting the mall at a time like this?"

FLORENCE WATCHED THROUGH the mesh opening in her face veil. The woman approaching her was dressed from head to toe in a white *abaaya*. She approached and stood there, looking about uncertainly.

"It's me," Florence said.

"God be praised," Laila said. "Look at us both. I feel like a guest on *Cher Azade*."

They sat by the ficus tree as the bourgeoisie, haute, middle and low of Matar ambulated past in the Muzak hush of the mall.

"I managed to elude my bodyguards by slipping out the back of the dressing room at Ralph Lauren. They are inept. God forbid someone should actually try to assassinate me. Well, what's all this enormous urgency about?"

Florence told Laila about Princess Hamzin. Laila absorbed the news in silence.

"I met her once. She's the prettiest of Tallulah's wives, not that that will help her. God, what *could* she have been thinking?" Laila sighed. Her head turned toward the Starbucks.

"Hundreds of years ago—perhaps a thousand—this area right here was a souk. Teeming with merchants and ships and caravans. Some of the first coffee ever drunk by Europeans passed through here. Now we have Starbucks. Thus do we progress. Well, Firenze, I must say, you seem to be very well informed about all sorts of things. What else do you have to tell me outside Starbucks? Have you gotten me mixed up in some sort of CIA operation after all?"

"I don't really know who I'm working for," Florence said.

"*That* smacks of evasion."

"I know how it must sound. But the truth is, I don't. There's this man who calls himself Uncle Sam—"

"I really don't want to hear this," Laila said angrily. "If I'm going to end up in a prison cell, I'd rather not have anything they want. You might have told me, Florence."

"That's what everyone tells me these days." For once, Florence was glad to be wearing a veil. She felt tears welling up. "I'm sorry. I'd been looking for the right moment to tell you."

"It's not that I hadn't wondered," Laila said in a slightly softer tone. "It did occur. I mean, I'm not a fool. But it was all going so well that I concluded it couldn't possibly be a CIA operation. They always turn out so badly. And now . . . So, your Mr. Bobby, then—it was him in the garage."

"Yes. It was self-defense."

"It always is. What was he doing there in the first place?"

"Checking out Maliq's car. He found out it was rigged. The black smoke, the miracle, it was a fake to provide an excuse for his religious conversion."

"So . . . we're to have a coup, then?"

"I can arrange to get you and your son out of the country," Florence said.

Laila stood. "Thank you, but I think you've been enough help as it is."

CHAPTER SEVENTEEN

Florence returned to her office, thoroughly depressed, to the news from her secretary that "your uncle" had called.

"He didn't say which uncle. He seemed to think you'd know."

Florence did know; and she knew furthermore that it was not a call she wanted. She dialed. Uncle Sam picked up halfway through the first ring, never a good start. She could hear the hissing of steam from his ears.

"What in the name of all that is holy do you think you're *doing* over there?" he spluttered.

"I see Bobby has given you a fill."

"A fill? Is *that* what you call it? Jumping Jehoshaphat, you can't go revealing this information on *television*! Do you have any idea how sensitive it is?"

Florence felt a certain weariness. It occurred to her that she had spent most of her time in the government arguing. "I told Laila I'm with the government," she said.

"What? You did . . . what?"

"As long as you're mad at me, you might as well be really mad."

"Why would you *do* such a thing?"

"I was tired of deceiving her. I think she knew anyway."

"Florence," he said, his tone quite changed. "I'm pulling you out of there, effective immediately. You've done a dandy job. But you're tired. You need some stateside time. Better still, a couple of days in Paris or London, shopping—on your uncle's dime. How does that sound?"

"You sent me here to start a revolution. Now you want me to go shopping?"

"Oh, for heaven's sake, lighten up, young lady. I'm not trying to make some big chauvinistic point. If you'd rather go to a museum, go to a museum. I'm all in favor of culture."

"That's very progressive of you."

"Florence, if you put this story about the princess on the air, it will— Oh, how do I explain?"

"In English?"

"English. Very well, I'll give you a perfect English parallel. In World War Two, Churchill found out the Germans were going to bomb Coventry. But if he warned the people in Coventry, the Germans would find out the British had broken their code. So he let the Germans bomb Coventry. And people died. But he won the war."

"In other words, one has to be ruthless."

"Exactly. Exactly."

"Thank you, Uncle Sam. You've clarified the situation for me."

"I knew you'd understand. I'll send the plane for you. Gosh, you must be just knackered. And what a job you've done. What a job. Think of a week in a suite at Le Bristol on the rue du Faubourg St. Honoré. My favorite hotel. Sleep late, massage, the *museums* . . ."

"It sounds wonderful."

"I'll be there when the plane lands. I'll be the one holding a sign at baggage claim!"

"Bye, Uncle Sam."

FLORENCE CALLED IN Fatima Sham and handed her the script for the broadcast. Fatima read it. Her eyes shot up from the script.

"I haven't seen anything yet on this. Is it exclusive?"

"Oh, yeah."

"Our source?"

"Reliable."

"Ah," Fatima said. "I see."

"This could be your big break, Fatima."

"Yes. It might even lead to a job in legitimate journalism. Florence, this seems a good time to ask."

"Shoot."

"*Are* we some sort of CIA operation?"

"I'm not really sure myself." Florence sighed. "That must sound terribly evasive."

"Well"—Fatima smiled—"it does, yes."

"We probably are, one way or the other. But it is also true that this girl in Kaffa is going to be killed if we don't do anything about it. And now you know everything I do."

"Oh dear," Fatima said. "And I thought we were doing such a jolly good job."

"I thought so, too. I should tell you something else. Reporting this story won't make you any friends in Wasabia. And the situation here could change. We've stirred up the adder bed. I'll understand if you'd rather not go on the air with this. I could do it myself, but that would give the other side ammunition to use against us."

Fatima looked at the script. "We can't just let them stone her to death. I'd better hit the phones, see what I can dig up." At the door, she stopped and said, "Whatever happens, good for you, Florence."

FLORENCE CALLED GEORGE and Rick into her office and shut the door, then raised Bobby on the phone and put him on the speaker.

"Bobby, I want you to get George and Rick out of the country right away."

"Why?" After a pause, he said, "I thought you told Uncle Sam you weren't . . . What's goin' on, Florence?"

"Bobby, please, just for ten minutes, pretend that you work for me? I want them both out of here tonight. Can you arrange for that water-taxi service of yours?"

"Aw, hell, girl, I can't just order up a nuclear submarine like it's Chinese takeout."

"Submarine?" George said, paling. "Stop *right* there. I don't do submarines. I'm claustrophobic."

"It's a big submarine, George," Florence said.

"It would have to be as big as the *Queen Mary 2* and stay on top of the water."

"George," Florence said sternly, "twelve hours from now, the most beautiful sight in the world to you might just be the conning tower of a U.S. fucking submarine. Bobby?"

"What?"

"Get them out of here. Sub, camel, hot-air ballon, I don't care. This is a high-priority exfiltration. All right? Can I count on you? Hello, Bobby?"

"I'm *here,* goddammit." After a few moments, his voice came back over the speaker. "You boys there?"

"We're here," Rick said, speaking for the stricken-looking George, who had clearly begun running the horror movie in his mind, starring himself, descending the ladder deeper, deeper . . .

"Okay, listen up. You know the Café Winston, on the Esplanade by the open-air fish restaurant? It's three-fifteen now. Be there in one hour. No later, understand? Do not go to your apartments. Do not take anything from the office with you. Just walk out the front door. Leave separately, ten minutes apart. Each of you carry a newspaper or magazine under your arm. It'll make you look casual. Walk, don't run. Don't look over your shoulder. If you see someone followin' you, it's probably one of my people. Everything will be fine. When you get to the café, order a coffee and sit tight. Pay for the coffee when it's put down. Leave a normal tip. You'll see two white Mercedes Amo taxis pull up, a few minutes apart. Each will have a strip of yellow tape on the radio antenna. George, you take the first cab. Renard, the second. Take your newspaper with you. Have you got that? You want me to repeat it?"

"No, we've got it," Rick said.

"George, you there?" Bobby said.

"What?"

"It's gonna be all right. You're gonna be all right. Do you have some Valium or somethin' on you? Never mind, I'll have some in the cab. You'll be all right. Hey, there's lots of, uh, people like you on subs."

"Claustrophobes?"

"No, you know, uh— Never mind, you'll be fine."

"Bobby?" Florence said.

"*What?*" he snapped.

"Thank you."

Bobby clicked off.

"He's not really thrilled with me at the moment."

"For God's sakes, what's going on?" George said.

"You're both going on R and R. You've both done a spectacular job. I'm proud of you." She felt herself choking up but managed to swallow it.

"Firenze," George said, "*what* is going on?"

"It's about to get messy. I'd rather not have to worry about you two."

"Hey, hold on, I can handle it," Rick said. "You're talking to the man who put on a golf tournament in North Korea with O. J. Simpson."

"Rick, we're beyond spin. Look, we're about to lose the backing of whoever the hell it was who sent us over here. That makes our situation here, as they say at the old State Department, nonviable. This is when you evacuate nonessential personnel."

" 'Nonessential'?" Rick said. "Is that what I am?"

"You're the most brilliant—and twisted—mind in the business. And you're leaving in fifty-five minutes."

"Why can't we all leave?" George said.

Florence looked at her two boys. "I'm coming, too. I'll meet you on the beach, but I have to take care of some things."

They left. On the way out, she heard George telling Rick, "I'm not going on a submarine. There's not enough Valium in the world."

When they were gone, Florence burst into tears, but, efficient girl that she was, she briskly got it over with and plunged back to work.

CHAPTER EIGHTEEN

"*Good evening. I'm Fatima Sham for TVMatar, and this is the six o'clock* report. Princess Hamzin, second wife of King Tallulah of Wasabia, has been sentenced to death by stoning. Her crime: petitioning her husband and his ministers for basic women's rights. I spoke this afternoon by telephone with Prince Jerbil al Jakar, minister of Wasabi external affairs."

A still photograph of the minister appeared on-screen, accompanied by a recording of the telephone conversation.

"This is a monstrous lie! There is no truth at all to it. It is lies. All lies! Who has told you this terrible lie? Some villain."

"Will you make the princess available for an interview with us?"

"The royal household does not give interviews. No, this is a gross provocation. This is an attempt to interfere in our sovereign affairs. This will not succeed. No, no."

"Can you produce proof that the princess is alive?"

"Of course she is alive! Everyone is alive! Everyone is happy. Good night to you, madame."

There followed the sound of a phone being slammed down.

"That was Prince Jerbil al Jakar, minister of Wasabi external affairs," Fatima continued. "The Wasabi practice when stoning women to death is to match the size of the stones to the severity of the offense. In cases of adultery, small stones are used to prolong the execution. It is not known what size stones might be used on a royal wife for the crime of petitioning to improve the situation of women. I spoke with Grand Mufti Adman Ifkir, one of Wasabia's leading religious authorities."

The tape rolled. "Grand Mufti Ifkir, thank you for speaking with TVMatar."

"Yes, I am here. God be praised."

"This sounds like a very serious offense Princess Hamzin has committed."

"Oh, most serious, most serious. There can be no punishment severe enough."

"What about stoning? That's pretty severe."

"Only if you use very small stones."

"Why not just cut off her head?"

"No, no, no. That is too quick. Too quick."

"So what size stones would you recommend?"

"The smallest. Like this. These are the best. Like the ones we throw at Satan in Mecca during the hajj."

"Those *are* small. Wouldn't it take a very long time to kill a woman with stones that small?"

"Yes. That is the point. It's a mercy. It gives her time to repent of her crime."

"Thank you for taking the time to speak with us."

"You are welcome."

Florence said through the intercom into Fatima's earpiece, "That'll get their attention. Good interviews."

"Florence," said a control-room assistant. "The sheika Laila. Line two."

"Christ, Florence," Laila said, "what are you *doing*?"

"What I came here to do."

"Does that include destabilizing the entire region? Giving Wasabia an excuse to invade us? And you, you'll be long gone, won't you? Last seen climbing aboard an American helicopter." She hung up before Florence could answer.

FLORENCE STAYED AT her post in the control room through the night and into the next morning, monitoring developments. There's no better place, really, to monitor developments. All the world came to her on dozens of screens. On the one in front of her was a grim-looking man identified in the Chyron as PRINCE BAWAD, WASABI FOREIGN MINISTER. Florence watched the husband of the late princess Nazrah, whose midnight dash to freedom had set off this chain of events. He looked distinctly unamused as he made his way past a scrum of bawling reporters outside the United Nations. "There is not one word of truth in this libel." He scowled, before disappearing into a limousine, surrounded by nervous security men.

On another monitor, Florence watched a crowd of women outside the Wasabi embassy in Washington, holding signs saying WASABI PIGS and RELEASE PRINCESS HAMZIN.

Well, Nazrah, Florence thought, *look what a great fuss you've created.*

Another monitor showed a press briefing in progress at the State Department in Washington.

"I have nothing for you on this at this point in time," the spokesman said, more lugubriously than usual, to a forest of raised hands in front of him.

"Has the secretary spoken with the Wasabis about this?"

"Not to my— As I said, I have nothing for you on this."

"What is the princess's current status?"

"You're free to ask their foreign ministry."

A French reporter asked, "What can you inform us about the relationship between the U.S. government and TVMatar, which has broadcast this provocative story?"

"I'm not aware of any connection."

"But the funding, it comes from the CIA, no?"

"I wouldn't have any comment on that."

Florence found herself thinking about George and Rick. She imagined them all on the rubber boat, on their way out to the waiting submarine, guarded by Navy SEALs with black faces. George would be complaining. She smiled, thinking of Bobby telling him about all the hunky sailors he'd meet.

She decided to check in. She dialed Uncle Sam on the secure cell. It rang several times, and a recorded voice told her she had reached a nonworking number. They were destroying the connective tissue. She was alone now.

Toward four in the morning, she got exhausted and needed to rest for at least an hour or so. There was an escape hatch in the ceiling of the bathroom off the control room. Bobby's people had installed it. She opened it and climbed up onto the roof of TVMatar, which had a view of the city and the Gulf. She lay down and looked up at the night sky over Matar. She knew that on any given night in the Middle East, many people were sleeping on their roofs—to escape the heat, or the secret police. In a part of the world where they come for you in the middle of the night, it is a sensible sleeping arrangement. The only problem is that sometimes, along with the stars falling, come bullets raining down. Arabs love to fire joy shots into the air to celebrate life's victories: a wedding, the birth of a son, the news that a new martyr has ascended to heaven.

Florence drifted in and out of restless sleep until dawn, then climbed back down to the control room to the news that the Wasabis had produced evidence that the Princess Hamzin was alive and well.

Triumphant evidence. The princess was not only alive and well but shopping for jewelry, in Paris, no less. French television was showing footage of her, taken through the front window of Hermès. The images showed Princess Hamzin handing over an American Express card for a $150,000 diamond bracelet. The news announcer came on with a smirk and said, "Evidently, the princess prefers to *wear* stones."

Florence scanned the other monitors. They were all showing the same footage. It was followed by Prince Bawad, a picture of smugness.

"The world can plainly see," he said, stroking his goatee, "what an oppressed life our royal princesses lead."

For the next hour, Florence watched a succession of talking heads on dozens of television shows. One, an anthropology professor at the University of Chicago, said that the U.S. had no business trying to impose feminist values abroad, for the reason that many, perhaps even the majority of Arab or Indian or African women, "don't want to be liberated." "How would *we* feel," he asked thoughtfully, "if one of *those* countries tried to impose *its* values on *us*?"

Florence was pondering whether the majority of, say, Arab women were content with the status quo when her cell phone rang. It was Laila.

"I shouldn't have said what I said."

"You don't have any apologies to make to me," Florence said.

"I take it you've seen the images? From Paris?"

"Yes."

"Well?"

"There are two possible explanations," Florence said. "The first is that the information was wrong. The second is that we saved her life."

"I must say, it wasn't quite my idea of Arab suffrage, forking over an American Express card for a hundred-and-fifty-thousand-dollar bracelet at Hermès."

"You saw the expression on her face. She looked doped."

"Is that what you're going to say on television?"

"I don't know." Florence wished Renard, master of spin and counterspin, were here. "I've been outmaneuvered."

"Would you care to know where the New Saladin stands? I think he's about to institute lapidation in Matar—for TVMatar executives. Will we be issuing an apology?"

"To those bastards? Over my dead body."

"I wouldn't say that in the Middle East, if I were you. Better issue something. I'll try and fend off the New Saladin, but you'd better get cracking."

Florence stared at the bank of glowing TV screens in front of her and summoned Fatima.

"Fatima," she said, "the day will come when you practice legitimate journalism. But that day will not be this day."

"GOOD AFTERNOON FROM the TVMatar newsroom in Amo-Amas, I'm Fatima Sham.

"A source close to the Wasabi royal family has confirmed to TVMatar that the princess Hamzin was in fact sentenced to death by stoning for the crime of disrespect. He further confirms that because of negative world reaction to this news, along with mounting international outrage, the royal household is attempting a cover-up. Last night, according to the source, the princess was drugged and put aboard a Royal Wasabi Air Force plane and flown to Paris, where a staged shopping expedition was mounted to make it appear that she is thousands of miles away, buying expensive jewelry, and not facing a horrible death. We bring you this exclusive interview with the Kaffa palace insider.

Because he fears for his life, we agreed not to show his face and to identify him only as 'Abdul.'

"Can you tell us what happened?"

"They were going to stone my lady to death. With little small stones. Oh, terrible. Then came the report on the television—praise God! The king Tallulah's minister became fearful and said, 'Oh, this will make a terrible, terrible impression on the royal image! We must wait and kill her when no one is paying attention.' So they came with big needles filled with drugs and stuck her, like this." Abdul jabbed his arm. "And took her to a plane to Paris."

"How do you know all this?"

"I was there! I saw. With my own two eyes, praise God that I am allowed to keep them. There was a French person."

"What French person?"

"Oh, very French. An old French person with gray hair. He has been in the palace here many times. The royals listen to him all the time. They think everything French is good. He tells them what to do, and they do it. He tells them, 'Bring her to Paris, we will make it look like a shopping trip.' "

"So you're saying the television images of the princess shopping, they were all fixed to make it look like she's in no danger?"

"Yes, but she is in great danger! Still! When no one is paying attention, they will kill her. My poor lady!"

"Abdul, thank you for telling us this. You are very courageous to come forward. One final question: You say the French have a lot of influence with the Wasabi royals?"

"Yes. Many times I have listened to the princes and the king on the telephone, many times with the French saying, 'You must help us get back the coastline that the English villain Churchill took from us. We will give you oil and navy bases.' Many times I have heard these conversations. Many, many times."

"Thank you. God keep you safe. When we return, we'll have a report from our correspondent in Paris."

Florence sat back in her chair in the control room. Too bad Renard hadn't been here to watch it with her. She felt certain he would have been proud of her. She was particularly pleased with the French element.

Laila rang. "Wow. How on earth did you find Abdul? What a coup."

"He works in the cafeteria here," Florence said.

"Aha." There was a pause. "Well, *that* will win us an Emmy for hard investigative news. I think I won't share that part with the New Saladin. Oh, it's coming back on. I don't want to miss a word. I'll call you at the commercial."

"Welcome back to TVMatar News, I'm Fatima Sham. We now bring you this exclusive report from Rita Ferreira, our Paris bureau correspondent."

"Yes, Fatima, I'm standing outside the gates of the Onzième Bureau, a little-known branch of the French intelligence service. We tried to speak to officials here about a *report* that they have been funneling money secretly to Matar's mullahs, in an attempt to start a coup in the tranquil Gulf nation and replace its benevolent and popular ruler, the emir Gazzir Bin Haz, with a fundamentalist Islamic dictatorship."

The screen showed the reporter trying to thrust a microphone through the window of a dark sedan driving out the gate.

"TVMatar, hello! *Bonjour!* Is it true that you are trying to start a revolution in Matar?"

The car kept going. The screen showed two gendarmes approaching, waving the camera away. "*Allez! Allez!*"

"We are with TVMatar, here to ask questions."

"No. You must go. Go. Go now."

"But we want to speak with someone from the Onzième Bureau, to ask about their plans to destabilize our country."

"You must ask to the Foreign Bureau. *Allez!*"

CHAPTER NINETEEN

"I *think," Laila said over the phone, "that you'd better get over here to the* palace. The French ambassador has requested an audience. The New Saladin's spine could use some stiffening. It's the *only* part of him that isn't normally stiff. I'll send a car."

Florence was driven through the tranquil, baking streets of Amo-Amas to the palace. She walked on lapis-lazuli-flecked tiles past cool alabaster fountains and shaded terraces and mosaic corridors, past bodyguards in ceremonial dress, and into the emir's audience room, where the Lion of Matar awaited. The Lion was frowning.

"*Well,* Miss Intrigue," he said, "you've made me very popular. Everyone wants a meeting with me suddenly. The French ambassador, the Wasabi ambassador. Your American ambassador. Even the Russian ambassador. What can he want, I wonder? I should just invite them all at once. It's been a long time since we've held a grand diplomatic audience. I don't know whether to thank you or have you deported. I could just have you escorted to the Wasabi border and tossed across. I'm sure King Tallulah would be delighted to have you as *his* guest."

"I regret having caused His Majesty such consternation."

"Oh, pish. Now, what's this about the French buying my mullahs? Is this true?"

"Yes."

"And how do you know this arresting fact?"

"I'm in the news-gathering business."

"Are you with the CIA? I want an honest answer now."

"Not that I am aware, my lord."

The emir stared. "What do you mean, not that you're aware? What kind of answer is that?"

"A vague, honest answer. There was a man, but he's vanished. So now it would seem that I'm an employee of TVMatar. Which is to say, I work for you."

"Stop throwing sand in my eyes. This man, who is he?"

"I was never sure. He represented himself as being with the United States government. He was possessed of great resources, certainly. Enough to make all this possible. The initial funding, the gift of Your Majesty's helicopter . . ."

"I want an answer!"

"Darling," Laila said, "calm yourself. You'll give yourself a rash. Florence is trying to explain. Though I must admit I'm confused, too, at this point. But TVMatar is fully independent. *You* own it, darling. Morever, you're doing very, very well by it. You're now the largest broadcaster in the Arab world."

"Yes yes yes, but was this *funded by American intelligence*?"

"Darling," Laila said, "if it had been, do you really think it would have worked this well?"

"Good point," Florence murmured.

"I don't know that it's turned out 'well,' " the emir said. "And don't try to deceive me with your honey tongues. I want to know—right now, this instant—*was this an American operation*?"

"Yes," Florence said. "I regret deceiving you. But I do not regret what we've done."

The emir looked from Florence to his wife. "Did *you* know about this?"

"No," Florence interjected. "I deceived Laila, too. I deceived you both."

The emir sat back in his divan seat and tapped his purplish lips with a fingertip. "Then I have no choice. There will have to be an arrest. And a trial, and then . . . Look at the position you've put me in. I hardly have a choice."

"Darling," Laila said, "let's think this through before we do anything hasty. Florence has admitted to working for some esoteric division of the U.S. government. But TVMatar is entirely controlled by us. And it's made Matar, and you, a voice on the world stage. We're a long way from fig oil and the Churchill tax.

"And now Florence and her curious mice seem to have exposed a French plot to replace you on the throne with your odious little brother. So she's made you independently rich and important, and is trying to keep you on that throne. And you want to arrest her. You do what you think is right, but if you insist on this idiotic course of action, all you'll be saying to the whole world is 'Gosh, wasn't *I* a booby! This American woman managed to pull the wool completely over my eyes!' So much for the New Saladin. But it's up to you, darling."

The emir rubbed his forehead.

Laila glanced over at Florence. "Are you *still* a U.S. agent?" she asked.

Florence imagined she was giving a press briefing at the State Department. *I have nothing for you on that at this time.*

"Florence?"

"No. No, I don't think I am at this point."

Laila turned to the emir. "There. So why the fuss?"

The emir regarded the two women standing in front of him warily. "If I find," he said, "that you two were in collusion, there will be consequences. Severe consequences."

"Shouldn't we give some thought to what you're going to tell Monsieur Valmar?"

In due course, the French ambassador was announced. Laila and Florence withdrew through a separate door before he was ushered in.

"You might have given me some warning that you were about to admit to being an American spy," Laila said crossly.

"Not a spy, Laila. I was never that."

"Whatever. The situation seems stabilized for the time being. But *au revoir,* Switzerland of the Gulf."

"Yes," Florence said. "It's starting to feel more like the Middle East."

FLORENCE RETURNED TO TVMATAR. Her cell phone rang. She picked up, frowned; recognizing the voice.

"What do *you* want?" she said.

"That's not a very friendly hello," Uncle Sam said. "I've been trying frantically to get you."

"Really? How odd. I called you several times and got a nonworking number. I had the distinct feeling that I'd been thrown overboard."

"These phones. They drive me cuckoo."

"Oh, please. What do you want? I'm very busy."

"We need to talk, Florence."

"Talk."

"In person. I'm sending the plane. Again. I can have it there in two hours. This isn't a request, young lady."

"I don't work for you anymore." She heard a sigh. "I'll send you a formal letter of resignation, if you prefer. I told them all about you."

"Told who about me?"

"The emir. Laila. It felt wonderful."

"Oh, goodness, Florence. *Why* would you do such a thing?"

"I got tired of lying. Sorry."

"You've got clientitis. Look, it happens. Practically every ambassador we send overseas, they end up lobbying for the country instead of the U.S. Fortunately, there's a cure."

"Oh? What?"

"You get on a plane and come *home*. And by the second day, you wake up and it all seems like a dream."

"I'll come home when I'm finished here."

"You *are* finished there. What do I have to do—send in Delta Force to get you? Don't think I won't. Florence, *don't make me come down there*."

"Goodbye, Sam. Thank you for everything."

"Is it the sheika?"

"What do you mean?"

"These rumors—are they true? Are you, how to put it, having a *thing* with the sheika?"

"This is absurd."

"We're picking up a *lot* of chatter about this, Florence. It's very dangerous for you. You know how Arabs can be. The whole manhood thing."

"Unlike us, say?"

"You know perfectly well what I'm saying. We have to get you out of there. I mean *now.*"

"Rely not on women,
Trust not to their hearts,
Whose joys and whose sorrows
Are hung to their parts."

"What are you talking about?"

"It's a verse from *The Arabian Nights*. Look, I made a promise to stay, to see this through."

"Promise? Promise to whom?"

"To my lesbian girlfriend, Laila."

"Florence—"

"Goodbye, Sam."

Florence felt a sense of weightlessness after ending the call. She stared at the cell phone, the one Bobby had given her, her link to her now former employers, still warm from Uncle Sam's spluttering. It rang again. She was about to press TALK, but then paused. She knew that cell phones were a popular means of assassination in the Middle East. The Israelis had pioneered it. A few grams of C4 plastic explosive packed into the earpiece.

Would they do that . . . to her? Florence put the phone down and backed away from it while it continued to chirrup.

"Ah!" She started.

"Sorry, Florence." She had backed into her assistant.

"Are you all right?"

"Yes, fine."

"We can't find Fatima."

FATIMA SHAM, THE ANNOUNCER, hadn't shown up for work. They'd called her apartment, her cell phone, her boyfriend, her mother. She'd disappeared.

Florence called Laila.

"I'll call Colonel Boutros," Laila said. "When was she last seen?"

"Last night, when she left the studio."

"All right, I'll get on it. Meanwhile, Gazzy's pumped up like the Michelin Man. He gave the French ambassador what-for over funding the moolahs. M. Valmar looked very pale, leaving. Gazzy hasn't felt this empowered since he exiled his mother. I hope we're not creating a Frankenstein."

WHILE THE AUTHORITIES searched for Fatima, Florence tried to concentrate on directing TVMatar's coverage of events. There was a lot to cover.

Maliq had reentered the fray. He had called for his followers to assemble at the racetrack for "prayer." The emir had denied him a permit for the assembly. The mullahs were now denouncing him for "selling out Islam to the infidels." Gazzy had responded by throwing a few of them in jail and impounding their Mercedeses. He issued a statement pointing out that by law, public assembly in Matar must be granted by the emir. It went back to the third emir (1627–41), who scholars now think suffered from agoraphobia, a rare condition in deserts, but nonetheless.

The French were suavely denying, with dismissive waves of the hand, funneling money secretly to Matar's moolahs. They were also denying the very existence of an Onzième Bureau. Meanwhile, the Onzième's agents were busy planting stories throughout the Arab media suggesting that the Bin Haz family was now a wholly owned subsidiary of the United States government.

Princess Hamzin, looking hollow-eyed, had moved with her burly male entourage from Paris to London, where she was widely photographed at Harrods and other deluxe emporia. American Express was reaping a windfall from the shopping spree. The Wasabis were still furiously demanding an apology from TVMatar for its "odious mischief-making."

In other news coming out of the Middle East: Palestinian schools were now offering online correspondence courses in suicide bombing; in Israel, American archaeologists had discovered a first-century scroll underneath the Old City that purported to be a certificate of marriage between a Nazarene carpenter named Yeshua and a former prostitute named Mariah, from the town of Magdala. This caused a great sensation for months, until carbon-dating and an investigation traced the document to the publicity department of a New York City publishing house.

THREE DAYS AFTER Fatima's disappearance, a package was delivered to the front desk of TVMatar. After it was determined not to contain a bomb, the package turned out to contain a videotape. It showed Fatima buried in sand up to her neck, being stoned to death with small rocks. The tape was twenty minutes long. Everyone who watched it wept.

Florence brought the tape to Laila. She could not bring herself to view it again, so she left the room while Laila viewed it.

She waited outside on the terrace, looking out over the Gulf in the moonlight, her skin misted by salty droplets from the fountain that spouted out the royal crest. Laila emerged, pale and shaken. Neither woman spoke. The two of them stood by the balustrade overlooking the gardens, listening to the waves lap the shore and the onshore breeze rustle the fronds of the date palms.

CHAPTER TWENTY

It's a miserable business," said the emir. "I'm not saying it isn't, but we have no proof."

"Proof," Florence said angrily. "Who else could it have been?"

"What are you trying to do? Start a war? It's horrid and regretful, and I will get to the bottom of this matter. But you will, under no circumstances, broadcast this videotape. That would only play into the hands of whoever did this."

"Emir," Florence said, "this woman was a citizen of your country. She lived under your protection. Are your people now fair game, to be hunted like gazelle at the pleasure of poaching Wasabi raiders?"

"Of course not. And I'm not sure I like your tone, madame."

"Forgive me. I forgot that I was addressing the New Saladin."

"Your situation here is complicated enough without adding insolence. Laila, perhaps it would be best if you showed our guest out."

"Gazzir," Laila said, "you can't just let this pass. It may have been an act of retaliation, but it was also a test of your resolve."

"What would you have me do?"

"At least show the world what they did to this woman."

"But we don't know *who* did it."

"Then just show it," Florence said, "and let the world draw its own conclusion."

"It *is* a war you want, Madame CIA," the emir said. "I'm not going to give you one. You came here to make mayhem, and now you have it. You don't have the stomach for it? You should have stayed home. You're lucky it wasn't you on that tape."

"What a thing to say, Gazzir," Laila said.

"No," Florence said. "He's right. It should have been me."

"I'm not going to start a jihad just to satisfy your cravings for martyrdom. Now, I have a very full schedule. You may both retire."

Laila walked with Florence to the car. She whispered in Florence's ear, out of hearing of her bodyguard, "Coffee tomorrow, ten o'clock."

FLORENCE'S NEW GOVERNMENT "bodyguard" did not follow her into the control-room bathroom. The next morning at nine o'clock, Florence took the *abaaya* that she kept in a drawer in her office. She went into the bathroom and up the escape hatch, out onto the roof, down a fire escape and walked the three blocks to the single-car garage that housed what Bobby called the "safe car." Theoretically.

She held her breath, starting the ignition. The car didn't explode. Twenty minutes later, she was at the mall outside Starbucks, where, under the ficus, a familiar figure in white awaited, holding two grande nonfat lattes.

"It's impossible to drink through this damned mouth mesh," Laila said.

"Use your straw."

"Yesterday after we left him, he took a telephone call from— Oh God, now *I'm* the spy. You're not still working for them, are you, Florence? You have to tell me."

"No. It's just us now."

"All right. He got a call from King Tallulah. I listened in on the whole thing."

"How?"

"I had the system fixed so that I can. I'm not an idle snoop, but when you have a young son to look out for, as they say, knowledge is power."

"What did the emir and the king discuss?"

"The Pan-Arab summit in Bahrain. Tallulah said how much he was looking forward to seeing him there. *Ever* so excited about it. *What* a great honor for Matar. Et cetera. I wanted to scream."

"Did they discuss Fatima?"

"It was dealt with in the way they have. 'Such an unfortunate business.' 'Yes, indeed unfortunate.' You see, the score had been evened. So there was no point in pressing it. No honor to be gained. Let the feasting commence. I had a vision of them under a tent together, chins glistening with sheep fat and buttered rice. It was awful, Firenze. I loved him once. Even with his harem. But after listening yesterday . . . no. I cannot give my love to such a man."

They sat in silence. Florence said, "They're trying to get him out of the country. The Pan-Arab meeting. That's when it will happen. That's when they'll make their move."

"Yes."

"Would he listen to you?"

"At this point? He might think it's a cabal you and I cooked up to cheat him of assuming the mantle of the New Saladin."

"So, Laila, how shall we proceed?"

"I need to get my son out before anything else."

"Do you want help?"

"Best not. But I'll need a day or two. My sister is in England. I've kept bank accounts. Against a rainy day. It doesn't rain much in the desert, but when it does, the floods can kill."

"Forty-eight hours, then."

"Firenze, I know you said you'd see it through with me. That was all very gallant of you, but . . . What I'm trying to say, darling, and not being very articulate with, is that it might be better if you left Matar now."

"Not yet. I have to do this first. Then I'll leave with you. Anyway"—Florence smiled—"I can't watch it all on a television screen at the Frankfurt airport. I've gotten too used to being in the control room."

"Oh dear," Laila said. "What will become of us?"

"That's what Nazrah said that night in the Fairfax Hospital."

They stood and walked toward the elevators.

"I'd kiss you goodbye," Laila said, "but we mustn't scandalize all the nice bargain hunters at the mall."

—

THREE DAYS LATER, TVMatar's viewers were surprised by the new face that greeted them from the six o'clock anchor desk. It was that of an attractive woman in her late thirties, with dark hair. She might have passed for an Arab, but her name was Italian-sounding.

"The person who regularly gives the news on this program," Florence began, "is Fatima Sham. Fatima disappeared following a broadcast in which she reported that the Wasabi royal family had sentenced one of its own princesses to be stoned to death for the crime of petitioning the king to stop the persecution of women.

"An extensive search by the authorities was undertaken to find Ms. Sham. The investigation produced no result.

"Then, four days ago, a videotape was anonymously delivered to TVMatar. You are about to see that videotape. Be warned: It depicts Ms. Sham being killed. If you have no stomach or desire to witness a young woman being slowly stoned to death, then you should not watch this. If there are children present, you should send them from the room.

"It is being shown on my initiative, and mine only, for one reason: to honor a brave woman who dared to speak out against a terrible injustice, and who for that was herself savagely murdered. The term 'martyr' has been debased and corrupted. You are about to witness an actual martyrdom."

Florence had instructed the staff to switch off the telephones and to bar all the doors to the control room. She also specified that the power source be switched to the emergency generators, so the broadcast would continue if the outside power was shut off.

The tape ran for its full twenty minutes. Though they had seen it before, the staff again wept. Florence had to struggle to keep her own composure. She had dispensed with makeup so her eyes would not become a caricature of muddy mascara.

It took a few moments after the tape ended before she was able to continue.

"It is not known precisely who did this deed. However, this method of execution is regularly employed in Wasabia.

"Fatima Sham was twenty-six years old. She is survived by her family, by her friends, by her colleagues and by millions of sisters throughout the Arab world. *Etemen aan mouwt'ha yekoon aindee manaa.*"

In minutes there was a pounding on the steel doors to the control room. The staff's blood was up. They armed themselves with fire extinguishers, axes, steel pipes, electrical tubing. Watching them, Florence felt mixed sensations of pride and futility.

"No," she commanded, "put those down." She unclipped her microphone, checked herself in the mirror and walked to the door. She gestured to a technician who had positioned himself to bash the invaders with a wastebasket. He opened the door. A half-dozen men burst in with drawn weapons.

Florence addressed them sternly. "Put your weapons down. We have none."

The security agents froze, startled by this unexpected temerity. Then one of them, apparently the leader, approached and cuffed Florence hard across the face. The blow caught her off balance. She fell. The staffer with the wastebasket moved toward the attacker and got the butt of a pistol in his face, breaking his nose and misting the air with blood. Florence, dazed, felt the cold snap of metal around her wrists. She was pulled to her feet and dragged out of the control room.

They hustled her into the back of a car and threw a blanket over her head. Whether this was to humiliate her or to keep her from seeing where they were taking her, Florence could only speculate.

She knew the location of police headquarters and, from the car's movements, tried to calculate whether this was the destination. After a quarter hour of turns that she could not follow, she had no idea where they were taking her. The leader sitting in the front seat did not respond to her questions.

It was only ten miles to the Wasabi border, and it was this directional scenario that was the least pleasing. But there was another possibility: that she might be on her way to the same fate that had befallen Fatima. Florence imagined the car stopping, the blanket being pulled from her head, the neck-deep hole dug in the sand, the basket full of small stones, a video camera mounted on a tripod. They'd want a record of this one, too.

Her face flushed hot, and she felt like she was going to throw up. But then the image of herself covered in her own mess, as she was executed, overrode her nausea. If this was to be her fate, Florence was resolved to meet it with such dignity as she could, head high, and serene, with maybe even a shouted "Fuck you!" at her killers. Well, perhaps something more elegant than "Fuck you!" She mused on her final words.

A half hour passed. Finally, the car slowed, made a series of turns and stopped. She heard voices. She was pulled from the backseat and, with each arm firmly grasped, was marched across a stone floor. She remembered from her State Department hostage training to notice every detail, but with the blanket over her head, it wasn't easy. She thought, *There's the floor, I might as well notice* that. But in the end, it was only a floor.

CHAPTER TWENTY-ONE

She was taken to a windowless room of ambiguous architectural purpose. It could serve as a cool cellar for fresh foodstuffs, Kaffir limes and Damascus melons. Such subterranean spaces had other, less pleasant uses. The thickness of the door that shut behind her, the sparseness of the furnishings before her—a wooden chair and table, an overhead lightbulb, a bedspring cot and plastic tub—bespoke austerity. The one item out of place was a video camera mounted on a tripod.

By her wristwatch, its face scuffed by the handcuffs, it was going on three in the morning when the door opened. The man confronting her wore Western dress that might have been a military uniform minus insignias.

"You are being deported," he said. He put some papers on the table before her. "Where you are deported to, it depends."

She read the papers. It was a confession in the form of a script. Presumably, she was to read it for the video camera.

In it, she admitted to an "unnatural and immoral relationship"—not with the sheika but with her TVMatar colleague Fatima Sham. Florence had become enough of a journalist to know a good lead paragraph. She read on. She was further admitting to trying to blackmail the Wasabi Royal House of Hamooj. Her "shameful plot" was to demand $20 million from them. When they refused—"as, God be praised, they should have"—Florence's lover Fatima Sham put on television the "wicked and untrue" story about Princess Hamzin. *Someone put a lot of thought into this,* Florence mused as she read. It went on to say that Florence and her "accomplices" then avenged themselves on the "honorable Wasabis" by killing Fatima in the gruesome manner depicted and sending a copy of the tape to Kaffa, saying they would put it on TVMatar and blame them for it if a ransom of $40 million weren't paid. Again, the "upright" Wasabis held fast. But then "the police"—the script did not specify whose police—caught her. She could no longer live with the shameful things she had done, so she was recording this "true confession." It concluded with an apology to the emir of Matar and the king of Wasabia for perpetrating such vile doings while a guest on "holy" soil.

"Well," she said finally, looking up at her dour jailer, "I seem to have been very busy."

He pressed the record button on the video camera. "Begin," he said.

Florence looked into the camera. "My name is Florence Farfaletti," she said. "I'm an American citizen. It appears that I am being held in some basement somewhere. It's a bit damp, but otherwise tolerable. Have a nice day."

The man pressed the stop button. "You won't like it in Kaffa." He came toward her. Florence recoiled, thinking he was going to strike her, but instead, he unlocked her handcuffs.

"You run a television station," he said. He pointed to the video camera. "So, here is television camera. In two hours I come back. Make the film."

She used the next hour to explore every inch of the room. She tried to pry a piece of wire from the cot, with the idea of fashioning a tool to pick the door lock, but gave up after five minutes. There were problems with this approach, the first being that she did not know how to pick a lock. They'd taught her the rudiments of the skill during her weekend of hostage training in Virginia, but she had never really gotten the hang of it. She thought of buying herself some time by sabotaging the video camera, but that seemed like feckless temporizing. Perhaps if she kept talking but never quite confessed until the tape ran out—a video Scheherazade, with the tape counter stopped at 1001.

She wondered what was going on back in Washington. What was Uncle Sam doing? Pulling strings or erasing computer files? Or sitting down to a martini and medium-rare porterhouse with onion rings at the Palm?

She missed Bobby. She missed George. She missed Rick. George and Rick wouldn't be much good, but they'd cheer her up. She shut her eyes, headachy with fright and fatigue, and dreamed of the conning tower of a U.S. nuclear submarine breaking the glass-still surface beyond the snaky beach. Where was Laila? The hours passed.

A FEW MINUTES before seven A.M. by the scuffed watch, she heard the sound of the door being unlocked. Her heart was pounding. The door opened, admitting the jailer and another man, a torturer by his looks. The jailer went to the video camera and examined the counter. It was still set at 003. His face creased with displeasure. He nodded to the torturer, who took out a nine-millimeter pistol and pressed the muzzle against Florence's forehead. It was as cold as a doctor's stethoscope. She swallowed and closed her eyes.

"You make confess?"

"No."

"Kill her," the jailer said.

Florence shut her eyes. She smelled gun oil. She wondered what they would do with her body. Feed it to the sharks beyond the reef? The crabs would finish it off. She saw her own bones, bright white, phosphorescently aglow against the blue of the water, resting placidly at the bottom. *Get it over with.*

The hammer snapped forward against the action. Florence emitted a little shriek and opened her eyes. The men were smiling cruelly, but there was the unmistakable element of defeat in their eyes. They left. She stood and kicked the plastic bucket across the room. It ricocheted off the wall. Then, from terror and exhaustion, she passed out.

In the dream, she was thirsty, very, very thirsty. She was biting down on her lips to draw blood to drink. She was in the desert. It was a furnace. In the attack on Aqaba, it was so hot that Lawrence's hands blistered on the metal of his rifle. There was a submarine. *A submarine in the middle of the desert? Don't ask. Go aboard—listen—they're calling you.*

"WHAT DAY IS IT?" she said to Laila.

"Thursday."

Florence had been in the subterranean room for five days before the door flew open and in rushed Colonel Boutros of the Royal Matar Constabulary, along with two of his men.

"God be praised, you are safe, madame. Are you grievously injured? What did they do to you? Did you see their faces? Can you give a description?"

When they brought her out, she saw that she had been in the basement of some abandoned factorylike building on the edge of Amo-Amas. She asked Colonel Boutros at least a hundred questions on the drive to the constabulary headquarters. His answers seemed guarded. And when they arrived at the HQ, there was a crowd of reporters with cameras waiting. Colonel Boutros preened, posing with Florence. "God be praised, we have found her!"

A television reporter thrust a microphone at her and said, "Flor-ents, will you now announce an end to the sexual jihad by Matari women?"

"To the what?"

"You did not know?"

"I have been locked in a cellar for five days."

"The women of Matar made jihad on your behalf. Against the men of Matar."

"How did they do this?"

"After you were taken, the sheika Laila went on the television and called upon the women of Matar not to make relations with their husbands until you were returned. There are many men in Matar grateful for your return."

Florence was digesting this when she heard sirens. A forty-foot-long white limousine bearing the royal crest and accompanied by a motorcycle escort arrived. Fetish, the emir's man, was inside, all greasy smiles. "Praise truly be to Allah that you are returned to us safe!" Then it was off to the palace.

After being given a room to clean up in and fresh clothing, Florence was admitted to the emir's ceremonial chamber. As she walked in, there was a flash of light that caused her to flinch. An official photographer. The emir stood—that *was* unusual—and walked over to her. He embraced her and kissed her tenderly on the forehead as the camera flashes continued, bathing them in flickery strobe light. Laila looked on.

"*Dear* sister!" he said, "what a time you have had, and how worried we were!" He continued to pose for a few more pictures. Then Fetish waved and the photographer was gone and it was just the emir, Florence and the sheika. There was tension, Florence noted, between husband and wife.

"How are you feeling, dear Florence?" he said. "I am appalled, appalled that this could have happened. And yet"—he lowered his voice to a gentle lecturing tone—"you were very naughty to do what you did. This is not the American Super Bowl, where you can put just anything on television. You have no idea, no *concept*, of what trouble you caused me with my neighbors. They moved tanks—tanks!—to my border. Your own government was most anxious. *Most* anxious. They were no doubt thinking, *Oh God, not* another *Kuwait.* There were *many* conversations between Washington and Kaffa and Amo-Amas. I don't want to look at my phone bill. Well, it's all fixed. For now. Sit, sit, for heaven's sake. Do you want some tea? Something more than tea? Whiskey? I could use one myself. Thank God for the diligence of Colonel Boutros."

Florence looked at Laila, who gave her a glance, as if to say, *Just play along.*

"Yes," the emir said, straightening slightly. (Always sit up straight while lying through your teeth.) "It was his men who found you. And just in time. God knows what evil things they had planned for you."

Florence said, "Thank God for Colonel Boutros."

"Were you able to see their faces?" the emir asked solicitously. "We will hunt them down. They will know no peace. Or perhaps they have already fled across the border."

"My captors—they were . . . Wasabi?"

"Of course. No Matari would do something so barbaric."

This brought a grunt from Laila. The emir stiffened. He said, "Laila was very concerned for you. As were we all. She went on television and told the women of Matar to withhold . . . normal marital relations until you were found."

"It worked for Aristophanes," Laila said tartly.

The emir grinned. "It certainly gave us inspiration to find you. All of Matar—especially the males—rejoices in your return. Which must, alas, be brief. Under the circumstances, I think it would be best if you departed Matar.

I shall be sorry to see you go, Florence. How you have enlivened our drab little kingdom by the sea. But before you go, one or two matters."

"I would have thought at least three or four, sire."

"Eh? Ah, your terrible ordeal has not dulled the wit. Excellent, excellent. Now, if you would make a little statement."

"That's what my captors wanted me to do."

"Oh, nothing like that," the emir said rather too quickly. "Just something to make peace between me and the women. You see," he said with a tight glance at Laila, who was viewing him with distinct coolness, "the impression was given that our government was insufficiently concerned by this terrible abduction. Of course, nothing could be *further* from reality. You will correct this impression before you leave?"

Florence eyed the emir coolly. "As Your Grace commands."

"You are very simpatico, Florence. It's the Italian in you. I have always *adored* the Italians, though they were very naughty under Mussolini. So you will make peace between me and the women. Good, good. Well then, I must take my leave of you. How can I repay what you have done here? You must come back and visit. Oh, I almost forgot, a present."

The emir clapped his hands. Fetish appeared holding a black box. The emir opened it. It was a medal, lushly done in enamel and gold in the shape of a lion's head, above two drawn swords, the emblem of royal Matar.

"The Order of the Royal Lion of Matar, First Class," the emir said proudly, putting it around her head. "This is the first occasion ever it has been given to a woman."

Florence looked at Laila, who was rolling her eyes.

Florence bowed slightly. "It is a great honor, sire."

"Hurry back, my dear. Hurry back. Darling, will you see Florence off?"

FLORENCE AND LAILA spoke softly on the way to the car.

"Sexual jihad?" Florence said.

"Don't knock it. It worked. No Matari male has been laid in five days. Other than my husband. Powerful incentive, that. Still, if it hadn't been for your Mr.

Thibodeaux, you might still be in that room. He went into very high gear after you were taken."

"Bobby? Is he—"

"Outside. He's got himself a new identity. It's rather daring. Do be sure to compliment him on it."

CHAPTER TWENTY-TWO

Florence heard the crowd before she and Laila walked out the front door of the palace. "What's this?" she said to Laila.

"Your fans, darling."

There were thousands of them, mostly women. When they saw Florence, they began to ululate in the way of Arab women, though it had been rather a very long time since this tradition had been observed in progressive Matar. They began to chant, "Flor-ens! Flor-ens!"

To the object of this homage, standing on the marble steps, it sounded like the name of some household air freshener. They surged forward, swarming around her, touching her, grasping. She was presented with flowers. Palace security tried to push them back without success.

Laila had seen to it that cameras were there to record it all, as well as a TVMatar truck to feed the footage to a satellite 250 miles up and back into millions of televisions. Lately, Laila had been thinking like the producer of a reality TV show, a fact that appalled her somewhat.

"Flor-ens! Flor-ens!"

Laila shouted into Florence's ear, "I think you'd better address them, darling, or they'll never let you out of here."

"But—"

"Remember to thank Gazzy, or you *will* never get out of here."

Florence blushed and swallowed, her mouth dry as dust. She felt more exhausted than triumphant, but she raised her hands to quiet the crowd, and into her mind flashed, unavoidably, the image of Peter O'Toole scampering whitely across the top of the dynamited Turkish train. Try as she might to shake it from her head, she couldn't. The movie wouldn't stop playing. The next image was of the wounded Turk firing the pistol shot into O'Toole's shoulder. Now she looked down at the surging crowd with fear. Though most of the women wore Western dress, there were a few dozen wearing *abaayas*. Maybe the University of Chicago anthropologist was right: Perhaps some Arab women didn't want to be rescued from oppression. Florence weighed this terrible possibility along with how simple it would be to kill her right now. How easily a gun could be concealed beneath the veil.

The fear emboldened her. She gestured forcefully for the crowd to quiet. It did. She opened her mouth to address it and—was dumbstruck for words. It was then that she realized tears were streaming down her cheeks.

"Darling," Laila said, "*do* pull yourself together."

Then Florence heard a voice, a male voice, southern-accented. It said, "Goddammit, girl, you gonna say somethin' to the folks or just stand there blubberin' like you won the Miss America contest?"

The voice seemed to be coming from a woman dressed in an orange *abaaya*. Florence looked over at Laila, who was smiling.

Florence's impulse was to leap into the arms of the orange apparition, but this was, she decided, not an appropriate crowning gesture at a moment of feminist triumph—leaping into the arms of a CIA Muslim drag queen.

"Well?" it said. "Come on. Don't got all day."

Florence raised her arms higher, and the crowd quieted.

"God be praised, sisters, I am glad to be back with you. I am sure that your husbands are glad, too!" They liked that, the crowd. "I am grateful to you, and to the sheika Laila."

Laila waved and said sideways, "*Don't forget Gazzy.*"

"And of course to the emir," Florence said, "the Lion of Matar, the New Saladin . . ." Florence tried not to burst out laughing. "Champion . . . and *protector* of Arab women . . . throughout the world!"

"Aren't you laying it on a bit thick, darling?"

Florence's expression was not lost on the Lion of Matar, watching on television in his office. *Bitch,* he thought. But the crowd was roaring, and that, in the end, was what muttered. At least the bitch would be on an airplane in a few hours, gone for good.

The crowd was chanting, "*Flo-rens! Flo-rens!*" The Lion of Matar took the television remote control in his plump, bejeweled hand and pressed the off button.

"I'VE NEVER KISSED a woman," Florence said to Bobby.

Laila had arranged for them to be driven separately to Florence's apartment overlooking Marlborough Square. They'd have a few hours together before the flight out.

"I never slept with a lesbian," Bobby said. "Wanted to, just never quite got around to it."

They made love again. Afterward, Bobby stood by the balcony looking out over the square. It was early evening. The lights of the town were coming on.

" 'Bout time to go, Flo."

Florence smiled. She was wrapped in bed linens and very happy. It had been a long time since she had made love. "Do you have to call me that? Call me *Flor-ens.*"

Bobby looked back at her over his shoulder. "Knew that was gonna go to your head sooner or later."

She couldn't take her eyes off him. He reminded her of Steve McQueen, blond and coiled and dangerous. His pistol was on the bedside table.

"Tell me how you found me," she murmured.

"Already told you."

"Tell me again. I like being rescued."

"I've got . . . Aw, I can't tell you this stuff, Flo. Come on, time to get dressed now."

"More love first."

"We'll do it on the plane."

"Is it a nice plane? Is there a bed? I want to make love all the way home. How did you find me? I'm not leaving till you tell me."

"Could make you leave."

"I'll chain myself to this bed."

"Thought you'da had enough of chains by now."

"Tell."

Bobby looked at her, love-warm in bed, the sheet draped over her as if on a marble statue. He sighed, a gesture first experienced by humans a hundred thousand years ago when the first man gave in to the first woman.

"Fetish," he said.

"Anything, darling."

"*No.* Fetish—the emir's guy. I got to him."

"Got to him how?"

"He works for the French. I found that out and told him if he didn't tell me where they were holdin' you, I'd tell the emir. He coughed it up real quick. I got word to Boutros. He and I . . . That's how."

"How did you find out Fetish works for the French?"

"Can we talk about him on the plane? The French girl in Um-beseir, Annabelle, real dish, joined the harem just about the time of Maliq's religious conversion? *She* works for the French. I got to her."

"Got her or got *to* her?"

"Whatever."

Florence threw a pillow at him. "I'm sorry you had to go through such *hell* finding me."

The explosion knocked Bobby backward onto the bed. His instincts took over instantly, and he covered Florence's body with his. Half the ceiling came down on them.

Florence's face was pressed against his chest. She could feel his heart pounding.

"Get dressed now," he said. He slipped on his trousers, took his pistol and approached the balcony, crouching. The flames from the street below reflected on his bare skin.

"Looks like your revolution's started, Flo."

CHAPTER TWENTY-THREE

Florence crawled to the balcony and peered over the rail with Bobby.

"Car bomb," Bobby said. "Big mother."

"Laila," Florence said. She dialed on Bobby's cell. The building shook from another explosion, smaller, more distant. That was followed by a half-dozen more around the city. *Boom, boom, boom, boom*—nearly identical intervals.

"It's coordinated," Bobby said.

Laila picked up. "Florence? Something's happening. Thank God I got Hamdul out."

"Are you all right?"

"Just scratched up. The windows blew out. We're on fire. Needless to say, no one is trying to put it out. They're too busy running around shrieking uselessly. Where are you? Your place?"

"Yes. There are explosions all over the city. Bobby says it's coordinated."

"Get out of there, fast. There's shooting on the grounds. Wait. Hold on, I hear something."

Florence heard rotor blades.

"It's the helicopter," Laila said. "The one you gave him. Nice of him to tell me we're leaving."

"You better go," Florence said. The sound of the rotor blades became louder over the phone.

"Florence!" Laila sounded stunned.

"I'm here."

"They're leaving—they've lifted off! I can see him. He's sitting next to the pilot!" The rotor blades grew louder. "That pig! That fat, adulterous, odious, cowardly—"

There was an explosion.

"Laila? Laila? *Laila*?"

"What's going on?" Bobby said.

"Laila!"

Bobby took the phone from Florence and listened. He disconnected. "Time to go." He handed her the orange *abaaya* that had been his disguise at the rally. "Put this on."

She looked at the garment.

"Flo, it's not a fashion statement."

She put it on slowly. It smelled of him. Bobby yanked the sheet off the bed, took out his spring knife and cut a slit in it and threw it over his head. "Trick or treat," he said. "Come on."

They took the stairs instead of the elevator. It was eight floors down to the lobby. He opened the door cautiously and looked into the lobby. Florence leaned back into the concrete wall, trying to get her heart to stop pounding so hard. She heard a noise.

Four men banged through the lobby door. They wore Western clothing. They spoke. Florence caught the accent.

They spoke loudly, in unafraid tones, and carried drawn pistols. They made for the elevator. Bobby slowly closed the door and held the bar handle of the fire door, manually locking it.

"Wasabi," Florence whispered to Bobby. He looked questioningly at her. "He said 'hlonek' instead of 'shlonek.' Trust me—they're Wasabi. Probably *mukfelleen*."

They went down to the basement and found a rear stairwell. There was a small wire-mesh window in it. With his hand already on the handle, Bobby looked through the window, then quickly darted to the side and threw the bolt home, locking the door just as someone tried to open it from the other side.

They retreated back up to the second floor and emerged into the corridor.

There was a door at the far end that opened onto a small balcony above an alley. They stood on the balcony and looked down. There was a large Dumpster filled with garbage bags.

"Can you do this?" Bobby said. Florence nodded. It was a twenty-foot drop into the Dumpster.

They landed to a commotion of squeaks. Florence felt things squirming under her. Rats. She stifled a cry. Bobby beat at them with his fists. He pulled garbage bags over the two of them until they were concealed. Florence lay there, rodents stirring under her. The garbage had been there for days, putrefying in 110-degree heat. Bobby reached over and held her hand. He whispered, "Best way to get to know a country."

The balcony door above them banged open. They heard two voices. Florence held her breath. The door closed. It was quiet again. They lay there for ten minutes. Bobby whispered, "You want dessert, or shall I get the check?"

They hauled themselves out of the Dumpster and made their way toward the waterfront, trying to stay in the shadows. The city was alive with the noise of explosions and small-arms fire. Bobby and Florence came to a grassy public square and ducked into a clump of trees at the corner.

"If we get stopped," Bobby said, "act hysterical, like you're scared shitless."

"Not a problem. Where are we going?"

Bobby thought. "Airport's out. The harbor."

"Is your water taxi operating?"

"You bet. In an hour, we'll be in our own submarine, drinking French champagne and screwin' our brains out."

She didn't believe him, and then it hit her—he'd come back for her on his own. He was operating solo.

"We'll head for the water," he said. "Where there's water, there's boats; where there's boats, there's gettin' the hell out."

"You came back on your own, didn't you?"

"We're gonna be fine. I've been through more Middle East coups than you've had hot breakfasts."

They came to a corner. Bobby looked around it and jerked his head back. The street was blocked by an armored personnel carrier with a mounted machine gun. The markings on it were Matari.

They moved along Soames Street, parallel to the waterfront. Bobby again peered around a corner and motioned her back. All the streets leading to the harbor were blocked.

"They don't appear to be encouragin' visits to the waterfront tonight," he said. "Time to find out what's goin' on."

They continued along Soames until they came to an appliance store with television sets and microwave ovens in the window.

"Keep an eye out." Bobby produced a tool and fiddled with the lock. It clicked open. He pushed the door open gently, listening for an alarm to go off. They entered.

Against a wall were fifty or so televisions. Bobby went behind the counter and began flipping switches. All fifty sets flicked on, bathing them in blue screen glow.

"Be a good place to watch the Super Bowl," Bobby said. He began flicking several remote controls at once, causing blizzards of pixels.

"Channel Forty-five," she said. The TVMatar channel.

He flicked. Normally, at this hour, TVMatar would be showing *Mukfellahs,* the situation comedy about the inept crew of religious police. Instead, there was a grim-faced announcer, a man, sitting behind the news desk. They knew instantly what it meant. The announcer was dressed in the clerical garb of a Matari moolah, and he was speaking Matari, not English. The first words Florence could make out were "criminal," then "infidel," then "provisional," followed by "Imam Maliq" followed by "God be praised." None of these buzzwords was reassuring. Again she was struck by how incongruently malevolent "Allah the merciful, the compassionate" could be made to sound coming from human lips. Then she heard her own name mentioned, and hot as she was under the *abaaya,* Florence felt a chill. She learned from the television that she was at large somewhere in the city, that all decent citizens should be vigilant, for she was dangerous, an enemy, an agent of Satan.

Bobby was standing by the door with his pistol drawn, in the event the alarm was silent and an enraged Mr. Mohammed Dera'a, whose name appeared on the sign above, was on his way to reassert proprietorship of his goods.

The moolah continued his announcements. The holy soil of Matar was—

praise God—under new rule. The decades of corruption and decadence so vile in the eyes of God the merciful, the compassionate, the wise, were over. A new dawn was proclaimed (though technically, it was only eight P.M.). A revolutionary Islamic republic was proclaimed. *Praise God.* Citizens should remain indoors until the last vestiges of the former regime could be "cleansed"—another sunny word made sinister.

Up on the screen came Gazzy's face. He was in sunglasses, grinning and waving at the photographer. The picture had been taken in what newspaper captions like to call "happier times."

"The imam makes the following announcement. The emir Gazzir Bin Haz, blasphemer, betrayer and tool of imperialist infidels, is dead. *Allahu akbar.* He was fleeing the royal palace like a coward when his American-provided helicopter stuck a tree and crashed. The former sheika . . ."

Florence held her breath.

". . . is in custody. Already she is repenting of her crimes against God the mighty and the people of Matar. Long life and blessings upon our glorious beloved imam Maliq, beloved of God, sent by God, savior of Matar's holy soil."

Florence began dialing.

"What you doing?"

"It's the Middle East. I'm trading."

Bobby sighed. "Baby, you're not bein' part of the *solution.*"

She dialed the main palace number. A voice answered, authoritative.

"This is Florence. Do you understand who I am?"

"Yes."

"I wish to speak with the imam Maliq."

"Impossible."

"I have something he wants very badly."

"Speak."

"I will convey that to the imam," she said sharply. "Put him on the telephone. Do it now, or you will feel his anger upon your back." In moments of drama, Arabic tended toward the archaic.

Bobby mouthed the words: "They're tracing the call."

Florence paced back and forth in front of the TV screens.

"Flo," Bobby hissed. "What the fuck you doin'?"

"I'm responsible."

"Aw, jeez, dammit, girl!" He banged his hand against the glass door. "You're *always* responsible! You want to be a martyr? Why don't you just strap on some explosives and go blow up a damn bus!"

"Fuck you."

"This is the imam Maliq," said a startled voice, "and fuck *you,* madame!"

"Not you. It's Florence calling."

"What do you want?"

"To trade. Me for the sheika."

"Why should I trade? You will be dead or captured before dawn."

"Just put her on a plane. The moment it lands and I see her on TV, getting off, I'll turn myself in. I'll confess to whatever you want."

Maliq laughed. "You will confess in *any* event."

"Look, Maliq, you're bringing the veil back to Matar. Yes?"

"Certainly, but what does this have to do with it?"

"There are two and a half million women in Matar. How long will it take you to look underneath every veil to find me?"

"There is no rush. My days of racing are over, God be praised."

"Come on, Maliq, do you really want to wait that long before chopping off my head?"

"*Imam* Maliq, if you please," he said almost flirtatiously. "Cut off your head? No, no. I have something else in mind. All in good time. And now I must go. It seems I have a country to run."

The television sets were showing file footage of Maliq addressing a crowd. He looked rather stylish for an Islamic religious leader, but then his clerical garb had been designed in Paris.

There was a long glass counter of cell phones and GameBoys and other electronic items. It was locked. Florence found a metal bar by the cash register for threatening robbers. She picked it up and began smashing through the glass.

Bobby watched. "Flo, what are you doin'?"

"Launching the counterrevolution."

She gathered all the cell phones into a plastic shopping bag. She pointed to another locked glass display case full of video equipment. "Break that, would you, please?"

Bobby went to the display and smashed it with a single blow of his pistol butt. Florence pulled out several video cameras and put them in the now bulging bag.

"That one, too." She pointed.

Bobby obediently broke another case. "Mr. Dera'a isn't gonna be real happy."

Florence gathered up some battery-operated televisions. Having completed her looting, she grabbed her orange *abaaya.* She kissed Bobby on the cheek. "Goodbye, baby," she said.

"What are you talkin' about?"

"Bobby. A man, a Westerner, blond, wanted for killing one of the new ruler's men in a garage? How long do you think you'd last in the new Matar?"

"I got *my* veil."

She smiled and stroked his cheek. "You'd do me more harm than good."

She put on her orange *abaaya* and picked up the bulging shopping bags. She looked like any Muslim woman who'd spent the afternoon at the mall.

Florence put her head out the door, looked both ways, cast a backward glance at Bobby and left.

He gave her a head start, then put on his own *abaaya* and followed.

CHAPTER TWENTY-FOUR

*The coup in Matar, or, as the State Department was calling it, "the develop-*ing situation in Matar," had taken the United States government completely by surprise. The White House gamely asserted that it had been aware "for some time now" that a violent takeover had been in the offing, and they had been working "behind the scenes and around the clock" to avert crisis. This, however, was a soufflé that refused to rise.

On Capitol Hill, the cries of "Who lost Matar?" grew louder and louder. Senators pounded their podia, demanding answers. The president declared that he, too, wanted answers. The CIA said that although it would have no official comment, it, too, perhaps even more than the president and the senators, wanted answers. The secretary of state said that there might in fact be no answers, but if there were, he certainly would be interested in hearing them. The secretary general of the United Nations said that he was reasonably certain answers existed, but first the right questions must be asked, and then they would have to be translated, and this would take time.

There were those who urged caution, and those who urged that now was a time not for caution but for boldness. Then there were those who urged a middle course of cautious boldness. There were extremists on both sides: the neo-isolationists, whose banner declared, "Just sell us the damned oil," and the neo-interventionists, who said, "Together, we can make a better world, but we'll probably have to kill a lot of you in the process."

Privately, the American president was said to be torn—between dispatching an aircraft carrier (perhaps the most dramatic gesture available to a president, short of actually landing on one); and dispatching a nuclear submarine. A distinguished naval historian pointed out on public television that submarines are every bit as lethal as aircraft carriers, but, being underwater, are harder to see and therefore "less visually impactful." It was, as another historian said on public television, "a time of great ambiguity." And yet about even that much, reasonable people differed. One fact, however, asserted itself stubbornly, insistently, over and over, until it could not be ignored or swept or channel-surfed away: that nearly one third of America's imported oil, without which there would be much shivering in January, now flowed through a country ruled by—as one more historian put it on public television—"a race-car driver turned ayatollah, installed by France." On this point, there was little ambiguity. The question was, what to do about it? France had played her cards with élan and panache, savoir faire and a heaping helping of je ne sais quoi.

Within days, snippets of film taken in the late Gazzir Bin Haz's "summer" residence at Um-beseir had made their way onto the Internet and television. Canal Quatre in Paris aired a documentary about the emir's harem that would have made Casanova, the authors of the *Kama Sutra* and, quite possibly, the Marquis de Sade blush. The film had been (apparently, since no one would take credit for it) shot by some hidden camera. (Annabelle had been a busy girl, indeed.) In one particularly riveting sequence, the emir of Matar was seen spooning beluga caviar onto the breasts of a pair of (admittedly delectable) Russian ladies named Tatiana and Svetlana, and then gobbling it up, pausing only to take puffs from a hookah that seemed to contain more than mere tobacco, and gulps from a bottle quite clearly labeled "Southern Comfort" while periodically shrieking, "God be *praised*!" True, every man worships God in his own way, but sich vignettes made it somewhat difficult for the exiled noblesse of Matar, now dug into their bunkers in Cannes, Gstaad and Portofino, to assert convincingly—between swigs of Chivas and Cristal—that the late emir had been guided by a decent respect for the opinion of mankind.

Expensive media consultants were duly engaged by the exiled Bin Hazzim to make the case that life in Matar under the emir, decadent and even downright naughty as he may have been, had been more benign than the Matar that the neo-conservative Maliq had in mind. Religious converts often try to make up for lost piousness with heightened fervor. Maliq's motto was a perverse paraphrase of Saint Augustine: *Oh God, make me bad—right now.* Within days of taking over, he had revoked driving privileges for women; reinstituted the veil; made it illegal for women to leave the house except with a male blood relation; and decreed female laughter punishable by twenty lashes, on the theological grounds that if a woman laughed, she was probably happy about something, and that would not do.

The citizens of Matar did not embrace this new pietism with open arms, but then Maliq had never said he cared what they thought one way or the other. A large construction crane was driven into Robespierre (formerly Churchill) Square, and several counterrevolutionary Matari citizens were duly suspended from it by the neck. Several women, frisky enough to venture out in broad daylight without their heads covered—and, if you please, without male chaperones—were swiftly made an example of. It was quite obvious, declared the *mukfellah* official who announced their sentences, that they had been on their way to fornicate with loathsome blackamoor cooks. There was no actual evidence of this, but the advantage of a religious judiciary is that you don't need evidence. The unfortunate women insisted that they were just going out to pick up milk and the dry cleaning, but you can't be too careful.

Much as he enjoyed a flogging or beheading, or even the occasional stoning, Maliq could take or leave them. He would much rather watch NASCAR and Formula One racing on television (though he now had to be a bit discreet about this). It was his Wasabi patrons who were behind all the chopping and lashing. They insisted. And since it was they who had put him on his throne, Maliq had no choice but to play along.

TVMatar and his late half brother Gazzir—whose helicopter had been brought down by a rocket-propelled grenade, not a tree—had caused the House of Hamooj nothing but ridicule and humiliation. Now it was payback time; time, moreover, to set an example for all the Wasabi women back at home who had gotten all sorts of dangerous ideas from all those months of watching TVMatar.

How different was its programming now! Recipes, tips on how to please the husband, how to keep from being trampled during the hajj, comedies about greedy Israelis and fat infidel Americans. Thursday nights at eight, *Everyone Loves Imam!*, with Maliq reading aloud from the *Book of Hamooj* and giving his own unique textural interpretations. True, ratings were a sliver of what they once had been. But then you need to give new shows time to build.

France, Wasabia's co-partner in the Maliq instauration, was not altogether thrilled by this grim state of affairs. But as the Ministère de Pétrole (Ministry of Oil) was about to sign an *entente economique* (sweetheart deal) with Wasabia for a 20 percent discount, France was not disposed to make too loud a *bruit* (noise) about it.

Confronted in the men's room at the UN Security Council by the U.S. permanent representative, the French permanent representative shook his head and rolled his eyes and said, "Yes, yes, yes, but what can one *do* with these people—they are *impossible,*" leaving the American representative with an even more deeply beetled brow and requiring further instruction from Washington.

France was also about to sign a mutual security pact with Matar, providing her with a deep-water naval base in the Gulf. The new government in Paris was manifesting neo-Gaullist (some said neo-Napoleonic) designs in the Proche-Orient, where the tricolor had once flapped proudly in the breezes. All the insults of 1922 were finally being avenged. Another distinguished historian—there seemed to be no end of them—said on public television that France was no longer content to sit back and watch the United States screw things up in the region. Did not France have her own proud history of screwing things up? Look at Algeria, Vietnam, Syria, Haiti—Quebec—all still reeling from their days of French rule. Clearly, France was ready and eager to show the world that she, too, could wreak disastrous, unforeseen consequences abroad, far more efficiently and almost certainly with more flair than America.

There was, meanwhile, yet another wave of anti-French sentiment in the United States. French maître d's were assaulted by gangs of thugs, champagne was poured into gutters, baguettes were angrily torn in two and hurled across restaurants, Peugeots were splattered with vegetables and their windshield wipers bent. The French embassy in Washington, once the scene of glittering soirees, was attacked by a mob of evangelical Christians hurling (innocent) frogs. One member of Congress introduced a bill calling for exhuming and repatriating the remains of American soldiers buried in Normandy. "Digging Up Private Ryan."

The cries of "Who lost Matar?" grew more clamorous, despite polls showing that for two thirds of the American people, the more relevant question was "Where exactly *is* Matar?" However, when informed by the pollsters that "perfidious Frogs" and "filthy Wasabis" had taken over the country in order to "make America look bad" and "drive up the price of oil," Americans by a distinct majority responded that their government must do "something" about it, as long as it wouldn't cost too much and could be done from thirty-five thousand feet. There was little appetite at this point for another Pentagon "boots on the ground" intervention in the region.

Such, at any rate, was the situation two weeks after Florence left Mr. Dera'a's appliance store carrying her shopping bags of electronics.

RENARD AND GEORGE were back in Washington following their watery exfiltration off Blenheim Beach. The submarine had been smaller than advertised, and its medical officer had had to sedate the claustrophic George with a hypodermic before they could get him down the hatch. The submarine transferred them to an aircraft carrier. They were flown off the carrier—along with crew mail and the corpse of a despondent, homesick sailor who had committed suicide by drinking the hydraulic fluid of an F-14—to Bahrain, and from there by commercial aviation to Rome, and from there on to Washington, where they arrived to find that all traces of their mission had been deleted, as if by a single stroke on some master keyboard.

The Alexandria safe house that had been their staging area was now occupied by a middle-aged couple who insisted that they had bought the house on the Internet six months before, and who didn't seem disposed to argue the point with the two forlorn-looking men on their doorstep. George and Rick felt like sailors who come across a ship in the middle of the ocean, eerily empty of human presence but for cups of still-warm coffee and cigarettes burning in the ashtray.

George telephoned his old desk at the State Department and got through to Duckett's deputy, who said he was under the impression that George had been transferred to Guatemala City. They didn't seem to care whether George came back to the Near East desk. George found himself in a bureaucratic Sargasso Sea.

When he and Rick went separately to get money from their ATMs, they each found in his checking account the inexplicable but not unwelcome sum of $1 million. It could have had only one source: the now vanished Uncle Sam. This was, evidently, their severance pay. The sudden largesse left them confused, all the more so when, a few days later, the sum disappeared from their accounts only to reappear the next day, doubled. They debated the meaning of this now-you-see-it-now-you-don't deposit and concluded that it was a message: Keep quiet, or all this money will go away for good. Behave, and it might double.

The discovery that they were millionaires twice over left them temporarily elated, then profoundly depressed, for by now the cataclysmic events in Matar had played on their television screens, and their thoughts were not on how to spend this munificence but on what had happened to Florence.

They were sitting glumly in Rick's apartment off Dupont Circle one evening, eating Chinese takeout and drinking Alsatian beer and watching a television news program in which several Middle Eastern experts, each beamed in from a different city, were screaming at one another about the need to remain calm, when the host interrupted his guests to say that the network's Manama bureau had received a videotape, apparently taken inside Matar. Inasmuch as the country had been sealed off from outside media by order of the emir Maliq, the announcer was excited by what was about to be shown.

Rick and George put down their Kung Pao chicken and intently watched Rick's spiffy new fifty-five-inch plasma-screen home-entertainment system. Rick thought they might as well spend some of the money, to the dismay of a censorious George, who had not yet decided on the moral propriety of spending the mysterious deposits. Their maxillofacial muscles gaped as a grainy simulacrum of Florence came on-screen, accompanied by scratchy but quite audible sound.

"I speak from inside occupied Matar. An iron veil has descended upon the country. The sheika Laila, widow of the late emir, is being held prisoner by the usurper Maliq and his Wasabi and French puppetmasters. Women are being tortured and executed. But their spirit is unbroken. They cry out to the civilized nations of the world. Do not allow the forces of corrupted Islam, which make a mockery of a great religion and of its founder, the prophet Mohammed. They cry out to you: Freedom! Freedom! Freedom!"

The announcer said that not much was known about the person on the videotape, other than that she had apparently once worked in some capacity at TVMatar, the formerly pro-women's-rights satellite network. It was thought that she might be an American citizen, a fact that, he pointed out, "could complicate the situation as far as the United States government is concerned."

CHAPTER TWENTY-FIVE

The scaffold had been erected in the center of the mall over a fountain so that the spectators could see.

Florence maneuvered her way as close as she could to the platform without drawing attention. She had contrived a shoulder harness for the video camera, which was tucked under her left arm. A small hole cut in the *abaaya* provided an aperture for the lens. There are advantages to a system that forces its citizens to cover themselves from head to toe.

At each corner of the platform stood a *mukfellah. Mukfelleen* had been trucked into Matar from Wasabia in great numbers, to enforce the religious codes. They were like secret police anywhere; they liked a bit of bowing and scraping. When Florence—accompanied by the required male escort—passed one in the street, if the *mukfellah* was looking especially sour, she would bow and say, "God be praised, brother, for your presence here!" Her male escort, his Western features obscured by *gutra* and large sunglasses, would tug at her and say, "Come along, sister, do not disturb these well beloved of Allah at their blessed labors." To reinforce the illusion that she was just another Matari wife, Florence carried a wicker basket full of fruit and other fresh items from the market. Underneath the produce was a nine-millimeter pistol, and the more she saw of the *mukfelleen* and their blessed labors, she more she yearned to use it on them. Whatever misgivings she may have had about Bobby killing Maliq's man back in the garage were gone now. Her weeks in occupied Matar had taught her how to hate.

The crowd stirred. The captain of the detail pushed his way through to the scaffold. Four *mukfelleen* stood at the corners of the platform. They called for silence and respect.

The captain climbed the steps of the platform and read the sentence. The woman, one Ardeesha, had been caught not only driving a car but trying to escape Matar. The imam Maliq, blessings be upon him and his holy work, had compassionately commuted the sentence from death to one hundred lashes. Allah is merciful.

Ardeesha was brought out, trembling and whimpering and begging for mercy. She was tied down. The *muk* brought the four-foot-long rattan cane down again and again on the writhing black shape on the platform. She screamed throughout the first thirty blows and then fell silent. The women closest to the platform began to cry and beg for mercy. The whole business took about ten minutes.

When it was over, the *mukfelleen* captain who had read the sentence praised the imam's compassion, and the order was given for the crowd to disperse. Most of the audience's male escorts had been smoking or having coffee at Starbucks. They gathered up their charges and left. Some decided to remain and do some shopping. The mall's shopkeepers took advantage of the Punishment Day crowds and announced sales. Florence's male escort collected her, and together they left. As they walked past the *mukfelleen* guard at the mall's entrance, her escort did not compliment him on his blessed labors.

They got into their car and drove off in silence. Florence pressed the PLAY button and watched to make sure she had gotten it on tape. Bobby listened to the sound of the cane blows coming from the camera's speaker and said quietly, "Turn it off."

Amo-Amas teemed with Wasabi Friendship Troops. Maliq had also requested French soldiers, but Paris, already having enough to explain at the United Nations, demurred; France did, however, dispatch hundreds of advisers to help with *le infrastructure*. Thousands of Mataris had fled (mostly for the South of France), producing the usual brain drain.

Bobby and Florence drove north, off the main roads. Traffic slowed to a crawl. Bobby leaned his head out the window and saw police vehicles ten cars ahead. Roadblocks and identity checks had become the norm. Florence removed the tape from the video camera hidden underneath her *abaaya* and substituted a tape containing images of children playing on the beach. Were the camera confiscated, the images would be innocent.

The basket of fruit was between them. They edged forward toward the police.

"God be praised," Bobby said to the policeman, who leaned in and demanded his and his wife's papers. Bobby's Arabic was without accent and he had darkened his skin with cosmetics. He looked as Matari as the next man.

The soldier did not return the greeting. He examined their papers, flipping through the pages of the Matari passports. "Where are you going?"

"Home, with your permission."

The policeman lingered over Florence's passport. "Wife?"

"I've got three. But this is the good-looking one, so I took her to see the punishment at the mall. So she won't get ideas. A good example our imam sets."

The policeman looked closer at Florence, who sat staring straight ahead. "What's in the basket?"

"Figs from the Mashuff Valley." Bobby held the basket to the policeman. "Have one, as a token of our thanks for protecting us from our enemies. They're delicious."

The policeman reached for the basket's handle.

"Brother, please." Bobby grinned. "They're for the children's supper." He moved his left foot, with its ankle holster, within reach.

The policeman hesitated. He picked the plumpest figs off the top and gave the basket back and waved the car forward. "Go," he said.

"And Allah be with you," Bobby said. He edged forward and muttered, "Asshole."

There were no more roadblocks, and half an hour later, they reached their drab concrete house in the Sherala district, one of Amo-Amas's poorer neighborhoods, a place of broken glass and spiked walls, starving dogs and Filipino "guest" workers who had been granted permission by their Matari employers to live outside the home. There was an enclosure for the car.

Inside, Florence made duplicates of the videotape. She took off the hated *abaaya*. Bobby aimed the camera at her.

"This footage that you are about to witness was taken inside occupied Matar on March twenty-seventh at the Chartwell Mall, which the usurper Maliq has turned into a place of public execution . . ."

When they were finished, Bobby put a copy of the tape inside a packet of cigarettes and drove to the airport. On the way, he called Fouad, a ground-crew chief with Air Matar whom Bobby had recruited years ago. Seven hours later, the tape was in Nicosia, Cyprus, and in the hands of an Armenian named Hampigian, with whom Bobby had also been doing business for years. In another eight hours, it had arrived at the CNN bureau in Rome. Within an hour, following a conference with headquarters in Atlanta that included the chairman of the board, the tape was broadcast.

Among the millions who watched were Renard and George. They had set up a makeshift command center in Rick's office, using more of Uncle Sam's severance pay. The tape made for very difficult viewing. Even the cynical Renard was unable to speak after it was over. George had to get up and leave the room after five minutes. But then few people in the West had watched a woman being slowly beaten to death.

The network was flooded with phone calls, mostly from people appalled that it would show such a gruesome thing—the worst, some said, since the pictures of Americans torturing Iraqis at Abu Ghraib prison. But there was intense interest in the American woman who had taken the footage, obviously at great personal risk. She was now an object of official curiosity—in Washington, Paris, Kaffa and Amo-Amas; indeed, all over the world. Naturally, the media couldn't resist. They dubbed her "Florence of Arabia."

IMAM MALIQ, BELOVED OF ALLAH, emir of the Royal Kingdom of Matar, high prince of the House of Bin Haz, sharif of the Um-Katush, was less than pleased to hear that Delame-Noir of the Onzième Bureau was in Matar and requesting an "audience." It did please Maliq that he had put it that way, "audience" being more august than "meeting."

Still, he felt that Delame-Noir was condescending to him. He didn't like

Delame-Noir to begin with, and now that he had achieved the throne, if there was any condescending to do, by Allah, *he* would do it. He was in no mood for one of Delame-Noir's interminable pedantic lectures about the historicity of Hegelian dichotomies. Nor did Maliq desire to be reminded that it was Delame-Noir who had put him on the throne with the scheme of transforming him from a cheating race-car driver into a religious leader.

King Tallulah and Prince Bawad had been imperious beyond belief, reminding Maliq in every phone call, every e-mail, every meeting that it was their troops, their *mukfelleen,* their money and, God be praised, their oil that had put him on the throne. Between Paris and Kaffa, Maliq was tired of being grateful. Dammit, *they* should be grateful to *him*! Had he not selflessly put himself forward, giving up a brilliant career as a race-car driver, to restore Matar to its glory? (Assuming Matar had ever actually been glorious.) Had he not risked all? What if the coup had failed? Where would he be now? In Gazzy's dungeon, supplementing his diet with beetles. No, he'd had quite enough of their telling him, *Now, here's what else you can do for us today.*

"We will not see the Frenchman," Maliq petulantly announced to Fetish, the aide de camp he had inherited from his brother and who had come highly recommended by Delame-Noir. A certain air of pronouncement-making had crept into Maliq's speech of late; this often happens, alas, when one becomes dictator.

"But Holiness—"

"I have spoken, Fetish."

Since Fetish was also on the payroll of Delame-Noir's Onzième Bureau, he pressed as gingerly as he could. "Great Imam—would it not be wise to grant the Frenchman a few minutes? He has traveled a great distance."

"Bah! You make it sound like he crossed the Nefud Desert on camel. He came in his own private jet. It's got a bed in it, a kitchen and a two-star Michelin chef. We ourselves have flown in it. It is—damn thy impertinence, Fetish. It is not for us to explain ourselves!"

"I am but dung beside Thy Augustness, lord, beloved of Allah, protector of the one true faith. However, in my despised humility, I ask, should not my lord receive the Frenchman just for a brief time?"

Maliq made a growling noise but knew Fetish was right. "Ten minutes.

Make sure you come in after exactly ten minutes and say, 'Imam, you are urgently needed by . . .' Well, by someone important."

"How truly wise and benevolent is my master. Allah truly—"

"Oh, just *get* him, Fetish."

Maliq paced in his office, fingering his worry beads. Delame-Noir was shown in.

"*Altesse!*" Delame-Noir bowed ever so slightly. He looked Maliq up and down, rather—Maliq thought—like a malevolent tailor. "In your person, the magnificence of the Bin Hazzim and the purity of the true faith have found their most sublime embodiment. How lucky is Matar to have so wise, so puissant, a ruler. This does not happen every day. Indeed, not since your second cousin's great-great-great-uncle Ali Hashim bin—"

"Yes, yes," Maliq said. "Matar is once again a holy place. God be praised. So. Here you are."

"I have come to pay you homage, *mon emir*. To see the new crown jewel of the Matari in his setting."

"Ah? Well. Good. Here I am. So. *Very* busy time."

"Oh, yes." Delame-Noir grinned Gallicly. "It is truly work, establishing oneself as the unquestioned authority. But you *have*, yes yes, you have. And now maybe it's time to give the signal that, okay, we take our religion seriously, we are very observant, very strict, but we're not going to beat to death *all* the naughty women in the mall outside the Starbucks? Surely?"

Maliq sighed. "We didn't know this Florence woman was going to take a video of it."

"All the same, it's not such a good image for the new Matar, *mon imam*. They are playing it on the Internet now. It's very— Speaking personally, I find it very difficult to watch. It's like a Mel Gibson movie."

"The Internet is an instrument of Satan."

"The theology I must leave to the theologians," Delame-Noir said. "My concern, it's for you. Because this is not good publicity. Look, myself, I don't really care. We chopped off a lot of heads during our revolution. For a while it's fun, and an amusement for the riffraff, but if it goes on too long, it's not good for business."

"What are they going to do, not buy the oil?"

"No, no. Oil they would buy from anyone. From Satan. But why give yourself such a bad image in the world?"

"It's not my image you're worried about. It's yours."

"From you, wise imam, there is no keeping secrets. But okay, yes, this is making everyone look not so good. Not that France cares what the world thinks, still . . ."

Maliq threw up his hands. "It's the Wasabis who insist! Tallulah himself—he calls me every day to say he's sending more *mukfelleen* to help me 'purify the country.' I tell him, 'Thank you, you are too generous, but we don't need any more religious police.' And the next thing I know, Fetish informs me that another five hundred have arrived—by bus! What am I supposed to do?"

Delame-Noir nodded sympathetically. "It's not easy being imam."

"If it weren't for me, the *muks* would be holding twice as many executions and beatings."

"Clearly, I have misread the situation. *How* can I apologize to you? How can I help?"

"Just tell me," Maliq grunted, "what am I supposed to do."

"Perhaps there is a solution. Look, why don't you say to Tallulah, 'My dear king, we have had the iron fist, now it's time for the handshake, eh? We have made the people tremble. They are making pee-pee in their *thobes,* they are so full of respect for you. Now we have a very obedient people. And now it's time for the making pleasant.' Eh?"

"They're Wasabis," Maliq said. "They don't *make* pleasant."

"At least get this publicity off *your* soil."

"How?"

"Here is a statistic that I happen to possess. It's very secret, so please don't tell who told you. Do you know part of the reason Wasabia is sending you all these *mukfelleen*? Because they don't have enough to do there, because the population is so scared of them, they don't do anything wrong. They don't even go outside the house anymore. And this has translated into an unemployment situation among the *mukfelleen*. Tallulah is very worried about this, so he see it as a golden opportunity to get them out of his country and fully occupied. This is what is going on with the *mukfelleen*. And it's not good to have out-of-work executioners, eh? They get ideas.

"So, why don't you say to Tallulah, 'Okay, in return for your assistance with the change in regime, I am going to send you all our naughty women of Matar to help with your *mukfelleen* unemployment situation.' If they want to chop off the women's heads and make the bastinado, then at least it's happening in Wasabia, where they expect this barbarism, not here in the former Switzerland of the Gulf, eh?"

"But what about this Florence woman? I can't have her running around loose. It undermines our authority."

"No, no." Delame-Noir smiled. "This we cannot permit. Perhaps for this, too, I have a suggestion."

CHAPTER TWENTY-SIX

Florence could tell from the look on Bobby's face that it was not good news. He ripped off his *gutra* with disgust and tossed *Al Matar* on the table. Florence saw the front-page headline above the fold:

FORMER SHEIKA CONFESSES TO IMMORAL RELATIONSHIP WITH AMERICAN FLORENCE SPY-PROPAGANDIST

Bobby said, "They probably didn't bother to torture her. Just made it all up."

Florence read the last paragraph aloud: " 'The decision about how to punish her foul sins rests with the highest authorities. Acknowledging the enormity of her crimes, the former sheika has herself stated that strict implementation of *shari'a,* as interpreted by our blessed imam Maliq—a thousand blossoms fall upon his immaculate person—is commensurate with her crimes, too unspeakable to detail here.'

"Aw, *shit,*" Florence finished.

"It's a trap. This is the bait."

Florence started to gather up her things. Bobby watched her. "Does this mean that we're takin' the bait?"

"I can do this alone."

"God-*dammit,* Flo."

By the time they left their shabby dwelling, they resembled a thousand married couples—she determined, he furious.

They drove to a car park in the Mirdam district, one of Amo-Amas's most crowded, a place of market stalls and outdoor eateries abutting the playing fields where soccer games and camel and horse races were held. It bustled still. Even the grim asceticism that had settled on Matar had not entirely stifled the ambient noise of buying and selling.

Bobby's ego had now recovered at least to the point where he was speaking to Florence. "If he picks up right away," he said, "make it real quick. If he offers to put Laila on the phone and tells you to hold, hang up. You can always call back on another cell. But if they're expectin' the call, and they sure as hell will be, we've only got a couple minutes before the place'll be swarmin' with *muks.* I don't know how much technical assistance they're gettin' from the Frogs, but let's assume they are, so whatever you've got to say, say it fast.

"The call will be taped. And they will take anythin' you say and splice it so it'll sound like you're admittin' to everything from lesbian orgies to pissin' on the Kaaba stone in Mecca."

They parked the car and got out and blended—Bobby's favorite pastime—into the late-morning crowd. It was as good a place as any to make a call that would be immediately traced: thousands of people, half of them veiled, traffic, two-way streets, dozens of ways in and out.

Florence took out one of the cell phones that she had stolen on the night of Matar's "liberation," as it was now officially called. Bobby pressed a wad of sticky wax on the back of it and returned it to Florence. The wax made it feel lumpy and strange in her hand. She dialed the emir's private line.

It picked up after two rings. She identified herself. Maliq came on within moments. They'd obviously been expecting the call. Bobby chewed gum and looked at his watch with the air of a nervous coach.

"Well, Maliq," Florence said, "are you ready to take your seat at the table of civilized nations?"

"What *are* you talking about, Florence?"

"I'm doing what you wanted me to—answering that notice you put in the paper today."

"Ah. Still want to trade, then? I shall require a down payment."

"What did you have in mind? A hand? Tongue? The whole head?"

"Since you like to make tapes, you'll make a tape of your confession. On it should be included all your admissions, all your crimes—the U.S. government's role in plotting against Matar, against Islam, against me personally, your unnatural relationship with the sheika. Everything."

"The thousand and one crimes? I'll need a very long tape. And after you have it?"

"She will be flown to Cyprus. And you will surrender yourself."

"What guarantee do you have that I would surrender after the sheika is set free?"

"You want her to live a long and full life, yes? With her son?"

"All right. Hold on a moment, would you, Maliq?"

She left the connection open. Bobby took the phone from her. He stepped off the curb and bent, as if to tie his shoe, and affixed the phone to the underside of a car that was stopped for a red light.

They moved off and again blended into the crowds. Moments later, there were sirens and a helicopter overhead, then several black sedans full of *mukfelleen* sped past them in the direction of the innocent vehicle.

"I HAVE COMMITTED offenses against the state and . . . I have . . ." Florence stared into the lens of the camera Bobby held. "My name is Florence. I am American. I have had a . . . relationship . . ."

"Would it help if I set it up on a tripod and let you do this alone?" Bobby said.

Florence sighed. "No, let's try it again. What take are we on?"

"Eighteen or nineteen. Lost count. Okay, rollin' . . ."

"My name is Florence. I am American. I am an enemy of the regime of Imam Maliq." She looked at Bobby. "How was that?"

"I think they're going to want more than that."

"This film—you're sure it works?"

"Like a charm. Used it dozens of times."

"Okay, then." She brushed a strand of hair away. "Do I look all right?"

Bobby rolled his eyes. "Fabulous. Rollin'."

"My name is Florence, and I have committed many offenses against the country of Matar and its glorious leader, the imam Maliq bin-Kash al-Haz . . ."

". . . FOR THESE TERRIBLE offenses, I deserve whatever punishment Imam Maliq, in his great wisdom, counseled by the holy mullahs of Matar, in accordance with shari'a, should decide upon. May my sins be cleansed, and may Allah forgive me for my transgressions. Long life to Imam Maliq. Long life to the new Islamic Republic of Matar."

Fetish switched off the VCR.

"Hum," Maliq grunted, pleased.

"Congratulations, Imam," Fetish said. "A great success."

"Yes. 'Twas, rather. You don't think she was acting too much?"

"No, sire. She looked most fearful and penitent. Very convincing."

"She's not bad-looking."

"Truly, a waste of beauty, Magnificence. Shall I have the tape copied and distributed?"

"Oh, yes. Make many copies."

"And shall I make the arrangements?"

"Which?"

"With respect to the sheika, Great One. The plane—to Cyprus?"

"Of course not."

"Ah? The imam would pray first, then have me make the arrangements?"

"You may make the arrangements, Fetish, when I *tell* you to make them. Is this difficult to comprehend? Is thy hearing afflicted?"

"No, Holy One. It is all quite straightforward. Forgive thy humble servant's obtuseness."

"Your what?"

"Stupidity, Imam."

"Ah. You may leave us."

Fetish went off to a quiet corner of the palace apartments to relay by cell phone to his other employer, M. Delame-Noir, the developments and lack thereof.

—

FROM ANOTHER CROWDED part of the city, Florence placed another call to Maliq. Bobby, now even more impatient, kept time with his watch.

"You have your down payment," she said when Maliq came to the phone.

"Yes. Do you have a television in whatever stink hole you're in? It's going to be playing tonight. But if you miss it tonight, you can watch it tomorrow night. Or the night after that."

"Will I also see on television the sheika disembarking from a plane in Cyprus?"

"Well, you see, there's a problem."

"What 'problem,' Maliq?"

"She's not well to travel. She has had quite the time of it, you see. Why don't you visit her? We'll put you in an adjoining room. You can make love through the bars."

"So, Maliq, still the cheater?"

"No, Florence, still the winner."

Florence pressed END and dropped the phone in the gutter, where it broke apart as it tumbled into the sewer drain. She and Bobby joined the throng and walked off. Above, they could hear a helicopter approaching.

"IMAM, THERE IS a problem with the tape," Fetish said.

"What 'problem'?"

"There is nothing on it."

"What are you saying?"

"I sent it directly to Jahar, the head of the television station, for duplicating and broadcasting. But he says that when they went to duplicate it, it was—empty. There was nothing on it."

"This is impossible, Fetish. You and I watched it together."

"I cannot explain, Imam."

Maliq picked up his phone. Jahar came on the line and tremblingly reported that, regretfully, alas, there was nothing on the tape. Maliq called him an imbecile and a fool and, what was more, a traitor. Jahar, sweating profusely, said that the tape was being examined most rigorously by TVMatar's top technicians, and if anything could be found on it—other than nullity and blankness—he would immediately advise His Most Holy Worship. Maliq slammed the phone down with such force that it cracked.

"Filthy deceiving bitch!"

"Holiness," Fetish said, "she is not worthy of thy wrath."

"Trickery! Foul women's deceit!"

"Calm thyself, Holy One, lest thy heart burst."

"Fetch the sheika! Bring her here, the slut! Immediately!"

"Master—"

"Fetish," Maliq seethed, "do you know what an *oubliette* is?"

Fetish did not, but he was certain it was no pleasant thing.

"It is a hole, Fetish, a very deep hole, found in French châteaux and prisons, for the hurling into of troublesome people. And there they are forgotten—*oubliés*. I'm having one installed beneath the palace. Would you like to be the first to try it out?"

Nothing so concentrates the mind as the prospect of being hurled into a pit. Fetish scurried off like a crab to call Delame-Noir.

Delame-Noir was a man of refinement, but on hearing Fetish's report, he uttered a low *"Merde."* Upon regaining his composure, he instructed Fetish to delay, whereupon Fetish began babbling about *oubliettes*. It had been some time since Delame-Noir had heard the word, but now that he was reminded of it, he was inclined to dig one himself, deep enough to accommodate the entire Matari royal family; or the whole country, for that mutter.

"IT'S BECOME EASIER now that film is digital," Bobby was saying. "There's an algorithm embedded in the chip that activates the erase function when you hit PLAY. So you can only play the tape once, and it won't duplicate. Can come in kinda handy. I've used it a lot."

Florence hadn't said much since dropping the phone into the sewer.

"Look, Flo," he said, "you tried. You did everythin' you could. He was never going to let her go. Even if he wanted to, the Wasabis wouldn't let him. The only thing they want more than Laila's head on a stick is yours."

"Algorithm," she said absent-mindedly. "It's an Arabic word. It comes from 'Al-Khawarizmi.' Mathematician, twelve centuries ago, in the days when they were great. They're going to kill her, Bobby."

"Maybe the French'll intervene. This PR can't be doin' them any good. They may be assholes, but they don't like lookin' like assholes."

"No, they'll kill her."

"Maybe it's time to go home, Flo. We're not makin' things any better here at this point."

She looked at him. "Are you scared?"

"To be scared, you gotta not want to die. I haven't really cared about that, since there wasn't really anyone I'd miss that much. Up to now. If you see my problem."

"You don't sound very happy about being in love."

"I've got mixed feelings about it, frankly. There are better places than the Middle East to lose your edge."

"THE FRENCHMAN is here, Holy One."

"What? Who does he think he is, just showing up? And where is the sheika? I told you to bring her here."

"Yes, she's coming. They had to . . . wash her. She was not presentable, sire. Being in the cell without amenties . . ."

"I didn't ask you to give her a bath, Fetish."

"My stupidity is a boundless as the Nafta Desert, oh lord. Forgive me."

Maliq made a growling noise.

"In the meantime, will you not admit the Frenchman, sire?"

"What does he *want*?"

"I don't know, Imam." The introduction of the *oubliette* had altered Fetish's posture: his spine was now bent in permanent bowing.

"Five minutes. Do you understand, Fetish?"

"Thou art truly benevolent."

Delame-Noir was ushered in. "The imam is indulgent to see me on such short notice."

"We are *very* busy, monsieur. What is it you wish to see us about?"

"We have made an intercept of the Americans' communications, sire. I thought you would want to have it from my lips, personally, rather than over the telephone."

"Yes?"

"It is very sensitive."

"Yes, yes, yes. So?"

Delame-Noir lowered his voice. "I gather my lord yesterday had a telephone conversation with Prince Bawad, the Wasabi foreign minister?"

"How do you know that? What if I did? I'm the ruler of Matar."

In fact, the French had a tap on Maliq's phone, thanks to Fetish. But best to pretend that it was the dreadful Americans.

"I am not criticizing, Imam. But it would appear that the Americans were listening *in* on this conversation. They are very technically, well— They are clever at this, at least. The vicissitudes of modernity. *Always* someone is listening. As for me, I understand, it is none of my business. But now, because of what we have learned, it becomes in a way my business. You grasp the essence of my discomfort?"

"Concerning what?"

"We have the recording of the conversation, thanks to the American eavesdroppers. I gather Prince Bawad was very—how to say it?—authoritarian with you?"

"I can hold my own with *Prince* Bawad," Maliq said stiffly.

"Of course you can. To me, it seems very rude the way he treated you. Very imperious, very bossy. Calling you—forgive me, Great Imam, for I am only quoting, eh?—the son of a kitchen slave, a cheater at automobile racing, and saying that if you don't do exactly as the Wasabis say—what were his words, exactly?—'we will remove you from the throne like a rotten fig.' A strange figure of speech, I agree. He is not so adept at the diplomacy, the prince, for a diplomat."

"Bawad is a toad. From now on, I deal only with Tallulah."

Delame-Noir shrugged as only a Frenchman can. "Yes, but Bawad is King Tallulah's nephew, and they are very close. I don't think that the prince would have said these things to you if his uncle the king did not approve."

"What of it?" Maliq said impatiently.

"*Mon imam,* the point is that the Americans are in possession of a tape recording of this conversation. And my conclusion is that if you execute the sheika Laila, the Americans may use this as a pretext to become involved directly. Florence has stirred up much publicity in the United States. In the world."

"And what are the Americans going to do? Not buy oil? Bah."

"Perhaps they will leak the tape of Bawad ordering you to kill her. And how is that going to look if it's played? Making it seem as though you are just a puppet of the Wasabis. Who wants this? The Wasabis, perhaps they don't care. But we, France, as your allies and true friends, this we do not want." Delame-Noir smiled. "We want a *strong* imam in Matar. An *independent* imam! Not one who must ask permission from the House of Hamooj every time he wants to go to the bathroom. Of course, it goes without saying that you may *always* depend on France."

Maliq threw up his hands. "What am I supposed to do? They want this sheika dead. And they want the Florence creature even more, and they blame me—me!—for not catching her. Florence tricked us, you realize. I asked her to make a tape, just as you told me, and she tricked us, the slut-bitch. It plays once and—*poof,* nothing, gone like a djinni."

"This was my own stupidity, Great Lord," Delame-Noir said soothingly. "You played your part with brilliance and subtlety, and we—no, I alone myself—let you down by not anticipating that they would resort to this CIA trick. I curse myself. I will not sleep tonight for—"

"You're overdoing, Dominique."

"Yes, I suppose I am."

"What am I supposed to do now? You say the Americans will use this tape of the conversation between me and Bawad?"

"I fear they might, yes."

"Why don't I call in the American ambassador and tell him his country better start building windmills to keep them warm this winter?"

"But my lord, is it wise to inform the Americans that you know about this? We have them exactly where we want them."

"We do?"

"But yes. Instead of making threats to the Americans, you say to them, 'Look, my hamburger-eating friends, we know the sheika works for the CIA.' "

"She does?"

"No, but you tell the Americans that you *think* she does, and this will make them very nervous. You tell them that she has confessed to everything. You say, 'And now the Wasabis, they are being very severe. They want me to chop off her head. You would think *they* are French! Ha! But I have decided that I'm not going to chop off her head. I'm going to give her to you—with the head intact. Do you know why, my American friends? Precisely to show the Wasabis that I am my own imam, my own person, that I don't take orders from anybody. And now here is what you Americans are going to do for me in exchange. First, I want to start hearing you say nice things about me in the United Nations. Second, I want you to stop saying all these terrible things about how France was very naughty to help me become emir. And third, I want you to send your people—your Delta Force commandos, who are very good—into Amo-Amas and remove this Florence woman of yours. Dead or alive, it's no matter for me, but it's time for her to go. I am not looking to make the next Joan of Arc. But if you don't come and get her, I will deal with it very soon. And finally, if you don't help me with these things, you Americans are going to have a very cold winter, yes?' "

"Hmm," Maliq said. "Do you think they'll go along with it?"

"My dear imam, you must understand—the Americans are idealistic to the point where they must lower their thermostat two degrees. Then they become very practical."

CHAPTER TWENTY-SEVEN

Florence and Bobby were in the middle of shooting another "Osama"—the name they had given Florence's videotapes—when they heard an electronic chirping. It startled them, since the phone had been turned off, and cell phones as a rule do not ring when they are in the off mode. And now this one was ringing.

Florence moved toward it. Bobby said, "Couple of grams of C4 can make for a pretty bad headache."

He took the phone from her and walked to a far corner of room. Florence watched him. He took a breath, held the phone at arm's length and pressed the TALK button. He exhaled and held the receiver a foot from his ear.

"*Salaam.*" He listened, his eyes darting sideways nervously. "I'll give her the message," he said with an edge in his voice, "if I see her."

Florence mouthed: *Who?*

Bobby mouthed back: *Uncle Sam.*

She held out her hand. Bobby cupped his over the receiver and whispered, "Keep it short." He gave her the phone and began gathering up their things. She recognized by now the rhythms of another hasty departure.

"Well, well," Florence said into the phone.

"Young lady, do you have any idea what sort of problems you're creating back here?"

"Didn't you tell me at our first meeting, 'If you can't solve a problem, make it larger'?"

"I didn't tell you to make it *this* large. We'll talk about it when you get home. The last thing we need is for you to be captured."

"First get Laila out."

Uncle Sam sighed. "What did you have in mind? An amphibious assault on the palace, or *Black Hawk Down: The Sequel*? Have you been outside lately? There are more Wasabi troops in Matar than there are citizens."

"It's not a request."

There was a pause. "I'll do what I can."

"Not good enough."

"It will just have to be."

Bobby motioned to Florence: *Finish up.*

"Oh-one-four-five hours," Uncle Sam said. "That's one-forty-five A.M. I'll have the water taxi on station, the usual place. Is Omar Sharif there? Put him on."

Florence numbly handed the phone to Bobby. He listened, grunted a few "yeah"s and hung up.

"Somethin' wrong here," Bobby said. "Come on, time to go."

"Did you tell him about us?"

"What about us?"

"That we're sleeping together?"

"I . . . might have. Come on, that doesn't matter right now."

"Why would you have told him that?"

"Because he asked."

"When did you tell him we were sleeping together?"

"*After* we started sleepin' together. Flo, we gotta go."

"Why would you tell him?"

" 'Cause he asked me if you were a *dyke*. The rumors. He didn't know what to believe. He was tryin' to get you to leave the country, and you wouldn't, so he—"

"Assumed I was a lesbian. So is that why you slept with me? Is this part of your mission? Sexual preference observation officer?"

"Of course not. Goddammit, Flo."

"Don't you goddammit. If anyone gets to goddammit, it's me."

"Flo, we gotta go. I got a bad feeling about that call."

"I thought we were being exfiltrated by submarine."

"Maybe. Will you just get your stuff, girl?"

In a huff, Florence gathered her things, consisting at this point of her pistol, cell phones and hated, smelly *abaaya*.

They got in the car. Instead of driving off, Bobby circled around to the front and parked two blocks away, facing the front of their little house.

"What are we doing?"

"Eliminatin' possibilities." Bobby was slumped low in the driver's seat, watching the house through small binoculars. His right hand rested on the butt of the pistol tucked into his waistband, beneath the folds of his *thobe*.

A quarter hour later, a sedan approached the house from the far side, slowed and stopped. Four men got out. They wore the distinctive black and blue *thobes* of *mukfelleen*. They carried pistols instead of standard-issue whips. Bobby peered intently through his binoculars.

"Well, sum-bitch. Goddammit."

"*Mukfelleen?*"

He handed Florence the glasses. "See that heavyset guy in front with the mustache? His name is Anbar Tal. He's a captain in the Royal Matar Air Force Security Service. I recruited him."

"He's . . . CIA?"

"Last I checked."

"Why is he approaching our house with all those men and pistols?"

Bobby peered through his binoculars. "The body language somehow isn't conveyin' to me *We're here to help.*"

He slipped the car into reverse and slowly began to back away.

Florence looked in the rearview mirror and saw the men in black and blue *thobes* approaching their car from behind. Bobby instinctively floored the accelerator.

There were two loud *thumps* from behind, and then the men in *thobes* were on the trunk of the car, and not happy about it. In the next instant, they were on the hood, and even less happy. Then they were on the ground in front of the car, limp and beyond caring one way or the other.

The car was now speeding backward at thirty miles per hour. Ahead, in the receding distance, Florence saw the five *muks,* led by Anbar Tal, running toward them, aiming their pistols. It took a second for Florence's overworked brain to process that this stance was preliminary to worse developments. She processed this critical insight a quarter second before the first bullet smashed through the windshield, leaving her *abaaya* coated in safety-glass crumbs. Crouching in her seat, she heard more vitreous explosions, accompanied by obscene mutterings from the driver's seat. Then there were even louder explosions, which after a moment she realized came from nearby. Bobby was driving backward and firing out the window with his left hand.

"Could use some help," he said.

Florence had fired a gun only once, many years ago, during her brief State Department training course. Though she had gripped a pistol many times in the previous weeks, it now felt strange and unwelcome in her hand as she flipped the safety off and aimed out the window. She shut her eyes and fired.

There was a loud metal *thunk,* followed by an explosive hissing and a vertical jet of steam. She had shot through the hood of their car and punctured the radiator.

Bobby swung the wheel hard over and yanked the hand brake, turning the car 180 degrees, then shifted into drive and floored it. The problem was that an internal combustion engine, however expertly engineered by the finest automotive minds in Germany, is not designed to run, either efficiently or for long, once penetrated by nine-millimeter rounds. Steam hissed from the hood like water spewing from the spout-hole of an angry whale.

"You all right? Flo? You *hurt*?"

"I'm okay. Oh, shit, Bobby, I shot the car."

"Listen up. I'm gonna turn that corner. I'm going to stop. I want you to get out. Okay? Now, listen to me: There's a man who works at the live-chicken *souq*. He's got a booth, the name on it is ZamZam Best Chickens. Got that? His name is Azool bin-Halaam. He's worked for me. He's independent. No one knows about him, not CIA, not Uncle Sam, not the Frogs, no one. He can get you on the ferry to— Shit, come on, you, sum-bitchbastard!" Bobby was pounding the dashboard in the obscure hope that the engineers had installed a sensor there that, when pounded violently, would instruct the car's computer to ignore the fact that a nine-millimeter bullet had been fired through the engine's cooling system. Alas, the engineers had overlooked this feature.

"I'm not going to leave you here," Florence said.

"Shut up and listen. You tell Azool you're a friend of Cyrus from Cyprus. Got that? Cyrus from Cyprus. He'll get you out of the country on the ferry to Pangibat. Got that? ZamZam. Azool. Cyrus from Cyprus. Have you got that?"

They'd turned the corner. Bobby pulled the cranking car over and stopped. The street was blessedly teeming with pedestrians, some of whom paused to stare at the strange sight, a hissing Mercedes.

"Go, Flo. Please. Don't make me beg, girl, I'm too old."

She opened the door to get out, then closed it. She took her pistol and turned around and aimed through the rear window. "Just drive."

"Goddammit, woman."

"Just drive."

Spewing cusswords, Bobby stepped on the accelerator. A violent, bronchitic *hissss* issued from the hole in the hood as the last of the coolant evaporated. The car moved forward without conviction.

Looking back, Florence saw a dark sedan round the corner fast. Pedestrians bolted out of the way.

She braced the gun in both hands and kept her eyes open. The first shot shattered the glass of their own rear window, providing a clear field of fire. She aimed again and methodically emptied the magazine of eight rounds into the windshield of the pursuing vehicle. The car veered from side to side and then went off the road and onto the sidewalk and into the plate-glass window of a pastry shop.

"Better," Bobby muttered.

Florence ejected the spent clip and rummaged in her satchel for a fresh one.

Bobby turned off down a narrow street. The hissing had stopped. The temperature-gauge needle was hard over into the red, indicating meltdown. This and a loud knocking sound augured the necessity, sooner rather than later, of alternative transportation.

Bobby braked. They opened the doors and got out. A car similar to the one Florence had dispatched turned the corner. It accelerated toward them. Florence saw pistols aimed at them from the windows on both sides.

Bobby opened fire. A hole appeared in the windshield in front of the car's driver, another in front of the passenger. The car veered sharply to the right, into a lamppost, in the process shearing off an arm that had been aiming a pistol.

Florence gasped. Bobby came around and pulled her to her feet. They ran down alleys until Bobby, breathing hard, finally announced, "Okay, walk, just walk."

They walked, another Matari couple taking a leisurely stroll after shooting dead a half-dozen men.

The streets around them screamed with sirens. From above, they could hear the urgent whoosh and roar of rotor blades.

Bobby whispered to her, "Y'ever fainted?"

"No."

"Start."

"What?"

"Just *faint,* would you?"

Florence collapsed to the pavement as best she could without breaking a kneecap. Why, she had no idea. She closed her eyes.

She heard a male voice speaking Arabic, asking what was wrong.

"She is pregnant," Bobby said with perfect lack of sympathy or tenderness and exactly the right tone of annoyance.

"She shouldn't be outside in that condition," the man said.

"Don't I know it? Twelve times I told her, and a thirteenth, but she insists. She thinks exercise will give her a male child."

"God *will* that it be. Is she all right?"

"I think her time has come. We must have an ambulance."

Florence thought, *Clever boy.*

"I will call you one."

"Allah favors the compassionate. Thank you, brother."

While the man spoke into his cell phone, Bobby leaned down and whispered, "Now, why didn't I think of that?"

Matar had good infrastructure and civil services. The ambulance arrived within minutes. Florence had maneuvered her satchel underneath her *abaaya* so that her outline was appropriately gravid. The two attendants loaded her onto a gurney and into the ambulance. Bobby jumped in after her.

"Which hospital?" he asked an attendant.

"Churchill—I mean King Bisma. They changed the name."

"You better hurry unless you want to deliver the child right here." As the attendant went about rolling up the folds of Florence's *abaaya* in order to fasten the blood-pressure cuff, Bobby brought the pistol butt down on the back of his head. Then he reached through the doorway and pressed the muzzle of the pistol to the driver's neck and pulled back the hammer for that extra note of emphasis and said, "If you want to live, drive to the airport. If you'd rather die, I will drive."

The man emitted a squeak and began to beg for his life.

"Relax. Do as I say, and everything will be well."

The man continued to babble and wail. He had seven children. He was the sole support. He had missed prayers that morning. If he died now, he would not see paradise.

Florence stripped the unconscious ambulance attendant of his uniform vest, then bound his hands and mouth with adhesive tape, which ambulances have in copious supply.

Bobby told the driver, "Slow down and turn off the siren."

The driver obeyed, still blubbering. Bobby handed him the radio handset.

"Tell the dispatcher to put you through to Matar Air Medical Service at the airport. Tell him only that." He pressed the muzzle into the man's neck. "I speak Arabic."

The driver did as asked. A voice came on. Bobby took the handset from the driver.

"This is Dr. Mansour bin-Halibib, personal physician to Fetish al-Zir, assistant to the imam Maliq, blessings be upon his name. To whom do I speak?"

The voice came back crisp and subordinate. "Saif al-Utabi, Excellency, at your service."

"Very well. We require an immediate medical evacuation. One of the imam's wives has sustained a brain injury. We are en route to you. We'll need your fastest aircraft, with fuel for Cairo."

"But I've received no authorization, Excellency—"

"*I* am authorizing it."

"But Excellency—"

"If the imam's wife dies in this ambulance, I will tell him that it was because I was distracted by *unnecessary questions*!"

One advantage of totalitarianism: The lower down the food chain, the higher they jump.

"We will make ready for you," Saif al-Utabi said.

"We will be there in fifteen minutes. Inform the security personnel at the gate to admit us without delay."

"Yes, Excellency."

The ambulance driver looked at Bobby, goggle-eyed with fear.

The road to the airport went through mostly empty desert. Bobby put on the unconscious attendant's uniform vest. He instructed the driver to pull off on the far side of a billboard advertising the pleasures of Infidel Land; *Mukfelleen* censors had painted over the offending text. Florence held the gun on the driver while Bobby dragged the other man out of the ambulance and laid him behind the base of the billboard.

Back inside, he gave the driver instructions, conveying, as gently as possible under the circumstances, that if he did not follow them precisely, he would be meeting Allah sooner than expected, prepared or not.

Florence listened and said to Bobby in French, a language she guessed the driver did not comprehend, "They do have an air force. They'll shoot us down."

"I'm wide open to suggestions."

"What about the embassy? They have to take us in there."

Bobby snorted. "Oh yeah, they'd be just tickled to have us. Even if the marines didn't shoot us down, even if we did make it through the gates, then what? Spend the rest of our lives living in the basement being frowned at by embassy pukes? No, thanks. Right now a jet with medical markings sounds pretty good to me." Florence had to agree.

They were approaching the airport. Florence rigged herself up with every medical device in the ambulance—respirator tube, blood-pressure cuff, IV tubes, CoolPak pressure bandages—and lay back on the gurney in a passing imitation of an imam's wife with a serious head injury. Bobby took his seat in the front, reminding the whimpering driver that he had a pistol in his vest pocket. Bobby reached forward and flicked on the siren and lights, lighting up the desert around them in red, white and blue strobes.

There was a roadblock at the airport entrance.

"Stay calm, say nothing. I will do the speaking," Bobby said.

They slowed to a stop. Soldiers with machine guns blocked the way. One motioned to the driver to roll down the window. "Where are you going?"

"Air Medical Service," Bobby said. "What's the problem, sir?"

"That's for me to ask, not you. There's an alert."

"But sir, it's urgent, as you can see."

The two rear doors of the ambulance opened, and two soldiers looked in. Florence lay still on the gurney, clenching the grip of the pistol under her *abaaya.*

"Who is she?" the soldier said through the driver's window.

"The imam's wife," Bobby said. "His *favorite* wife. She's being evacuated to Cairo." He added gravely, "It's critical."

The soldier straightened. "We've had no notice of this."

Bobby said angrily, "Why do you tell me this? This injury was not planned in advance! Allah is merciful—don't expect the imam to be."

The soldier hesitated. Then, with a slight, contemptuous sideways gesture of his head, he indicated his permission to proceed. The ambulance's rear doors shut with a bang. The soldier in front stood aside. The ambulance moved forward.

"I think my blood pressure spiked," Florence murmured.

The driver appeared to be hyperventilating. Bobby patted him on the back and spoke to him in a friendly tone. "You did well, my friend, well. A few more minutes, and it will all be over, and you'll have a great story to tell your wife and chil—"

The driver's eyes rolled up under his eyelids. He pitched forward onto the steering wheel. The ambulance veered into the path of a service vehicle.

Bobby lunged for the wheel and swung it back, avoiding the oncoming truck by inches. Florence was thrown off the gurney in a tangle of medical appurtenances. "What the hell?" she said.

Bobby was trying simultaneously to steer the careening ambulance, reach the brake with his left foot and drag the unconscious driver out of his seat, a complicated endeavor under the best of circumstances. Florence struggled to free herself of tubes and crawl to the front. A crunching sound announced the fact that they had driven through a wooden barrier and were now going the wrong way on a one-way service road, which declared to even the casual observer that all was not well at the wheel.

With a grunt, Bobby succeeded in hefting the unconscious driver out of the seat and onto the floor, and then jimmied himself into the seat, reasserting control of the ambulance, which was now driving straight at a fuel truck. The ambulance had the advantage of a siren and flashing lights, forcing the oncoming vehicles off the road with angry blaring. But now other sirens asserted themselves. And as Florence groped her way over the unconscious driver to the passenger seat, she heard the squawk of voices over the radio—urgent, angry voices, addressing themselves to the driver of the ambulance and demanding that he halt.

"Hang on." Bobby spun the wheel and slammed on the brakes. The ambulance turned but, top-heavy, went onto two wheels. It tottered for what seemed a very long time, then fell back miraculously onto all four wheels.

Now, at least, they were facing the right way, although they had by this point created a spectacle of themselves, and with that came increased interest on the part of a dozen vehicles in the distance. Some had mounted heavy-caliber guns.

Bobby assessed the deteriorating situation in the clinical language of the professional: "We're fucked."

He turned up a ramp that announced DEPARTING FLIGHTS. The security vehicles were still hundreds of yards off but closing fast. It was evening, and the airport was crowded. There were dozens of vehicles in front and hundreds of travelers getting out and entering the terminal.

"When I pull up to the curb," Bobby said, "jump out. Blend like hell. You can make it. Remember, ZamZam Best Chickens. Azool. Cyrus—"

"—from Cyprus. Yes, Bobby, I know."

"Okay, then." He drove to the far end of the terminal, then pulled over to the curb. He'd turned off the siren and the lights. "Go, Frenzy."

"I'm stuck."

"What?"

"My foot, it's wedged."

Bobby leaned toward her.

"No, you can't reach it from that side," she said. "Go around. Quickly."

Bobby opened his door and bolted around the front. As he did, Florence jumped into the driver's seat, put the ambulance in drive and took off with a screech of tires. She caught a glimpse of him in the side mirror, standing on the curb. Then the police and military cars screamed past him in hot pursuit of her.

Ambulances are built for speed. She drove fast, drawing the pursuers away from Bobby. But police and military vehicles are also built for speed, and they soon closed behind her. They had apparently satisfied themselves that there was no imam's wife inside, for they were now shooting. The low overhang of the ambulance protected the tires, and her body was shielded by the metal bulkhead behind the driver's seat. But a volley of bullets ripped through the doorway and smashed through the windshield, turning it into a spider web.

Florence analyzed her situation as she drove. In minutes, she knew, she would be captured or dead. They'd drag her out and—what then? Interrogation. Torture. Execution. The Wasabis would want their licks. They would want her most of all.

She heard a noise and saw the helicopter. It was flying low, keeping pace with her. She saw the man with the rifle aiming at her. She looked at the speedometer. A hundred and ten. She was approaching a highway overpass. It could all be over in seconds, neat and clean. So much easier all around. Not a particularly glorious way to go out, smashing into the concrete strut of a highway overpass, but *so* much cleaner. No one screaming at her, no one hooking her up to a car battery, no beheading or being stoned.

She nudged the vehicle into the left lane and kept her foot down on the accelerator. She felt, suddenly, quite calm, almost thrilled to be in such complete control of her fate. She thought of Nazrah, who had set all these events in motion with her own car crash. Florence put her head down and aimed at the support. And then she heard the groan.

It was the driver. She had forgotten all about him. He was looking up at her in pure terror, babbling. He presented a pathetic spectacle, lying on the floor there, but then she remembered his seven children. If only he hadn't mentioned that. If only he'd been a little braver. If only he'd kept that to himself and . . . The overpass was seconds away.

She veered away from the concrete strut and sped under the overpass.

The helicopter was flying alongside her, low off the ground. She saw a man leaning out the side door. He was aiming a rifle at her.

He fired three efficient shots into her engine block. The windshield splattered with oil. The vehicle began to slow.

She caught a brief glimpse of the man as he lowered his rifle. She noted the blond hair and the telltale rolled sleeves of a French para. *Yes,* she thought as her vehicle slowed and was surrounded, *they always were very good at* le sniping, *the French.*

CHAPTER TWENTY-EIGHT

R*ick Renard was in his Washington office trying to persuade a portly* former U.S. senator, twice thwarted in his attempt to be elected president, to become spokesman for a chain of weight-reduction centers.

The senator was pretending that this was beneath his dignity, which it was, but he had another reason: He wanted more money. Renard, meanwhile, was pretending that helping obese Americans lose weight was a magnificently self-less humanitarian act, and if a distinguished man who had devoted his entire life to public service made a few dollars in the process, what reasonable person could object?

In the midst of this perfunctory Kabuki dance, Renard's assistant entered apologetically and handed Rick a note saying that George was on the line demanding to speak to him. No, it could not wait, and yes, it was urgent, very, very urgent.

"The White House," Rick said to the senator as he reached for the phone. "Do you mind?"

The senator understood perfectly well that it wasn't the White House, but he was flattered that Rick should elevate the lie to such a high degree. In Washington, you know how tall you stand by how low the other person is willing to stoop.

"No, of course not."

"Yes, Karl?" Rick said into the phone.

"It's Firenze," George said. "I think they've got her."

"Shit," Renard said. "Fuck."

The senator stared.

"I'll find out what I can," George said. "I'll meet you at your office as soon as I can get out of here. Duckett has me auditing eight-year-old visa applications, the swine."

Rick hung up.

"Is everything all right—at the *White* House?" the senator asked heavily.

"Oh, yeah. Yeah. You know how they are." Rick smiled. "Every time their numbers drop a point, it's panic city."

Rick got rid of the senator and told his assistant to cancel everything, then switched on all the TV sets and surfed those and the Internet until George arrived with what news he'd been able to gather. It wasn't easy, since Duckett had petulantly downgraded his security clearance. But George had friends.

The U.S. embassy in Amo-Amas had cabled a report about some kind of disturbance in the Dismalia Quarter: shootings, car crashes, an incident at the airport. Embassy communication monitors had picked up Matari police-radio chatter about *el imra'a amrikiya* (the American woman). They had also picked up French radio transmissions to and from a military helicopter, asking for and receiving permission to fire upon a fleeing vehicle. Half an hour later, a convoy of vehicles had driven at high speed through the gates of the Prince Wazba Air Base. Following Maliq's takeover, the base had been turned into a detention facility for Mataris who were bold enough to express the opinion that Maliq's coup was less than the greatest event in Matar since the coming of Islam. The vast majority of these complainants were—no surprise—female Mataris.

"Duckett disappeared into his office looking like a Komodo dragon had just crawled up his ass," George said, pacing back and forth. "He wouldn't give me the time of day. They've got her. I know it."

"I tried calling some of the old gang at TVMatar," Renard said glumly. "No one's left. All I got were hang-ups. One person actually called me an infidel. I want my old Matar back."

Renard's assistant came in. "Someone named Bobby for you?"

Rick and George practically knocked each other over, reaching for the phone.

"Bobby? Is she all right?" Rick said.

"No. They got her. Okay, just listen, I'm not gonna stay on long, on account of that double-dealin' lowlife Uncle Sam probably listenin' in. You there, Sam? You listenin'? You tell us you're arrangin' for a water-taxi exfil, and ten minutes later, Anbar Tal—*my* recruit—shows up to kill us. Well, listen to this: I'm gonna come back there. If I have to *swim,* I am comin' back there, and by the time I'm through with you, you'll be breathin' through your asshole and crappin' through your ears. You got that?"

Renard cupped the phone and whispered to George, "I think he's upset."

"All right," Bobby said, "is it on the news over there?"

"No, not yet."

"George there? Put him on. George, what's State doin'?"

"What they do best. Nothing. Just a few cables out of Amo. Duckett won't tell me anything. Bobby, what are they going to do to her?"

"I don't know, man. Put Renard back on. Rick, you remember that cell phone I gave you? The one I told you to keep in D.C.? Do you still have it?"

"Yeah, I think—yeah."

"All right. Use that to call me. I'll be in touch. You get started at your end."

"Started—on what?"

"You're a PR man, aren't you?"

"Well, yeah—"

"Start spinnin', man. Spin till you drop. Yo, George?"

"I'm here."

"Don't let those embassy pukes walk away from this."

"I'm on it."

"All right," Bobby said, "let's get her out of there. Shock and awe, boys. Shock and awe."

The line went dead.

"What did he mean by that last part?" Renard said.

"Oh, it's just knuckle-dragger talk. But for once I agree."

—

IT WAS A SMALL CELL, fairly clean; by cell standards, the very lap of luxury. There was a cotlike bed with a bit of foam for a pillow, a plastic pail for necessities—with a lid, very deluxe—a bottle of water, and a copy of the Holy Koran.

They'd hooded Florence after dragging her out of the ambulance. Before the hood went over her head, she'd had a last look at the French sniper who had put the bullets in her engine. He looked almost apologetic, giving her a little shrug as if to say, *But what can one do? Orders are orders. Hélas, chèrie.*

After the handcuffing and hooding were done, without apologies or shrugs, Florence was put in the back of a vehicle and driven off. Even with her instinctive inertial guidance navigation, she had no way of knowing where they were taking her. After an hour, perhaps more, the hood was removed, and she found herself blinking in a brightly lit room, somewhere—pray Allah—still in Matar, and not across the border in Wasabia. Not that there was much sunlight left between the two countries.

She was reading the Koran when she heard the key turning in the heavy door. In Washington she had met a man who had spent five and a half years being tortured and confined in North Vietnam, most of it in solitary, unspeakable conditions. He told her that even thirty years later, whenever he heard the sound of keys or a door being opened, his pulse quickened and his chest seized up.

The man who entered the cell wasn't wearing the black and blue uniform of the *mukfelleen*. One takes such comforts as one can.

Florence was hooded, manacled leg-and-hand and marched off. She guessed that the chains were for psychological effect, the likelihood of a woman overcoming her captors and breaking free being low. Florence clanked along the stone floor barefoot, trying to fall into a semblance of dignified rhythm. She was also trying not to trip and fall. Her situation was undignified enough as it was.

She was prodded forward with the end of what felt like a club into a cooler space. The thought came to her, not entirely unwelcome, that in a second the hood might be pulled off to reveal the executioner with his *seyef.* If you were going to have your throat cut, better that it be cleanly done and with some semblance of a ceremonial beheading, instead of with a rusty folding knife of the kind used on a *sekeen* sheep.

She found herself in an air-conditioned room reassuringly devoid of bloodstains or instruments of death or torture, facing a plain table at which sat three men, the center of whom she recognized right away as Maliq, emir, sheikh and imam of the Islamic Republic of Matar, blessings be upon him.

It took her several seconds to place the man sitting on Maliq's right. From the distinctive teal and maroon *gutra,* she knew him for a Wasabi, and by the scarlet trim of his otherwise plain *thobe,* for a member of the Hami Babb, the tribe that, since the time of Sheik Abdulabdullah "The Wise" Waffa al-Hamooj, founder of the Wasabi dynasty, had been entrusted with the duties of royal bodyguard. This was Salim bin-Judar, first deputy for the Ministry of Public Health, the euphemism that the Wasabi central government had decided upon for its secret police. This man she knew by reputation very well, and despite the honor of being in his presence, it caused her a distinct dryness of mouth.

The identity of the man to Maliq's left was all too easily discerned. The black and blue *thobe* proclaimed him *mukfellah.* His stare of pure hatred was the most intense Florence had ever seen from a human being—anthracite coals of smoldering fury—trained on a shackled American woman, an infidel who deserved to be consigned to hell to be gnawed for all eternity by Satan's foul jaws and stinking breath. Have a nice day.

"*Salaam,* Maliq," Florence said.

The *mukfellah* leaped from his seat and roared at her to show respect to the imam. But Maliq silenced him with a raised hand.

"*Salaam,* Flor-ents." He smiled and pointed to her manacles. "So, bracelets? The latest in fashion?"

"Yes, they're all the rage. But fashions change quickly, especially in Paris."

"Enough of the little talk. These men here are very important. And they are very angry with you. Yes, I would say, very angry. They want to deal with you directly. Shall I give you to them?"

"You'd better do what you're told, or your masters will be unhappy."

"I rule in Matar. Be certain of *that,* madame. Your CIA lover, Mr. Theebo, Tibu—"

"Thibodeaux. Surely your French is up to that."

"We have him. You don't believe me?"

"Have you ever told me the truth?"

"Then perhaps you would like to see the body. It's very unpleasant. He died in a most undignified way. Do you know how? Blew himself up with a hand grenade. Such a pity. We would have treated him with justice. Perhaps even given him back to your government, as a goodwill gesture. We are not the third world here, you know."

Though Maliq spoke confidently, Florence couldn't bring herself to believe him. Bobby was a grenade thrower, not a hugger. Still, her stomach knotted.

Maliq said gaily, as if this butterfly thought had spontaneously perched on his forehead, "Maybe you'd like to have the body in your cell? How cozy it would be for you." Switching to Arabic, Maliq said to the *mukfellah,* "When she's taken back to her cell, have the American's body put in with her. Then have the door welded shut. Seal them in. Let them rot together."

The man nodded, and for the first time during the interview, his face lightened into something like a smile. So he had a soft spot after all.

"No translation required, eh, Flor-ents? Come, come, what a look! You're a student of our history. In the days of my ancestor Jamir al-Kef, emir some hundred years ago, you recall what was the custom with women who had been very naughty? They were tied up, and a small hole was made in the stomach and the intestine pulled out a foot or two, then left in the desert for the dogs. You see what progress we have made in the new Matar! How liberal we have become!"

CHAPTER TWENTY-NINE

Just after two A.M.*, the door to Renard's office, where he and George were* furiously brainstorming, opened and admitted two unsmiling, burly men who looked remarkably like the sort the U.S. government dispatches when it desires to make an emphatic point. Once these two had secured the room with their scowls, they were joined by a third man whom Rick and George immediately recognized as their long-lost relative Uncle Sam.

"Hello, boys." Uncle Sam motioned to his men to wait outside. "No sense beating around the proverbial bush. We intercepted a call to this office from Bobby Thibodeaux last night."

"Oh, for the days when gentlemen didn't listen in on each other's telephone calls," George said.

Uncle Sam poured the dregs of the coffeepot into a cup, dusted it with powdered creamer, sipped it and winced. "Lord save us! You might have bought a decent coffeemaker with some of that two million dollars. Let me say what I have to say before this reaches my bloodstream and kills me.

"For starters, what Bobby Thibodeaux told you is simply, totally, completely cuckoo. He seems to be under the delusion that I dispatched a CIA assassination team to kill him and Florence. I don't know where he got that one. Well, actually, I do."

George and Renard listened in sullen silence.

"Why am I getting the distinct feeling that you don't believe me? Pardon me—but is this the United States of America, land of presumed innocence? All right, hear me out, fellows. I tried several times—*several* times, as you are well aware—to pull those two out of there. As you further know, Florence refused to leave without the sheika. Now, I don't know *what* was going on between those two, but never mind. My sole interest was in getting her out before a disaster of this—this—this mind-boggling proportion happened. And here we are.

"As I recall, the mission was to try to empower Arab women and bring about some kind of stability in the Middle East. There were those who said, 'Are you out of your mind?' Others said, 'We've tried everything else, why not give it a shot? What harm can it do?' Ha! And how did it all turn out? With a coup d'état—and how appropriate to use the French term for it—against the only stable country in the region. Not only did it not work, but it brought about the further enslavement of two point five million Arab women, along with the empowerment of a psychopathic race-car driver, to say nothing of a whopping increase in Wasabi oil prices that may well determine the outcome of the next U.S. presidential election. And did I mention France getting naval bases in the Gulf? Damn fine job, boys. Have a cigar. Your government is proud of you.

"*Meanwhile,* your erstwhile colleague Mr. Thibodeaux, who, by the way, I never wanted to be part of this mission—but never mind, what say do *I* have in the mutter?—has baked it into his fevered brain that I'm out to get him. I understand it's hot in Matar, and that heat can do strange things to a man, but goodness gracious, to treat *this* level of paranoia, you're better off with tranquilizers and a dart gun!"

George said, "Not to interrupt your splendidly indignant rant, but why don't you just tell us what happened? Or skip that part and tell us where Florence is. And whether she's even alive."

"I was getting to that, George. She's alive. This much we know. I am doing everything in my power—that is, what power I have left after this catastrophe—to get her out of there. But it's going to require one heck of a diplomatic balancing act, let me tell you. And if you two go barging in like a couple of bull elephants on steroids, acting on input from a delusional ex-spook—"

"Ex?"

"Completely ex. CIA fired him. And not for calling in that cruise missile strike on the Indonesian ambassador in Dar. Would you like to know why he was given the boot? For screwing the wife of the U.S. ambassador to Jordan."

"She was a notorious nympho," George said. "The woman was insatiable. She'd have sex with the elevator operator if the ride was more than three floors."

"Nevertheless, the ambassador didn't much appreciate it. And he was the president's chief fund-raiser."

"Enough!" Rick interjected. "Who cares who was screwing who!"

"Whom," George said.

"Whatever. What are you doing to get Florence out of there?"

"Look, fellows, the less you know about that, the better."

"Oh, no," George said. "No, no, no, no, no. What do we look like, two mushrooms that you're going to pile manure on and keep in the dark?"

"George, I'm saying this for your own protection."

"You sound like you're putting on a condom," said Renard. "Never mind all that hooey. I want to hear, right now, right here, how you're going to get her out, or I promise you'll find yourself in such a public relations shitstorm that you'll be picking it out of your eyes for years."

"All right." Uncle Sam sighed as though about to divulge the formula for Coca-Cola. "We're working on it through the French."

"The French?" Rick and George said simultaneously. Rick added, "The *French?*"

"Believe it or not, they're almost as appalled by this new regime as we are."

"But they helped install it."

"The last thing Paris wants is to have its client chopping off the head of a feminist American hero. That's not going to help them sell Airbuses or Brie in the U.S.A. But you've got to let me handle it. Are we on the same sheet of paper here?"

"I still don't understand," George said. "Bobby told us you'd arranged for the water taxi, and suddenly, the CIA shows up shooting. The embassy cables from Amo confirmed there was a shoot-out and a chase and a capture. So—what happened?"

"I just can't go into that."

"Oh, do."

Uncle Sam gave another heavy sigh. "My call to Bobby and Florence was intercepted. We found that out after the fact."

"Intercepted by?"

"The French. They're the ones who sent the hit team, not me, for heaven's sake."

"The *French* sent the CIA to kill two Americans? This makes no sense."

"The man Bobby was referring to is Anbar Tal. He works for the Matar Air Force. And yes, he also works for CIA. Bobby himself recruited him. It also happens that he works for the Onzième Bureau. That's the part Bobby didn't know. He's a double agent. Triple, technically."

"So you're trying to get the French to help free Florence, and they're the ones who sent this multitasking thug to kill her? It still makes no sense."

"It's the Middle East, Rick." Uncle Sam shrugged. "I don't really understand it myself."

George said, "We're not going to sit on our hands while you sip aperitifs with the head of the Onzième Bureau. And frankly, I think you're more full of shit than a Strasbourg goose."

Uncle Sam said quietly, coolly, "You don't really have much choice in the matter, do you now, George?"

"Is Uncle threatening?"

"Uncle may not have as much grease as he did before his niece and nephews fucked things up seven ways from Sunday, but he is not without resources." Uncle Sam stood. "You fellows are in receipt of two million dollars each. In your personal bank accounts. Can you produce 1099 forms for those funds? I guess not. Did you happen to note the origin of the wire transfers?"

"Third Bank of Bangor."

"Very good. And Third Bank of Bangor, as any wet-behind-the-ears FBI rookie investigator will tell you, is a shell for Banc Mercantil de Grand Comore—in Moroni, that would be the capital city of the Comoro Islands, not to be confused with the angel Moroni. And who owns the Banc Mercantil? Sheik Adman Ifkir. Third cousin, on the Yemeni mother's side, of . . . guesses, anyone?"

"Osama bin Laden." George sighed.

"What?" Rick said.

"Gold star for George." Uncle Sam applauded noiselessly. "So it would appear that you two are in receipt of funds from a bank controlled by Al Qaeda. Won't that be fun explaining at your arraignment for treason? But I'm sure there are lots of lawyers here in town who would be happy to represent you for, say, six hundred dollars an hour. Let's see, two million dollars divided by six hundred—that might see you through the first year of legal bills. But heavens, what am I thinking? The government will have *confiscated* the money. Dear, dear, dear."

"You're a real prick, aren't you, Sam?" Rick said.

"You should see the people I report to," Uncle Sam said as he went through the door. "Definitely, a new coffeemaker."

BACK IN HER CELL, Florence had passed the fretful hours waiting for the sound of the door being unlocked and the remains of her lover to be tossed in, followed by the sound of the door being welded shut. Immuration, she'd had time to reflect, was the punishment meted out in Rome to vestal virgins whose chastity had been compromised. Though she could not remember whether they had been entombed alive with the corpses of their paramours.

But as the hours passed, nothing happened. She began to hope that it had all been some kind of bluff to keep her off balance—either that or just for kicks. At some point in the afternoon, her hands had started trembling uncontrollably.

As she was thus reflecting, the lights in Florence's cell went out, plunging her into complete darkness. A few minutes passed, during which she could hear her own breathing distinctly. She struggled against the temptation to cry out for a guard. An electrical failure? Prelude to a rescue? She was pondering this last possibility when she heard the lock mechanism on the door. She felt the outward suck of air as the door opened, and in the next instant, she was knocked backward by the force of a human body, inert and rank with the aftersmell of explosive, being hurled into the cell.

CHAPTER THIRTY

"Greatness, you honor me with this audience. Emir, you have lost weight! You look marvelous!"

Maliq was in no mood for Delame-Noir's triple-cream pleasantries. "The burdens of office. One yearns for the simpler life of the racetrack."

"Yes, of course, but you must *eat,* Great One. You will waste away to nothing. Was it not your great-great-great-great-uncle on your maternal side, the illustrious sharif Ehem al-Gheik, who received in annual tribute from his subjects in the Wazi Bikkim his weight in Tarfa pearls?"

"Yes, yes, yes. So, you wanted to see me?"

"I will send you my own chef. He was for many years at Taillevent. His Boudin de Homard Breton au Fenouil is not to believe. It is not blasphemy to say it is to taste paradise itself."

"I cannot have a French chef, Dominique."

"But why not?"

"I'm the *imam.* How would it look? I mean, really."

"I have known many well-fed imams in my time."

"I'm meeting with the mullahs in fifteen minutes. It never ends. What—you wanted to see me?"

"I regret, yes. I suspect my imam knows the reason."

"I told you, Dominique, it's out of my hands. It's a religious matter now."

"Yes, and you are the imam."

"It's also a security matter."

"And you are the emir."

"It's also a *tribal* mutter—matter—isn't it?" Maliq said petulantly.

" 'Tribal'? In what way?"

"One of the men she killed in the escape was a Hazi Agem."

"Yes. So?"

"*You're* the historian," Maliq said.

"I bow to your superior knowledge. Educate me on this 'tribal matter.' "

"For a hundred years, there has been a blood feud between my line, the Beni Harish, and the Hazi Agem. So you see?"

"Frankly, I do not."

"I'm in a delicate position. Most delicate."

Delame-Noir's hooded eyes blinked like a falcon's. His lips pouted with malevolence. He was a sophisticated man, and he was tired of playing with this gelatin-brained idiot whom he had, in a moment of weakness (and perhaps, he admitted, pride), decided to install.

"*Alors,* Maliq, you are the grand sharif of the Tribal Council. I don't mean to insult. But why, *mon vieux,* do you waste my time telling me these nonsenses?"

It had been a while since anyone had addressed Maliq as "buddy" or accused him of speaking rubbish. Alas, how quickly we become hostage to the kowtow. But tempted as he was to flick his *aasa* at the Frenchman, Maliq refrained. He refrained for the simple reason that he was terrified of Delame-Noir.

Delame-Noir had ordered more assassinations in his day than Hamas and Kim Jong Il combined. His legend was long and dark. It was he who had personally directed the sinking of the *Whalepeace,* the environmental vessel that had been protesting France's nuclear testing in Polynesia. Only Allah Himself knew what tentacles this eminence noir of a spymaster had throughout Matar.

"Understood, *mon vieux,*" Maliq said pointedly, "but if you don't want to waste my time *or* your time, why don't you go to Kaffa and explain it to Prince Bawad? *He's* the one who's demanding this woman's head. She apparently did something to annoy him back in Washington, something to do with one of his wives. You see my predicament?"

"Look, Maliq, you don't want to be seen as a Wasabi puppet, do you?"

"No more than I do as a French puppet."

"Sire," Delame-Noir said, "how have I deserved this insult? I spend all my hours worrying for you, from the first cry of the muezzin in the morning to the call to evening prayers."

"I know that I am in your debt, Dominique, but it is not in my *power* to hand her over to you. Look around—my kingdom is *bursting* with Wasabis."

Delame-Noir saw it was useless for the time being. He rose. "Very well, but let me implore you to keep this woman alive. You don't want an international martyr on your hands. It would be only a pretext for the Americans."

"The Americans aren't going to do a thing." Maliq snorted. "There's an election coming up. If they moved against me, Tallulah would shut off their oil. Anyway, their ambassador just sent me—this morning—an invitation to the opening of an Elvis Presley cultural exhibit. So I don't think they're planning to parachute soldiers onto my head for some crackpot lesbian CIA stirrer-upper of camel shit."

"Yes, but this crackpot lesbian stirrer-upper of camel shit is now a figure of international celebrity. Your Ministry of Informations can't just keep saying, 'Florence? We don't have no stinking Florence in our dungeon.' No one is believing it. Are you watching the television?"

"I have no time for television."

"You should create time, my dear emir, because they are saying some very harsh words about you." Delame-Noir threw up his hands. "I will speak to Bawad. But in the meantime, please, for your sake, keep this woman alive."

"Oh, she's alive."

"*Maliq.*"

"I said she's alive."

"You didn't put her in some hole with animals or snakes?"

"What do you take me for?"

"Scorpions?"

"Now you insult me."

"Then accept my profound apologies, Holy One. I should have known that as imam of all Matar, you are guided first and last by the precepts of the Holy

Koran, the truths revealed to the prophet Mohammed, blessings be upon his great name, by Allah the wise"—he paused—"the *compassionate*."

Maliq flicked at the air with his *aasa*. "Whatever."

Delame-Noir turned to leave. "Let me send to you my chef. As a token of fraternal love and respect."

"I could not accept such generosity," Maliq said. "It would be impossible to repay. And an Arab who is not in a position to repay hospitality is a poor friend."

Delame-Noir smiled. "A pity."

As soon as he was gone, Maliq summoned Fetish. "If he sends any food, any wine, anything, have it tested for poison. And tell Sharif bin-Judar to keep him under watch. I want to know everything he does. I want to know when he has bowel movements."

"But Great Imam, surely the Frenchman is our great ally?"

"We have *spoken*, Fetish."

"Truly, Majestic One. Thy words are like Tarfa pearls glistening in sweet water."

"Eh? What's that? Were you listening to us just now?"

"No, sire. May Allah strike me deaf and pluck the tongue from my mouth. I was only using a figure of speech—"

"Get Prince Bawad on the phone. And have the masseuse make ready. My head is coming off with pain."

"Immediately, sire."

Fetish scurried off backward, scalp prickly with cold sweat. He reminded himself of the ancient Matari proverb: *Dung beetles cannot crawl into shut mouths*. An English traveler centuries before had stolen it and rendered it less elegantly as *You never have to apologize for something you never said.*

FLORENCE COWERED IN a corner, unable to move toward the object now sharing her still-darkened cell. The smell made her gag. For a long time she cowered. Then, slowly, tenuously, she extended the fingers of her right hand and touched the body. What she felt made her recoil. The face and head were mostly gone. Finally, she reached out again and this time touched an eye dangling from its socket. She became ill. She forced herself to continue her forensic examination. She felt for the hands and found that these, too, were mostly gone, shredded. She wept silently as she probed.

The body was on its back. She thrust her hand between it and the cold concrete of the floor, feeling for the left shoulder blade. Some weeks before, she had felt there a inch-long ridge of thick scar tissue, the result, Bobby had murmured—his mind on other things—of a stab wound inflicted years before by "this Syrian fucker." The scar was right atop the shoulder blade. The knife, he said, had been deflected by the bone, and damn lucky for him.

Her hand was impeded by the tattered shirt, thick and stiff with blood, as well as the deadweight of the corpse. She maneuvered her fingers inside. Here the skin was not shredded or burned. Rigor mortis and death had made it cold and waxen. Her fingertips moved up, slowly, nervously. She held her breath as she reached the shoulder blade and continued.

There was no scar.

"WILL YOU STOP following me?" Charles Duckett said. "I've told you what I can."

"All you've told me," George said, still following the briskly moving deputy assistant secretary of state for Near Eastern Affairs (DASNEA), "is what I already knew from watching CNN."

"I'm not in a position to discuss it further."

"Charles, this is not a State Department press briefing, nor am I some reporter."

"I said I have nothing further for you on this."

"May I ask why my security clearance was suddenly downgraded? What's going on here?"

"I'm not in a position to discuss that, either. Now, if you'll let me proceed, I'm already three minutes late for a Procurement Committee meeting."

"Horrors, Charles! The world might stop spinning on its axis. But I'm not going until I get an answer: Are we doing anything about the capture, imprisonment and, quite possibly, torture of one of our own?"

Duckett was appalled at the prospect of being followed into the most boring meeting on the planet by an agitated, insubordinate subordinate. He peered at George over his glasses with the custard pugnacity of a life bureaucrat and said, as magisterially as he could, "You're out of line." In Duckett's pallid, formatted world, there could be no greater crime than being out of line.

"But don't you *care*?"

"Yes, I care. I care for process. I care for going through channels. I care for incremental, mutual steps that promote synergy over the long run and provide a platform for harmonious relations and partnering between—"

It was at this point that the spring inside George that had been coiling for sixteen years went *sproiiinnng*. He began choking Charles Duckett with the neck chain of his State Department ID badge.

"Are you out of your *eugghh*—"

Once Duckett's face had achieved a sufficiently livid shade of crimson, George leaned in to it and said, "If you don't tell me, I'm going to *kill* you. *And I'll make it look like the work of terrorists.*"

"Urgggh . . ."

"*You'll never put a cell phone to your ear again without wondering if it's going to blow your brains in.*"

George released the garrote around Duckett's neck. Duckett's complexion returned to its normal semolina hue.

"What the hell has gotten into you, Phish?"

"Not quite sure myself. Now—where is she, and what is this pathetic spineless bureaucracy *doing* about it?"

"They've . . . de-decided to adopt a hands-off posture." Duckett collapsed like a deflated balloon at having divulged this sacred piece of intelligence.

George stared. Duckett seemed to be trying to back through the wall. George reached toward him. Duckett cringed. George straightened Duckett's tie and collar.

"Better hurry. You're—omigod—*three* minutes late."

Duckett edged nervously away, clinging to the wall like a mountain climber negotiating a narrow ledge.

Ten minutes later, three men from Security surrounded George's desk. They took him to the office of the assistant deputy to the deputy assistant for

Internal Security Affairs and Inter-Human Resources. Duckett was already there, face flushed. He flinched when George entered.

"Did you attack Mr. Duckett?" the ADDAISAIHR said.

George looked at Duckett. "Oh, *Charles*, is *that* what you told them?"

"It damn well is! It's the truth!"

"Where do I begin?" George said with the weary attitude of a reasonable man having to explain something distasteful that he would, on the whole, rather not go into. "Charles—Mr. Duckett—made a pass at me in the corridor."

"What?!" Duckett roared.

"And though my sexual preference is well known and a matter of record within the department, he is, in addition to being my boss, simply not my type. Not to mention that he's married and has three children. I told him all this while he was trying to grope me, in the most *awkward* way, and I went about my business. And now here we are. Charles, I must say, I am disappointed in you."

"But—this is preposterous!"

"I don't want to file a sexual harassment suit. I really do not. I'm perfectly willing to let it go as a momentary lapse. But really, if you're going to indulge in this sort of lurid cover-up, I'm ready to swear out a complaint right here and right now. Do you have the relevant forms, Ms. Poepsel?"

The ADDAISAIHR looked at George, then at the blubbering Duckett. "Mr. Duckett," she said, "how do you wish to proceed? Do you want to make a complaint against Mr. Phish?"

Duckett, seeing headlines and his career passing before his eyes, let out a wan moan. "No. No . . ."

"Mr. Phish, do you wish to file a complaint against Mr. Duckett?"

"Let bygones be bygones, I say. But no more Mr. Grabby Groin, Charles—shake on it?"

"GOSH, THAT FELT GOOD," George said to Renard. "Poor beast hasn't had a day like that since CIA blew up his cultural exhibit in Quito. But there we have it. Official hands-off posture. She's on her own."

"No, she's not."

"We're not exactly a Delta Force hostage rescue team, are we?"

"Fuck it," Rick said. "If we're going to go down for the money, we might as well spend it."

"Why not?" George brightened. "Why fucking *not.*"

"To Damascus."

"To Damascus."

CHAPTER THIRTY-ONE

Highness!" Maliq said into the telephone with perhaps a bit too much fraternal royal bonhomie. His breath reeked from the brandy that he now found a necessary fortification for calling Prince Bawad bin-Rumallah al-Hamooj, foreign minister of the kingdom of Wasabia, beloved nephew to King Tallulah and, in all those capacities, Maliq's de facto boss. "May Allah shine upon thy countenance and make all that thou viewest pleasing unto the eye!"

Bawad reciprocated with a greeting so perfunctory, Maliq might as well have been a gas-station attendant. Since Bawad's promotion from ambassador to the United States to foreign minister, he had become even more grandiose. Too, he was painfully aware that the recent tectonic shift of power in the region had begun with the flight of his flightiest wife, the late Nazrah, back in Washington, D.C. That this Matari usurper, Maliq, had not already beheaded the hateful American woman Florence—along with her sluttish lesbian lover the sheika Laila—was intolerable. Bawad knew instantly from Maliq's fawning, lickspittle tone of voice what he wanted. And great merciful Allah, the Matari jackass was *still* prattling on.

"Is it true, Royal One, this glorious news that reaches my ear by the west wind?" Maliq was saying, Fetish having briefed him on the fact that Bawad's fourth wife, the ill-fated Nazrah's successor, had just borne him a male child, his forty-second or -third. "A male child, dear prince? My heart leaps like a gazelle uncaged, like a—"

"Eh?" Bawad interrupted. "Yes. So they tell me."

"But this is truly joyous news!" Maliq soldiered on. "And a male child! Allah be praised! May it grow to be as wise and as—heh, heh—*prodigious* as his worthy father!" Maliq waited. Silence.

"Did . . . the gift arrive?" Maliq said finally, swallowing what remained of his pride. He had sent a solid-gold baby crib, ordered from Wenphrew & Wenphrew, the London jeweler that maintained a special division for the making of solid-gold objects for bored oil potentates.

"Eh? What?"

"The crib?"

"I don't— Yes, perhaps. I will make inquiries."

"No, no, do not trouble thy august self."

"Well, Allah be with you. His Majesty, my dear *uncle,* bids me attend him. Thank you for calling."

"Uh, Highness, a word, if thou would grace me further. The American woman, Flor-ents—"

"Yes. His Majesty, my *uncle,* wonders why the matter has not already been dealt with."

"It is delicate, my prince."

" 'Delicate'? How is it 'delicate,' Emir Maliq? She is an American spy, a provocateur, an insurrectionist, an infidel, immoral, a seducer, a sworn enemy of Islam. A sworn enemy of *myself,* personally, who tried to humiliate me and, by extension, the *entire* House of Hamooj, may Allah keep it safe and always wise. *This* is the 'delicate' matter to which you refer?"

"Uh . . ." Maliq was keenly aware that Bawad had the advantage over him of a Cambridge education, to say nothing of a lifetime's experience of telling silky lies in gilt parlors. "Nonetheless . . ."

"Why is she still alive?"

"Worthy One, she *is* a figure of world concern—"

"What matters it?"

"No sense in making enemies of the entire civi—"

"The Americans have made it plain that they are embarrassed by her existence. The ambassador here in Kaffa has said this to ourselves personally."

"Ah? Oh? Well . . ."

"Look, Maliq, you're either going to rule Matar or not. His Majesty *is* counting on you. Thy name comes up in the council meetings with increasing frequency."

"Ah? Well, marvelous, marvelous . . ."

"I wouldn't put it quite that way."

"Eh? Ah. Why don't I send *you* the woman Flor-ents and the sheika? Then you can deal with them to your heart's content! Give them a good—"

"The crimes these two women committed," Bawad said heavily, "were done on your land. It was Matar's holy soil that was defiled—"

"Well, holy-*ish*. Hardly as sacred as yours. We bask in thy reflected glory . . ."

"No, Maliq, it is Matar that must be cleansed."

"It seems to me, Worthiness, that it was Wasabia these two were out to defile. I mean, Matar was already corrupt. And who better to mete out justice than your dear uncle? You should *hear* the things they've both been saying under interrogation about you and the king. I blush to repeat them. Frightful. Disgraceful."

"Hear me, Maliq," Bawad said in a tone of voice indicating the conversation was about to be ended, "His Majesty the King desires that this mutter—matter—be concluded. Promptly. Further, that thou thyself, personally, dispose of it. In a manner public, for all to see. So that the minds she has corrupted, in your country and in ours, will see how just and terrible is Allah's punishment. You *do* aspire to be an instrument of His Majesty and the One God? Don't you, Maliq?"

"Whatever."

"Eh?"

"Of course, yes. Yes, yes, yes," Maliq murmured.

"Good. I wouldn't want to think we made a mistake elevating you to such prominence."

The line went dead. Maliq hurled the phone at the gold and lapis mosaic on the far wall, where it splintered into little plastic and electronic pieces. Fetish heard the crash and entered, preemptively bowing and scraping. "Did thy conversation with Prince Bawad displease my lord?"

Fetish's master did not respond. He was drinking directly from the bottle of brandy. Not a hopeful sign in a Muslim spiritual leader, or indeed, of any denomination.

Fetish left Maliq to telephone Delame-Noir and make his report. But Delame-Noir, having been in the room with Prince Bawad throughout the call from Maliq, did not need to be briefed by his spy.

"He has the spine of a Red Sea jellyfish," Bawad said with disgust.

Delame-Noir smiled and opened his palms, denoting bemused frustration.

"It was a mistake putting him in," Bawad said.

"Respectfully, I disagree."

"Of course you do—he was your choice."

"Would you and the king really be happier with a strong, independent thinker on the throne of Matar? Puppets are better made from wood than steel." Delame-Noir's hands moved as if manipulating a marionette. "Much easier. Be content, my prince, Matar is your country now."

"Not forgetting your naval bases and your discount on crude."

"Our naval bases protect your new oil terminals. Historic synergy. Not since the days of Wadi Ben Salaam in the—"

"Yes, yes, but what about the women? Why doesn't the idiot execute them and get it done with?"

Delame-Noir shook his head. "With all respect to your eminent self and to the king, I think it would be a complete calamity to put these women on a platform and publicly cut off their heads. If you want to create martyrs, there is no better way."

"We know a thing or two about martyrs in Wasabia," Bawad said. He reflected. "Our embassy in Washington reports some pressure there for information about the Florence woman."

"Two of her former collaborators are making a media campaign. But it's nothing—as long as Matar's position remains 'We don't know where this woman is, so stop bothering us.' "

"Collaborators? They are—actively *campaigning*?"

"If I thought they were going to be a problem, I assure you I would act."

"Act?"

"We have no secrets, you and I. My contacts within the U.S. government assure me that they, too, are watching the situation there. Very closely. And the last thing they want is a huge publicity about her. 'Florence of Arabia'? No, no. She is at this point an extremely inconvenient woman. I think, to be honest, the Americans would be very content if Maliq would simply give the order to toss her into his new *oubliette*."

"Your contacts, they are CIA?"

Delame-Noir smiled. "*Mon prince,* asking an old spy to reveal his sources is like asking a whore to tell hers. It's a matter of professional vanity."

Bawad snorted. "The price of oil can go up as well as down."

"But I am telling you the substance of what I know. Which is this: The entire Florence operation was approved at the very highest levels of the United States government. Why? To embarrass *your* government. As punishment for your Israel position, for your independence, for your nobility. In any case, as with every other American foreign operation, it turned to absolute shit. But for us, for you, for France, it was a fantastic opportunity, which I must say you yourself brilliantly exploited. So we must not be *too* upset with the Americans. They have accomplished for us in a few months more than we were able to achieve in eighty years."

"They're not happy about it. Our ambassador at the UN reports that they're preparing a motion against Greater Wasabia for the Security Council."

"Which, I assure you, France will veto."

"They're already saying this was all France's idea. *You're* getting the credit for it."

"Have you heard one single statement from France, from one single minister, from any representative of the French government, taking credit for Wasabia's actions in Matar?" Delame-Noir said testily. "Not one word have we said."

"What about that Jewish senator in New York? He gave a speech yesterday saying this was all France's doing. He called Tallulah a 'Parisian tool'!"

Delame-Noir made a disapproving clucking noise. "Disgraceful. But what can you expect? This was the same Jewish senator who made the big fuss when we released an old man of ninety-four years—ninety-four!—because he had something to do with some concentration camp in World War Two. It's the same every time."

"I suppose it's too late to do anything about it," Bawad said, eyeing Delame-Noir carefully.

"About the senator? Really, Your Highness . . ."

"No—*Maliq*."

"Ah. I think that would not be a good idea at this point. Perhaps in time . . . Look, Matar has gone through enormous turmoil. A few months ago, it resembled Las Vegas. Now it's . . . a decent religious state. Not as much fun, to be honest, but okay. For now stability is of the essence. Later, if you are still unhappy with Maliq, I am always at your disposal." Delame-Noir smiled. "Your humble servant."

"Humble. Hah. But Florence?"

"She will not be a factor for too much longer. Of this I am confident. Anyway, people quickly forget. And I don't think she will last very long the way it is. It's not the Crillon, eh, where they are holding her. I don't think she is getting mints on the pillow every night."

MALIQ HAD NOT ridden many camels in his life. On the whole, he rather preferred the Italian leather seat of a Maserati or a Ferrari. But now the occasion demanded it.

Really, he thought, the demands on an imam and emir were beyond onerous. But better to ride the damned thing than to have to suck on a piece of its dung. What utter barbarians the Wasabis were.

One of the more unfortunate by-products of the new comity that existed between Matar and Wasabia was that Matar was now required to commemorate the anniversary of the Perfidy of Rafiq ("The Unwise"). King Tallulah and his council—Allah's blessing upon them—had dictated that the emir of Matar observe the occasion by riding the Camel Royal down former Winston (now Abgullah) Avenue while receiving the plaudits and ululations of his subjects as the *mukfelleen* dispensed lumps of the sacramental ordure for them to place on their unhappy tongues. It would not make for the cheeriest day on the Matar calendar, but the point would be made that Matar was now part of Greater Wasabia. Maliq had tried to persuade King Tallulah and Foreign Minister Prince Bawad that sucking on dromedary turds was not a ritual likely to enhance a sense of fraternity between the citizens of Matar and Wasabia. But Tallulah and Bawad were adamant: Tallulah because he had to placate his lunatic *mukfelleen*, Bawad because he was furious at Maliq's recalcitrance in the matter of chopping off the heads of the sheika Laila and the American busybody Florence.

And so Maliq found himself in a foul temper, sitting on a beast he loathed, having to play figurehead at an idiotic Wasabi ritual that would leave his subjects' mouths tasting—as the expression goes—like shit. Allah be praised.

Following dawn prayers, Maliq suffered himself to be hoisted onto the hump of Shem, the current Camel Royal. Shem was gorgeously caparisoned in gold and silver and jewel-colored tassels. Maliq wore the ceremonial robes of a high sharif of Matar, as well as the distinctive *farfeesh* of a grand imam of the Bukka. Into his waistband was tucked the *na'q'all*, the lustrously bejeweled ceremonial dagger that, legend had it, had been used by Sheik Alik "The Righteous" Makmeh to castrate five hundred English crusaders. (In deference to Matar's new ally France, the dagger used to castrate 150 French knights was not on display.)

As Maliq was lowered onto the saddle, Shem uttered a long, low, pained moan followed by a noxious emission of colonic gas that continued for nearly a full minute.

Maliq waved with annoyance at his nostrils and barked down at Yassim, the attendant to the Camel Royal. "By the Prophet, what have you *fed* this accursed beast?!"

"*Aashaah eshowkiya*, Holy One!" Yassim cringed. "The finest!"

"Next time give the fucking thing an enema before I am put on it! It is highly unpleasant!"

"Yes, Great One! May Allah bless—"

"Shut up. Let's get this over with."

Maliq and Shem, the latter still groaning and issuing a mephitic jetstream behind him, were led out of the courtyard onto Abgullah Avenue, where the sullen crowd of Mataris awaited. *Mukfelleen* were going down the line dispensing small lumps of dried camel excreta.

"This surely will make them love me," Maliq grumbled under his breath.

"*Urrrrnnnnnnnnnnneoooooooooooorrrrrahhhhh!*" Shem groaned.

"If he farts," Maliq hissed at the now trembling Yassim, who was leading the animal, "it's your head."

"But Magnificence—"

"Shut up. Pick up the pace."

Maliq waved noncommittally at the crowd. The crowd reciprocated. Ahead, a squad of *mukfelleen* was beating a man who was refusing to put the ceremonial dung on his tongue.

Oh, Maliq thought, *let this day be over.*

Maliq's royal court walked behind, their faces puckered from Shem's exhaust. Yassim tried to hide himself beneath his own robes. As Maliq passed a group of young men, Shem issued forth an epic gust that caused convulsions of hilarity. Since laughter was forbidden from dawn to dusk on the Feast of the Perfidy of Rafiq—and, according to Wasabi precepts, discouraged on all other days—*mukfelleen* were quickly upon them, dealing vigorous bastinadoes with their rattan canes. These particular howls of pain Maliq enjoyed, inasmuch as he did not enjoy being the object of their amusement. He was certainly the most miserable emir in the Middle East at this moment. Never had he felt more absurd. He was not a great drinker of alcohol, but once this ghastly ordeal was over, he was going to drink an entire bottle of brandy. Possibly two.

It was while Maliq was entertaining this palliative fantasy that the event happened, the event that became known (and is still known to this day) among Mataris—and a good many Wasabis—as the Revenge of Rafiq. It would take days of intense forensic investigation to determine what exactly had happened. But from the point of view of Maliq, what happened was as follows:

One moment he was scowling in the direction of the youths being beaten by the *muks;* in the next there was a very loud noise coming from directly beneath him, and he became aware of being propelled upward into the fierce morning sky at a rate similar to that experienced by astronauts launched into space, escaping—how does the poem go?—the surly bonds of earth. His ascent became dreamlike, understandable since at this point he had lost actual consciousness. He found himself happily swinging from star to star, like a delighted young child. Alas, this innocent, carefree state of mind did not last, and as Maliq regained consciousness, he was still a hundred feet or so up in the air and—alas again—earthbound at a rate commensurate with the implacable laws of gravity.

This part of Maliq's wild ride did not endure for long. He was saved—God be praised—from even more terrible injury by landing on what remained of the Camel Royal. If it was an inglorious cushion, it was at least softer than the unforgiving asphalt of Abgullah Avenue. Such of the emir's bones as remained unbroken were, doctors agreed, the result of his having landed on the lower torso of the formerly whole Shem.

CHAPTER THIRTY-TWO

Common as explosions are in the Middle East, it's not every day that the ruler of a nation is blown up by his own camel. Word traveled quickly around the globe, despite Matar's official news blackout.

Someone had covertly filmed the event. Indeed, the episode was so completely captured on tape that the authorities concluded that whoever made the film must have been involved. Within hours, footage of the emir lofting into the sky was being viewed avidly in Internet cafés, in airport waiting areas, in bars, on tens of millions of television screens—everywhere. Headlines ranged from the subdued (MATAR'S NEW RULER IS GRAVELY WOUNDED IN SUSPECTED BOMB ATTACK) to the less restrained (THREE-TWO-ONE-IGNITION-CAMEL!).

Undignified as it is to be blown up by your own Camel Royal, Maliq was more focused on the fact that his legs—legs that once controlled the fastest race cars in the world—now terminated stumpily above the knees. A team of crack French orthopedic surgeons had done what they could, but inasmuch as the legs had landed hundreds of yards apart, and much the worse for wear, there was only so much that could be done.

On a more positive note, the ceremonial silver saddle—used hundreds of years before by the emir Achmed bin Ulala'am—had protected the imam's vital parts, at least for the most part. A team of crack French urologists announced that Maliq might, in time, be able to sire a successor with some prosthetic assistance. The royal digestive organs, on the other hand, had undergone great trauma. There would be no more royal feasting on spicy foods, or on any food that required much chewing. Also encouraging was the news that a spleen, though nice to have, is not a necessity medically speaking; meanwhile, some minimal hearing had returned in the emir's remaining ear.

Expressions of sympathy poured in from world leaders, along with assurances of friendship and offers of assistance with the investigation. The United States, whose relations with Matar had deteriorated, volunteered a forensic explosives team, as did Russia, England, Italy and, oddly, Bulgaria. The U.S. offer was, of course, coldly spurned; the others were more or less politely declined. It was announced from the palace that Matar itself would conduct the investigation, by which it was understood perfectly that the matter would be handled by the Wasabis and the French.

THUS IT WAS that Major Bertrand Matteoli-Picquet of the Bureau d'Investigation Criminel National, found himself picking through the frankly unpleasant remains of the Camel Royal with an ultraviolet spectrometer and uttering the most useful word in the French language: "*Merde.*"

"What's the matter, chief?" his assistant said.

Matteoli-Picquet handed him the instrument. The assistant peered through it. His eyes widened. "*Oof,*" he said.

"What now?"

"Make the report. What else?"

The French technicians swiftly concluded their business so that they could proceed to the more important matter of lunch.

Twenty yards away, a man wearing the uniform of the Matar Department of Public Health—Crime Search Scene was hunched over yet more remains of Shem, including a piece of the ceremonial silver saddle and part of the emir's left shoe. These he diligently placed into a plastic container, which he duly sealed and marked. The French team paid him no attention; nor did the police who had cordoned off the scene. The man was just another technician poking through the appalling detritus.

The French team e-mailed its report—classified VRAIMENT SECRET (Really

Secret)—up the chain of command. The first stop was the Onzième Bureau, in the person of Delame-Noir. The French spymaster had immediately flown back to Amo-Amas from Kaffa to supervise the investigation.

When his eyes fell upon the word "Exuperine" in the first line of the report, Delame-Noir stopped breathing for several seconds. He was an unflappable man, yet it took a good quarter hour of pacing and sweating and cursing before he was able to compose himself enough to place the necessary call to Paris.

QUEER STREET IS the name of Washington, D.C.'s gayest bar. It was not a place that George normally frequented. Bobby had suggested it as a good venue for George to receive cell-phone calls. Bobby's reasoning was that U.S. government agents are reluctant to follow people into gay bars, especially really gay bars, for fear of being pinched.

George looked out the front window and saw the black sedan with two crew cuts inside. Precisely at three minutes past eight, the cell phone rang.

Bobby conveyed the information with the efficiency of his tradecraft. It took under three minutes. With all the efficiency of his trade, George memorized it verbatim. He hung up and went to one of the pay phones near the men's room and dialed a number at the *New York Times* Washington bureau belonging to Thomas Lowell.

Thomas Lowell had spent much of his career covering the Middle East for the *Times*. In fact, it was he who had coined the phrase "the Arab Street." (His first metonymic term for Arab public opinion was "Sesame Street," but the producers of the children's television program by the same name protested.) Lowell had then tried to coin the term "the Jewish Street," but it had not caught on. Still, he kept putting it in, and New York kept taking it out. He was currently back in Washington after being expelled from Wasabia, allegedly for having a bottle of Scotch in his hotel room; true enough, but the expulsion really had come after he wrote a column pointing out that Crown Prince Bahbar had had a Jewish girlfriend while attending the University of Southern California. Inasmuch as Bahbar was currently the deputy minister for anti-Semitism, this did not go down well in Kaffa's Arab Street, though it played rather well in the Jewish Street.

Lowell and George had known each other for years. They were able to converse in fluent Arabic. Lowell was most interested in what George had to say.

FLORENCE HAD BEEN in a completely dark cell for almost three days with a decomposing body, no food and half a cup of water, now gone. But for discovering that the body wasn't Bobby's, there was little pleasant about her situation. She had rationed the water, which she'd found under the cot in a cup that her jailers had probably neglected to remove. Her thirst raged. Though she was beginning to starve, the thought of food had no appeal. She kept thinking of the Ugolino scene in Dante's *Inferno*—the nobleman imprisoned in a tower with his beloved children, driven finally to cannibalism. Perhaps this was the particular madness toward which her tormentors were attempting to compel her.

She spent the time praying to any god passing overhead. When the terror crept closer, she tried to ward it off by translating every poem she could remember from English into Arabic, then into Italian, then into French and back into English. As the third day drew to a close, she knew that she was beginning to go mad.

It came as a blessing, then, when the door to her cell burst open and a furious guard—gagging at the stench—waded in and pulled her out. She sucked in lungful after lungful of nonfetid air as if it were pure oxygen. Two guards dragged her down the corridor. No manacles this time. Florence prayed—she couldn't help it—that they were taking her to her execution. She felt guilty about asking the Blessed Mother (Florence had been brought up Catholic) to grant this wish.

Her grandfather had written an unpublished memoir of fighting in North Africa in the 1930s. As part of Mussolini's attempt to style himself as a latter-day Caesar, Il Duce had sent his army across the Mediterranean to reconquer what had belonged, two thousand years before, to his forebears. Idiotic, to be sure, but all the same the one adventure of her grandfather's life, which up to then had consisted of being a traffic policeman in Florence.

Florence had found the manuscript when she was a young girl and had read it. There was an episode that came to her now, as she was being dragged along these corridors. Her grandfather's unit had been surrounded by Omar Mukhtar's forces. They faced death or certain capture and God knows what after that. Two of the young soldiers under her grandfather's command put their rifles in each other's mouths and simultaneously pulled the triggers. Her grandfather didn't try to stop them. Terrible things were done to captured soldiers, on both sides.

Moments later, an Italian armored column rolled over the hill and dispersed the attackers. Everyone in her grandfather's unit survived except the two who'd killed themselves. He wrote letters to their families saying that the boys had died glorious deaths in the service of the New Rome.

The guards heaved her into a room. She lay on the stone floor, gasping and trembling, her brain a kiln and her throat an oven, praying—no longer guiltily—for death. Surely Our Lady would understand.

A door opened. Footsteps. She felt arms lifting her onto a chair. And heard a voice speaking Arabic: "Give her something to drink." Another voice said, "No," but then a cup was shoved at her. She grabbed it and drank. She drained it at a gulp.

A voice barked at her, "I want the names of the plotters. Or you won't leave this room."

Plotters? What was he talking about? What she did know was that the prospect of not leaving this room was preferable to returning to her cell. She summoned the strength to focus on the man asking her these questions. She looked. Yes, this much made sense, it was Salim bin-Judar, head of the royal bodyguard. Next to him was another man. Her eyes were going in and out of focus. Crisp uniform . . . Colonel . . . Nebkir? Yes, that was it, Nebkir, from the Special Prefecture, a purposely obscure branch of the police set up by the British back in the 1920s. Ostensibly part of the Royal Police, only these men reported directly to the British governor. Florence had seen Nebkir once or twice during her visits to the palace. He usually hovered in the background. A curtain man. Forbidding-looking, yet he had always returned Florence's glance with a nod and sometimes even a smile.

Her mind was wandering. She wasn't thinking clearly. Her head was on fire. It was coming off. Focus, focus—

"*Who . . . are . . . the . . . other . . . plotters?*" Salim demanded.

They were going through the motions, she knew, so they could cut off her head. She wanted to speed up the process. Anything but being sent back to an airless tomb with a rotting corpse. She saw that bin-Judar was wearing a pistol.

"Why don't you," she said quietly, "shove the Koran up your ass? In your case, it would fit." There, that should do it.

Salim bin-Judar bolted from his chair and drew his pistol. *Good,* Florence thought. She closed her eyes and waited for the bullet. She heard male voices, loud and arguing.

"Don't you see," a voice said, "she's trying to provoke you."

"Infidel bitch!"

Florence opened her eyes and looked into Nebkir's. He was a sturdy, block-faced man with a pencil mustache and a neat goatee. A fastidious man, at peace with the world, but a killer when required. He spoke softly.

"Madame. There has been an attempt on the life of the emir. So you will perhaps understand that we are curious professionally to know what you know."

Salim bin-Judar murmured to Nebkir that he was giving away too much information. Florence wondered whether all this was planned. She decided to play her own game of counterdeception.

"The only plotter," she said, trying to summon what moisture remained in her body, "was Mr. Thibodeaux, the man you killed and put into my cell."

Nebkir said in a not unkind way, "His death, that could not be helped. Putting him in there with you . . . I assure you this was not my idea. But madame, I must speak plainly—there are people within these very walls standing ready, eager, even, to perform . . . unimaginable things upon you." He leaned forward and said with apparent sincerity, "Help me and I will try to help you. But I must tell you, before Allah, that I do not think you will leave this place alive."

"Then before Allah," Florence said, "I will tell you that I know nothing of any attempt upon the emir."

"Lies!" Salim al-Judar exploded. He lunged forward with the pistol, Nebkir pulling at him. Salim put the muzzle against Florence's forehead. How pleasantly cool it was to the touch, she thought. *Yes,* she thought, *pull the trigger—pull the trigger.*

"Tell!" he commanded.

"Salim!" Nebkir shouted.

It would all be over in a second, she thought. She closed her eyes and took a breath, perhaps the last she ever would.

"Tell!"

Then Florence felt a bolt of lightning inside her skull, and all went dark.

"Idiot! What fucking good did that do?" Nebkir seethed at Salim, who stood over Florence's body. Her temple was gushing blood. Nebkir took out his pocket handkerchief and pressed it against the wound.

"Let her bleed to death and give the body to the dogs," Salim growled.

Nebkir rose and thrust his face into Salim's. "*Rebi! Fool!* Did it occur to you that with all that is now happening, the Americans might intervene? And if the Americans come, do you think that I will take the blame for killing their woman? Do you want to spend the rest of your life in Guantanamo, jerking off to the sound of monkeys?"

CHAPTER THIRTY-THREE

By *some miracle understandable only to Allah the Wise, the All-Knowing,* Yassim, attendant to the Camel Royal, was not killed in the blast, though it was not likely he would be leading any more royal parades.

He lay on his bed in King Nadir Hospital, encased head to toe in a body cast, tubes running in and out, connected to an array of machines that emitted so many cheeps and squeaks that the room sounded like an electronic aviary.

Keeping vigil over him were two stern-faced officers of the royal bodyguard—Salim bin-Judar's men—and an agent of the Ministry of Public Health, as well as the obligatory *mukfellah,* wearing the trademark scowl of his ilk, his lips moving joylessly as he read from his worn copy of the *Book of Hamooj.* It was into this cheery scene that Delame-Noir, a shade paler than normal, uncertainly strode, accompanied by a French woman of efficient aspect wearing the white smock of a doctor and carrying an attaché case. Delame-Noir did not bother to identify himself to the Mataris. He was well known to them.

"Has he said anything?" he inquired.

One of the MPH men shook his head sullenly.

Delame-Noir announced in a collegial yet firm way that Dr. Rochet, the "eminent neurologist," had come from Paris and would now make her examination. So, if everyone would please excuse them?

"My orders are to remain," the MPH agent said.

Delame-Noir eyed him with Gallic *froideur.* "I will make my report directly to the emir. And to His Royal Highness King Tallulah in Kaffa. To whom do *you* report, sir?"

The room cleared efficiently.

Delame-Noir bent over and peered into Yassim's face. It bore the vacant but not displeased expression of one whose veins course with liquid lotus, bringing surcease from pain and blissful phantasmagorias of virgins on lush Technicolor riverbanks. Yassim was feeding on honeydew and drinking the milk of paradise—by the liter.

Delame-Noir nodded at his "eminent neurologist," one of the Onzième Bureau's chemical specialists, code name "Fleurs du Mal." She took from her case a hypodermic and injected ten milligrams of naloxone into the intravenous tube going into Yassim's arm. His eyes sprang open like window shades.

"*Ooooh.*"

"So, Yassim, you're alive?" Delame-Noir said. "God be praised. You had us worried, my friend."

"The pain—it is great, Excellency."

"Yes, yes, we will take away the pain in a moment, but first you must answer some questions. Okay?"

"What is this place?"

"You're in excellent hands. Good French doctors. Now, Yassim, the camel Shem—what did he *eat* before the parade of Rafiq?"

"The feed, Excellency."

"Feed? What do you mean? Grass? Hay?"

"The special feed. From the king. It was a gift from His Highness."

"Gift—a gift for a *camel*?"

"From His Royal Highness King Tallulah. In honor of the Perfidy of Rafiq. For the parade, Excellency."

"Who brought this 'gift'?"

"A man, Excellency."

"Yes, yes, of course, a *man,* but *who,* Yassim? Surely you don't accept food for the emir's camel from just any person."

"The pain, Excellency."

"I will make the pain go away. Who was this man, Yassim?"

"A servant of King Tallulah, Excellency."

"How did you ascertain this? How did you know?"

"He said so."

"Yassim!"

"He was very important-looking. He presented a letter from the king to me, to me personally. A great honor."

"Go on. Continue."

"The letter said that the feed was from his own royal stables, a symbol of the new friendship between the peoples of Wasabia and Matar."

"This letter, where is it?"

"In my room, Excellency."

Delame-Noir muttered imprecations under his breath.

"There was another man, Excellency. Your man."

"How do you mean, my man?"

"He said he worked for you."

"I sent no man to you."

"But he had papers—and a letter from you. He was French. There are so many French persons in Amo these days, helping to build the New Matar. The pain, Excellency . . ."

Delame-Noir reached into his jacket pocket and took out a photograph. It was of Bobby Thibodeaux. He thrust it in front of Yassim. "Is this your Frenchman?"

"Yes, Excellency. That's the man."

A FEW HOURS LATER, *The New York Times* posted a story on its website. The headline read:

EXPLOSIVE USED IN MATAR "CAMEL BOMB"
APPEARS IDENTICAL TO TYPE USED IN SINKING
OF VESSEL TIED TO FRENCH SECRET SERVICES

Investigators report traces of Exuperine in remains of royal camel, saddle and clothing of wounded emir

SPECIAL TO *THE NEW YORK TIMES*

By Thomas Lowell

Within an hour the story was being beamed by satellites into a billion television sets. One of these was in Maliq's apartments at the palace, which had been converted into a hospital wing so that he could recuperate at home.

Few world leaders like to hear grim news first from the television set, but in our modern age, this is often the way of it. Even American presidents hear disastrous tidings in this fashion, rather than from their generals and spymasters. Maliq furiously pressed his buzzer and bellowed. Attendants, doctors, bodyguards and spiritual advisers rushed in.

FROM THE POINT OF VIEW of France, the timing could have been better. The president of the republic was in Quebec to give support to a referendum that would require all of Canada to adopt French as its sole official language. Eager to assert the supremacy of the language of Corneille and Racine and Molière and—if you insist—Victor Hugo, the elegant Gaul instead found himself facing a phalanx of out-thrust microphones and a mob of clamorous reporters demanding to know if he had "personally approved the assassination of the emir of Matar."

The president "categorically and profoundly" denied these "absurd" allegations; and while he was at it, he denied "for the one thousandth time, okay?" that France had played any *rôle* in the sinking of the environmental vessel *Whalepeace*. He tried to steer the agenda back to the glories of the French language and why it was imperative that cattle ranchers in Alberta fill out their income-tax forms in it, but the reporters preferred to stay on the subject of Exuperine, a sophisticated high explosive manufactured only in France and—so far, at any rate—used only by the French military and secret services. The president was finally forced to take sanctuary inside the French consulate in Montreal, where, fuming, he growled to his aide, "Get Delame-Noir on the phone—*now*."

—

IN WASHINGTON, a group calling itself Friends of Free Matar and working out of the offices of Renard Strategic Communications was busy placing full-page ads in newspapers and magazines in the U.S. and abroad, heavily promoting Thomas Lowell's *New York Times* stories and calling for an international investigation into the situation in Matar. The ads played up a theme of Thomas's reporting, namely that Wasabia was being manipulated by France; indeed, that Wasabia was "a mere tool" of Paris.

According to Thomas's well-sourced reporting, Wasabia had been persuaded to back the coup in Matar "by the same secret services who now are planting explosives under the saddle of the emir." France, Thomas asserted, was determined to put "its own man" on the throne in order to "keep the Wasabis off balance."

Nor was that all: The advertisements proclaimed that French and Wasabi elements within Matar had captured both the American woman Florence and the widow of the late ("and much beloved") emir, the sheika Laila. The Friends of Free Matar proclaimed that the two women were being held in a "notorious torture center" outside Amo-Amas—"grim by even American torture and interrogation standards."

At the bottom of the advertisements were the words, in large, accusatory lettering:

WHY THE SILENCE OF THE U.S. STATE DEPARTMENT?

It all made for riveting reading—in Paris, Kaffa and Washington. The American president, not a man given to personal coarseness, was moved—having for once actually picked up a newspaper—to say at his regular morning intelligence briefing, "What the fuck is going on in Matar?"

That the situation was approaching a crisis was clear from the headline that appeared the very next day:

PEOPLE FOR THE ETHICAL TREATMENT OF ANIMALS
"INDIGNANT" OVER USE OF CAMELS IN ASSASSINATIONS

Calls for Treaty Banning Use of Camels in Political Killings

CHAPTER THIRTY-FOUR

Quelle ordure, Delame-Noir thought, pausing before being admitted to the emir's chambers. He pressed a fine linen handkerchief from the Pas de Calais to his perspiring brow. The past few days had not been good. He had taken calls from a furious president of France, a livid king of Wasabia and an apoplectic emir. But he was resolved to stand upright and look his best. Delame-Noir was, when all was said and done, a man of *une certaine dignité.*

The door opened, and he found himself in the familiar place. Yet how much everything had changed.

"*Bonjour, mon emir.* You look much better, I delight to say."

"What?" Maliq barked. "Eh?"

A doctor murmured to Delame-Noir that the emir's hearing was 10 percent of its former capacity. Delame-Noir sighed inwardly. He was, in addition to being a man of certain dignity, a man of nuance—an artist of the gesture and feint. Now he would be reduced to shouting his explanations at close range into the (remaining) ear of a purple-faced, legless Middle East tin-pot dictator. This, he knew, would be a grim uphill slog. The situation in Amo-Amas had deteriorated catastrophically.

After the report about the Exuperine appeared on television—*quel désastre!*—Maliq had petulantly refused two calls from the president of France. He had also refused calls from Prince Bawad, who was desperate to convince him that Wasabia was no "tool" of France. Maliq had even refused a call from King Tallulah.

The emir was fortified in his obtuse truculence by Salim bin-Judar, who had assumed the duties of vizier in addition to royal bodyguard. Fetish had been arrested. Not just arrested, but being interrogated by Salim's men, undergoing, as the French has it, *peine forte et dure*. He had made excuses for Delame-Noir and *la belle France* one too many times. Another calamity in the making. Delame-Noir could only pray that Fetish was made of stern stuff, but he knew from experience never to count on the fortitude of paid informers.

As for Maliq, he was, if no smarter than before, certainly more determined: no longer the callow vacillator but every inch—such inches as remained—Maliq the Formidable, to say nothing of Maliq the Paranoid.

He had sealed his border with Wasabia, put his military forces on alert, recalled his ambassador from Kaffa and expelled the French ambassador from Amo-Amas, along with all French nationals in Matar. When France dispatched a fleet of Airbuses to collect its citizens, Maliq denied landing rights. The French were forced to undergo the humiliation of standing on the municipal wharf in Amo in the baking heat and board—like refugees—several forlorn coastal freighters for Dubai. Not since Dunkirk had there been such an inglorious evacuation—and who cares more about glory than the French?

"I bring Your Greatness good news," Delame-Noir said.

"WHAT?"

"GOOD NEWS, EMINENCE. WE HAVE ESTABLISHED WHO PLACED THE BOMB."

Maliq scowled. His lips were coated in burn ointment, making his livid visage especially repellent. "Ennh!"

The meaning of "Ennh!" was unclear. Delame-Noir soldiered on. "IT WAS THE AMERICANS. THE MAN THIBODEAUX, THE LOVER OF THE WOMAN FLORENCE. HE WAS POSING AS—I REGRET TO SAY—A FRENCHMAN, ALONG WITH AN IMPOSTER PRETENDING TO BE AN EMISSARY OF KING TALLULAH. YASSIM—"

"Proof—what proof?"

"I QUESTIONED YASSIM, GREATNESS, BEFORE HE—"

"Bah. Bring him here. I will question the dog myself."

"I REGRET THAT IS NOT POSSIBLE, IMAM. HE HAS, *MALHEUREUSEMENT*, EXPIRED FROM HIS WOUNDS."

Yassim, that imbecile of imbeciles, had managed one final spectacular feat of incompetence: dying before he could corroborate what he had told Delame-Noir. Of course, Maliq knew very well that Yassim had died, but he wasn't about to make things easier for Delame-Noir, whom he blamed one way or the other for everything that had happened. It was, after all, Delame-Noir who had first suggested that Maliq take over the throne of Matar. Yassim's death had not only deprived Delame-Noir of his witness, it also made it appear that Delame-Noir had killed him. Had the Frenchman not arrived at Yassim's deathbed with some "eminent neurologist" from Paris and ordered everyone out? And was Yassim not dead a few hours later? All this had been duly reported to Maliq by the guards Delame-Noir had ordered out of the room, eager to assert their innocence and the Frenchman's villainy.

"Where is your *proof*?" Maliq demanded.

"I SHOWED YASSIM A PHOTO. HE—"

"Yassim is DEAD!"

"THEIR PLAN, MAGNIFICENCE, WAS TO MAKE IT APPEAR THAT WASABIA AND FRANCE, YOUR GREAT FRIENDS AND ALLIES, MADE THIS PLOT IN ORDER TO DECEIVE YOU INTO—"

"The explosive—where did the Americans get *that*? Eh? EH?"

"YES, THAT IS WHAT WE ARE AT THIS MOMENT INVESTIGA—"

"And why didn't your people have THAT in their report? Eh? *Eh?*"

Maliq now had Delame-Noir by the Achilles heel. Upon seeing the word "Exuperine" in the bomb squad's report, Delame-Noir had changed it to "Semtex," a more common type of plastic explosive manufactured in the Czech Republic and used by—well, practically everyone. It was this altered version of the report that he had forwarded on to the Matari authorities.

But unbeknownst to Delame-Noir, Colonel Nebkir had been conducting his own forensic analysis at the bomb site. His investigators, finding abundant traces of Exuperine in the remains of Shem, in fragments of the ceremonial saddle and in the shredded royal footwear, had passed along *their* report to the emir's men (and certain other people). Delame-Noir thus found himself in the unhappy position of being trapped in a lie the size of Montmartre.

When there is no way out, the only way to go is—forward.

"MON EMIR, THERE APPEAR TO BE FORCES AT WORK HERE BEYOND EVEN MY UNDERSTANDING. HOWEVER, I AM CONFIDENT—"

"Bah. Lies! It was FRENCH explosive that did this to me! Look at me!"

"WELL, PERHAPS IT WAS *MANUFACTURED* IN FRANCE, BUT I CAN ASSURE YOU THAT IT WAS NOT YOUR GOOD FRENCH FRIENDS WHO—"

"I have the report!"

"SIRE, DON'T YOU SEE? THEY ARE TRYING TO MAKE IT APPEAR THE WORK OF PARIS AND KAFFA. TO DRIVE A WEDGE BETWEEN YOU AND YOUR MOST TRUSTED FRIENDS AND ALLIES. TO BE SURE, THEY HAVE HAD SOME SUCCESS AT THIS DECEPTION, BUT . . ."

A doctor with a worried look entered and gave the emir an injection. Delame-Noir forged ahead with his explanations, all too aware of how awkward and unconvincing they sounded. Having to bellow did not help.

"This alleged letter from Tallulah to Yassim," Maliq said, momentarily calmed by whatever it was they'd injected into his veins, "where is it? Show it to me."

Delame-Noir sighed. Thibodeaux had outmaneuvered him here as well. A search of Yassim's room had produced a letter, all right—a thick, expensive piece of creamy foolscap—completely blank. The ink had vanished. One of the oldest tricks in the trade, and still effective, alas, assuming of course that the target was an imbecile like Yassim.

"THE LETTER WAS WRITTEN IN VANISHING INK, HOLY ONE. BUT I AM CERTAIN THAT A CHEMICAL ANALYSIS WILL SHOW BEYOND QUESTION THAT THE PAPER WE FOUND ONCE *CONTAINED* INK AND—"

"Enough! Enough pathetic, miserable excuses! You were supposed to protect me! And now look at me! How would *you* like to lose your legs, eh? *Eh,* French?"

Recognizing that this was a part of the world where the punitive removal of limbs was still practiced, the old Frenchman decided that the prudent course was retreat, immediate retreat. He was not a coward. He had fought at Dien Bien Phu and killed more Arabs in Algeria than anyone. He didn't mind dying, if it came to that—a final ritual cigarette before the firing squad, not such a bad way to go. But having legs sawed off to assuage the pride of a demented emir, no, this prospect Delame-Noir did not relish.

"REST, OH GREAT ONE. I SHALL *BRING* YOU YOUR PROOF, AND YOU WILL SEE WHO ARE YOUR TRUE FRIENDS."

"OUT! GET OUT!"

The doctor, frowning, leaned forward. "IMAM, YOU *MUST* REST!"

Delame-Noir retreated backward in the protocol of taking leave of royalty. At the door, he took a last look at the hysterical, legless emir who had once been his *chef d'oeuvre*. Maliq's face was one large, ointment-coated bruise, so empurpled that Delame-Noir thought for one ghastly moment that it might just burst.

CHAPTER THIRTY-FIVE

Florence awoke to light and the suspicion, lasting several seconds, that she was dead and that all this whiteness was the decorative motif in some waiting room on the near bank of the river Styx.

She became aware of a pain in her left temple and a bandage, and she knew that she was not dead. She felt metal around her left wrist: a manacle attaching her to the bed.

She was no longer in a dark cell with a corpse, or in a room with armed men bawling at her, but in a brightly lit, clean room on a cot covered with a sheet. They had bathed her, too. She no longer smelled of death.

Florence looked at the door and saw a face peering through the thick glass and wire-mesh window. The face registered that she was conscious now, and disappeared, leaving her a few more moments of tranquillity in which to try to assess her situation.

The last thing she remembered was a pistol being pressed against her forehead. Salim bin-Judar. Another person had been present, Colonel . . . Nebkir? The wound in her temple throbbed. With her free hand, she worked her fingers under the bandage, feeling sutures stiff as fishing line. Bin-Judar must have knocked her out with the pistol. Was she in some sort of prison hospital? Evidently, they didn't want her dead just yet.

The door opened, and Salim bin-Judar entered. He no longer looked formidable, oddly, but more like a harassed middle manager running late for a PowerPoint presentation on how to cut 8 percent out of next quarter's operating budget. He carried a clipboard.

"You're awake, then? Will you sign this now?" He handed her the clipboard.

"What am I confessing to today?"

"Your role in the attempt on the emir's life. You're to be executed tomorrow evening. Whether you sign this or not."

His casualness appeared studied. *There was something else I had to tell you—oh yes, we're killing you tomorrow night, having a few people over.*

All right, Florence thought. She, too, could be casual. "I'll sign whatever you want," she said, almost with a shrug, "but you must let me see the sheika."

"She's not here. She's somewhere else." It was obvious he was lying.

"Is she well?"

"Alive is well enough."

"Let me see her, and I will sign." She handed him back his clipboard. "I will talk no more of it. You hold no more terrors for me, Salim."

Salim stared at her. A flicker of something like respect crossed his face. In his career so far, he had informed sixteen people that they would be executed; none had taken the news so placidly. He left.

An hour later, the door to Florence's cell opened again, admitting two guards. They did not handle her roughly or manacle her, but covered her head with an *abaaya* and led her out of the cell. After walking down a corridor or two, she heard a series of doors opening and felt the immediate baking heat of outdoors. She was put into a vehicle between two men, one of whom had terrible body odor. They drove for under an hour. She was taken from the vehicle, felt again the oven heat of Matar—unless she was in Wasabia—and was taken inside, where it was cool again. They put her in a chair. In front of her, she felt a table. They left the *abaaya* on her, and having no mesh or eye slit, she could not see. Some minutes passed, then a door opened and she heard male voices. She had told Salim the truth: They had no terrors left for her. Her fear was exhausted.

Then the *abaaya* was removed. Blinking, she looked and saw, sitting across the table from her, Laila.

"Oh, my dear sister," Laila said, her eyes brimming with tears. "What have they done to you?"

Florence reached across the table and took Laila's hands in hers. Laila looked gaunt, hollowed out, aged, yet still beautiful. Her eyes, once gay and impertinent, looked hunted, if not defeated.

"And how are you, dear sister?" Florence said, and with that, they both burst into tears.

"This is hardly becoming," Laila said, brushing her tears away. "They'll say it's true—that we're a couple of desert dykes."

Florence smiled. The expression felt strange on her face. She realized that it had been a long time since she had smiled.

"So," she said, "we're still alive. How did we manage that?"

They were alone in the small room, though almost certainly being observed and tape-recorded.

"Do you know anything that's happened?" Florence asked Laila.

"I gather someone tried to kill Maliq."

"Yes." Florence nodded. "I'm to . . ." Her voice trailed off.

Laila's face turned fearful. She shook her head. "No, Firenze, don't do it."

"Have they asked you to confess to anything?"

"Corrupting Gazzy."

Florence smiled. "You always *were* a bad influence on him. In return?"

The two women stared at each other.

"A hundred lashes," Laila said.

"Oh, Christ, Laila." It was a death sentence. Did she know that?

"It's no worse than some of the schools I was sent to. They'll deport me after, I imagine." She forced a smile. "I'm hoping for the South of France, not some lugubrious sub-Saharan country. What about you, Firenze? What is to happen to you?"

"Deportation," Florence lied. "It seems I've finally worn out my welcome."

The door was opening. The guards entered.

They clasped each other's hands tightly. They both understood.

"See you in the South of France, then," Florence said.

"In the South of France. We'll get roaring drunk on champagne."

"Go with God."

"With God, darling. *Allah maa'ek yehfathek. Eshoofek biheer.*"

DELAME-NOIR WAS INFORMED over the phone by an icy voice in Paris that he was to return without delay. A jet was standing by, and this one the Mataris had granted permission to land. Delame-Noir understood.

He leaned forward and asked his driver for a cigarette. A good thing he was in the Middle East. Everyone smoked. He himself had not had a cigarette in over forty years, when he was overcome with shame at having pressed the burning end of one into the chest of a recalcitrant *pied-noir* prisoner in Algeria while trying to extract critical information. He lit this one and inhaled and leaned back in the leather seat with the serenity that comes from accepting defeat. He decided to place one last call, to Prince Bawad in Kaffa, more out of curiosity than anything.

Bawad immediately began to excoriate Delame-Noir in the harshest terms. Delame-Noir let the torrent of abuse go by him along with the passing desertscape. He was intrigued by Bawad's fear—it was so palpable.

"And what is the decision with respect to the women?" Delame-Noir asked, exhaling a lungful of smoke. How good it felt. What a pity he had given it up for so long.

"He's going to kill them tomorrow!" Bawad shrieked.

"You should be pleased, *mon prince.* After all, it's what you wanted for so long."

"Don't you see—this will only make things worse. Much worse! His Majesty is furious!"

"So why don't you do something?"

"The maniac has sealed the borders and expelled everyone. We *can't* do anything!"

"Where there are no alternatives, there are no problems. Do you know who told me that saying? De Gaulle himself. I knew him well."

"This is all your doing!"

"How is it my doing?"

"The only reason he's going to kill the Florence woman is because you kept talking him out of killing her! And now he hates you so much, he's going to kill her just to spite you!"

"It's true I always thought that to kill the women would be a terrible public relations mistake. I know how you people love nothing better than to chop off a head every now and then. So now you can enjoy your national sport." Delame-Noir exhaled another lungful of Turkish tobacco smoke. "I think you are going to find yourself in a very big pit of quicksand, *mon prince.* Give my regards to the king. *Au revoir.*"

Delame-Noir pressed END. Rarely, he reflected, had it felt so satisfying to hang up.

The jet was waiting. It was his own jet they'd sent for him, with all the comforts. There were two men inside, instead of Celine, the lovely woman who usually served him. Delame-Noir greeted them cordially. He was aware that everything he said, every action, every gesture, would be a topic of conversation the next day in various offices in Paris—indeed, for many years—and he was determined that these conversations would be conducted in tones of admiration and reverence.

"Come on," he said, "let's have a drink." He found the bottle of forty-year-old single-malt Scotch that Celine kept for him, poured drinks for his subdued guests, and as the jet lifted into the sky and headed out over the sparkling blue Gulf before turning west, he lifted his glass and said, "To the New Matar!"

The obituary appeared in *Le Figaro* two days later: Dominique Laurent Delame-Noir, seventy-four, army veteran, Croix de Guerre, Légion d'Honneur, widower, assistant subdirector of Near Eastern Affairs within the directorate of the Bureau des Affaires Étrangères, died of an embolism while walking his dog near his home in Brive-la-Gaillarde. Service and internment private.

CHAPTER THIRTY-SIX

Florence was pleased that it was not to be done at a mall.

All afternoon she had been tormented by the thought that she would have her head chopped off at a mall, and that her last earthly sight would be a Starbucks. There was no dishonor in dying, but she did not want to die in the middle of a 30 percent–off sale on women's shoes.

The vehicle stopped. She looked out the window and saw that she was in a town square. It looked like Randolph Square, now Yasgur Square. She used to go shopping here. There was a stand that sold wonderful peaches.

A crowd of several hundred had gathered around the scaffold, mostly women. They were moaning and whimpering softly in the manner of Arab women being forced to watch yet another abominable act. A moolah with a megaphone was haranguing them, educating them about Florence's villainy and godlessness and perfidy in attempting to kill the great imam, Allah's blessing be upon his mutilated body.

Florence looked nervously to see if Laila was there. She asked the officer accompanying her if the sheika was to be dealt with here as well. He told her no, that was happening at—the mall. Florence winced. But at least Laila would not have to witness her death; nor would Florence be required to watch them beat Laila to death in front of Starbucks. God is truly merciful.

A murmur went through the crowd as the executioner, a tall Matari of the

Qali Sad tribe—Matar's traditional executioners—moved through the parting sea of *abaayas* toward her, escorted by a moolah and a pistol-bearing captain of the Department of Public Health.

Executions in this part of the world, being commonplace, are not elaborate. Other nations and cultures like a bit of pomp and circumstance on the scaffold—a final statement, the blessing of a priest, the offer of a hood or blindfold, a cigarette (no longer allowed now, for reasons of health), a drumroll. The executions Florence had witnessed had been swift, businesslike affairs involving no more ceremony than the chopping off of heads at the chicken market, except for the obligatory complimenting of God for His greatness. This suited her. No point in prolonging it. The more quickly it was over, the less chance there was that she might lose her nerve and make some undignified show. She so wanted to make a good death. But she could feel the fear fluttering in her like a dark moth.

The headsman took her firmly by the arm and led her toward the scaffold. His attendant stood there, holding the sword. Florence prayed it was sharp. She had been troubled by another thought—that of an incompetent headsman, hacking away like a drunken butcher. It happened. One time in Chop-Chop Square, after eight or nine feckless strokes, a soldier finally pushed the executioner aside in disgust and finished the business with his pistol. She wished she had something of value with which to tip the executioner.

The moolah was still haranguing them through his megaphone. The crowd of women moaned. He took her to the center of the platform and pushed her to her knees. The attendant moved to blindfold her, but she shook him off. She had spent enough time under a hood. She would not have her last view in life be of the inside of a dark stinking cloth.

She knelt upright and looked at the crowd and smiled. Women began to wail openly. Florence looked down at the fresh wooden planks of the scaffold and saw, brightly outlined, the shadow of the executioner raising his sword to strike. She closed her eyes and tried to relax her neck muscles.

Then she heard gunshots, and she opened her eyes. The executioner went over backward, his sword falling with a clank onto the scaffold, nearly cutting her in the calf. She spun her head toward the crowd and saw, scattered throughout the crowd, dozens of women, their *abaayas* lifted, firing weapons at the police and guards. In the next instant, she felt herself being picked up and rushed off by two men. She was tossed into the back of a van. The doors slammed shut, and it roared off.

She lay there, heart beating madly, for a while and then lifted her head toward the front of the van.

"You want to keep your head down, Flo? Y'almost lost it back there."

IT WAS DARK by the time they stopped. When he opened the rear door, she burst out and hugged him.

"Come on," Bobby said finally, "checkout time. Look out for snakes. Whole country's crawlin' with snakes."

She walked across the sand on bare feet toward the water. She wondered whether Maliq's bureaucrats had gotten around to renaming Blenheim Beach. They waited, ankles in the lapping surf, Bobby watching, holding a machine gun.

Ten minutes passed. Headlights approached from the road.

"*Bobby!*" Florence called out.

He signaled with a small flashlight. The headlights blinked twice, then once more. Bobby sprinted up the beach toward them. A minute later, he returned, supporting with one arm a female form hunched over in evident pain.

Florence embraced Laila.

"Not so hard, darling." Laila winced. "The bastards got in ten lashes before all hell broke loose. I could use that drink now."

The three waited. Then there was the sound of an outboard engine, and they saw men in a boat with blackened faces and weapons.

Florence had never been in a submarine before. She expected to hear Klaxons and men shouting "Down periscope!" Instead, an attractive, unhurried officer in khaki smiled and said, "Ma'am, Your Royal Highness, welcome aboard." Then Florence heard over a loudspeaker, "Prepare to dive," and a moment later, there came another sound sweet to the ear, a cork being propelled from a bottle of champagne, though officially, alcohol is not served on U.S. Navy vessels. But under the circumstances . . .

EPILOGUE

Following the Arab Women's Uprising, Matar was plunged once again into turmoil, though not for long. Having cut himself off from his former Wasabi and French patrons, Maliq found himself isolated. Since politics, like nature, abhors a vacuum, Colonel Nebkir of the Special Prefecture—assisted by his patrons, Bobby's people—moved swiftly to fill it. Within a week, Maliq was forced to flee. There was karma in the manner of his departure: the race-car driver being driven into exile, cursing, in the back of a pickup truck. His present whereabouts are not precisely known. Some say he found refuge in Yemen; others, Mogadishu. It is not an especially heated topic of conversation.

After the Restoration, Laila returned to Amo-Amas with her son, Hamdul, who—God willing—will someday assume the throne. In the meantime, Colonel Nebkir administers the country, to the evident satisfaction of most Mataris, though it must be admitted that the promised elections keep being postponed for this or that reason.

TVMatar flourishes again under Laila's leadership, broadcasting with flair and humanity into the darker recesses of the region. The once again enormous advertising revenues go to the Fund for Arab Women, administered in Washington by a woman who bears a certain resemblance to the woman known as Florence Farfaletti. If it is true, as the eminent University of Chicago anthropologist insists, that many Arab women do not want to be "liberated," so be it; now, at least, many of their sisters have more of a choice in the mutter.

France once again found herself sans naval bases and discounted crude oil, but still and forever ineffably, irresistibly belle.

Wasabia found itself once again cut off from the sea and having to pay Matar the hated Churchill tax, now double the previous rate. King Tallulah blamed the dismal reversal of his country's fortunes on his nephew Foreign Minister Crown Prince Bawad. Under an obscure provision of Hamooji law, the disgraced prince was stripped of his wealth and prettiest wives and internally exiled to a region of Wasabia inhabited mainly by baboons (the country's only tourist site of any note). Vans stop, and the guides, shouting above the din of baboons, point out that the lowly mud hut in the distance is the dwelling place of Prince Bawad—yes, "that" Prince Bawad. It is said that his howls can be heard at night even above the baboon din, but this may be an exaggeration. Even Wasabis have a sense of humor.

George and Renard went into business together. Their firm, Renard Phish Strategic Communications, is one of Washington's top public relations firms, with clients all over the world. In one of those distinctly Washingtonian ironies, they were retained by the Royal Kingdom of Wasabia to improve the kingdom's image in the United States, an image in much need of repair. The two of them are so busy that George complains he is working far too hard; but then George is never really happy unless he has something to be unhappy about. In such free time as he has, he oversees the painstaking renovation of Phish House, which he purchased from the estate of his late mother. Already there is talk of a ghost.

Florence's little house in Foggy Bottom was quickly overwhelmed by media and curiosity seekers. Agents bearing book and movie contracts hurled themselves against her front door. America does not make life easy for its heroes. She escaped out the back on her motorcycle. They pursued her, but she lost them in the Virginia suburbs. With Bobby's help, she assumed a new name and identity. No useful purpose would be served by describing Florence's new looks, except to say that heads still turn when she walks down a street. The Fund for Arab Women thrives.

Following the submarine exfiltration, there was much debriefing by various government officials. They all professed ignorance, even skepticism, of the shadowy Uncle Sam figure Florence described to them. And yet the officials were forced to acknowledge that she could not have done what she did without the assistance of certain elements of the United States government. The more obvious this became, the less eager they were to pursue the matter. Could this have come from—the very top? The officials began casting nervous glances at one another. The silences grew longer and more awkward. Matar was once again the Switzerland of the Gulf, oil was flowing, America was—God be praised—spared the necessity of having to be more prudent about its gluttonous consumption of energy, the French and the Wasabis were back in their boxes. Why not call it a day and leave well enough alone?

"We're done," the chief debriefing officer said finally. He had never bothered to introduce himself. On the way out, he turned and looked at Florence and said, "Got dinner plans?"

Florence began to have dreams. Being shut up in a cell with a corpse for three days and escaping decapitation by seconds would qualify in any diagnostic manual as traumatic. She woke up trembling, though at least she could reach over and find Bobby. Lately, the dreams had featured Uncle Sam. It was bad enough to spend the days tormented by wondering who he was without having to encounter him in her sleep going, "Heavens to Betsy!" and "Goodness gracious!"

In the dream, she was driving her motorcycle at a very fast speed down the country road, and suddenly, he was standing in the center. She had to hit the brakes and go off the road into a tangle of briar and blazing yellow forsythia. The thick interwoven mesh of vines acted as a net. She hung there like an insect snared in a spiderweb, and there he was, grinning, standing over her, saying, "You're going to kill yourself if you keep driving like that, young lady"—at which point Florence woke with a squeak, and there was Bobby, who had seen all the horrors the world had to offer, snoring away contently.

It was over coffee one morning, after another of these disturbed sleeps, that a headline in the business section of the *Post* caught her eye. It was on page three. She might well have missed it.

WALDORF GROUP GETS $2.4 BILLION
IN ADDITIONAL WASABI FINANCING

She stared at the headline for a few moments and then read the story. There was nothing particularly remarkable about it. She knew all about the Waldorf Group. Everyone did. It was the Washington-based investment-banking firm with close ties to Wasabia. There were twelve directors on its board: three former U.S. presidents, secretaries of defense, state, commerce, treasury, two ex–CIA directors . . .

"Son of a bitch," Florence said.

"Unh?" Bobby said, shuffling barefoot into the kitchen wearing pajama bottoms, scratching his chest and yawning, sniffing at the air for traces of brewing coffee.

THE WALDORF GROUP'S offices occupy the two top floors of a Washington, D.C., office building that, fittingly, overlooks the White House. The view from the boardroom is quite spectacular, allowing the various directors to see many of the government buildings they once ran. The conference table is of rich burled walnut, the chairs luxuriously upholstered in Milanese leather. The ashtrays—many of the directors like to puff away on fresh Cuban cigars—are of the finest crystal. A map of the world, stuck with dozens of pins denoting Waldorf Group investment projects, seems to announce, "It's a big, big world, and it's all ours!" Today another pin would be stuck into Wasabia and, that done, the directors would enjoy drinks, a little chitchat, the latest off-color jokes—the current one involved two nuns driving through Transylvania—and then disperse variously into Secret Service–driven vehicles and helicopters and private jets. The board meeting might go a bit longer than usual, given the recent developments.

The chief executive officer was presenting an overview of the group's recent investment in a diamond mine near Yellowknife when the door opened and a woman entered.

She was blond, very attractive, dressed in a business suit whose lapel bore a Secret Service badge denoting to the dozen or so agents outside that she was cleared to be in this august company.

The CEO looked at the woman with surprise. Waldorf board meetings were not usually interrupted. His mouth remained open. He turned somewhat nervously to a man in his sixties sitting against the wall of the boardroom. This man looked at the woman. He stood, smiled and said, "Well, Florence, hello."

"Hello, Sam," she said.

"No need for introductions," Uncle Sam said.

The twelve men sitting around the table looked at Florence. The three ex-presidents smiled warmly, but then they had the most refined political instincts of those present. The former cabinet secretaries did not smile; the former intelligence directors frowned.

"Can we talk later?" Uncle Sam said. "We're having a meeting."

"No," Florence said, "we'll talk now."

"I really don't think—"

A door at the opposite end of the room opened, admitting a well-built man of steely aspect. He, too, wore a Secret Service lapel badge. He stood there, hands crossed over his chest, jaw set, staring at Uncle Sam.

"Hello, Bobby," Uncle Sam said. "Well, I guess everyone's here."

Florence said, "So, all along, I was working for a bunch of investment bankers?"

One of the ex-presidents said in a kindly, gentle voice, "One way or the other, Florence, we're all working for investment bankers."

"This group," she said, "got started with financing from Wasabia. Profits last year of eight hundred million dollars. Divided by twelve makes sixty-six million. You've been very successful, gentlemen. But the success depends on steady financing from your friends in Wasabia.

"Then the Wasabis start to have internal problems. Terrorism, too much power concentrated in too few people. Forty thousand crown princes. Vast unemployment and half the country under the age of sixteen. And if the kingdom crumbles and becomes an Islamic fundamentalist republic, there goes your financing. So, you want the kingdom to modernize, to reform. Not a bad goal in and of itself.

"Only they won't reform. They can't, because the power's concentrated, and because the royal family struck a deal with a fanatical religious sect hundreds of years ago. The royals got the power, and the fanatics got to keep things the way they were back in the good old Dark Ages.

"They need to reform, but they can't reform. And what leverage, really, do you have? There's only so much pressure you can put on them. Because one of your partners is Prince Bawad, ambassador to the United States. An old golfing, skiing, shooting pal of two thirds of the people around this table. And, if I may say, one of the most despicable human beings on the planet. But let's not allow emotions in. Women are so prone to doing that, aren't they?

"And then one day Bawad's wife tries to defect. We, of course, hand her back, because nothing must interfere with the flow of oil and investment capital. She's executed. And in the process, I become involved. I send in my proposal and cause a major freak-out at the State Department.

"And now you have a means of forcing reform on the Wasabis. All you have to do is push a few buttons, pull a few strings. Among the twelve of you, you've got a Rolodex bigger than God's. And here's the amazing part—it's actually all for a good cause. That doesn't happen very often in Washington, does it? Two good causes—women's rights, Waldorf profits."

"Florence," said one of the ex-presidents, "I think I speak for everyone here when I say that you did a marvelous job over there."

A murmur went around the table: "Hear, hear."

"I think I also speak for everyone here, Florence, when I say that we would much like you to come aboard."

"Hear, hear." Even the ex–intelligence directors were smiling now. Bobby, on the other hand, looked like he was about to reach into his jacket and take out his pistol and make history. What a headline that would be.

She said to him, "We're done here." Florence and Bobby moved toward the door.

"If you change your minds," Uncle Sam said, "you know where to find us. And we know where to find you."

20 October 2003–19 May 2004*
San Luis Obispo; Washington, D.C.

* Death of T. E. Lawrence, 1935

ACKNOWLEDGMENTS

A thousand and one thanks once again to Mr. Karp and to Binky Urban; and a thousand and two thanks to the delightful and mysterious T. Freifrau von G. Thanks also to: dear, dear Lucy; Tómas Salley; John Tierney; Eric Felten; Bill Hughes; Dr. Close; His Eminence Cullen Cardinal Murphy. Background-wise: Bob Baer; David Fromkin; Fetema Mernissi; Sandra Mackey; Sir Richard (F.) Burton. Inspiration-wise: Paul, Mark and Brooke, splendid Americans all, in an unsplendid world. Finally, respect and homage to Fern Holland, a real-life Florence of Arabia, assassinated in Iraq, March 9, 2004, age thirty-three.

ALLAH YEHALEEHUM, UHTEE.

ALLAH HUMMA YESKOONHA FASEEH JEENAANOO.

ABOUT THE AUTHOR

CHRISTOPHER BUCKLEY is the author of ten books and the founding editor of *Forbes FYI* magazine but is proudest of the fact that he recently had a ten-and-a-half-hour lunch with Christopher (no relation) Hitchens. He (Buckley, not Hitchens) was managing editor of *Esquire* at age twenty-four and has worked as a merchant marine and a White House speechwriter. He was awarded the Washington Irving Medal for Literary Excellence but lost it during the lunch with Hitchens. *Florence of Arabia* is his first and probably last Middle East comedy.